Forgotten Cowgirl

A Woman of Character in the Arizona Territory

JK HOFFMAN

ISBN 978-1-954345-22-5 (paperback)
ISBN 978-1-954345-23-2 (hardcover)
ISBN 978-1-954345-24-9 (digital)

This is a work of fiction. Names, characters, places, and incidents either are the product of the author's imagination or are used fictitiously, and any resemblance to any actual persons, living or dead, events, or locales is entirely coincidental.

Rushmore Press LLC
1 800 460 9188
www.rushmorepress.com

Printed in the United States of America

A factitious book, loosely based on real people and events.

DEDICATED TO THE MEMORY OF
MARVIN "JIMMY" PARSONS

CONTENTS

PART I

My Early Life 1886-1896

PART II

What Happened To Us Going To South Africa? 1896-1903

PART III

Spring Valley

AUTHORS NOTE

Thank you to all my readers who have supported me in my endeavor to remember this fascinating woman. She continues to astound me with her adventures and bravery. I hope that my research on her has just begun.

As to Lizzie's actual date of birth, I found three different days listed in various records. I went by the date on the headstone.

I want to thank Jacques Laliberte, my editor, and coach, through the final stages of this journey. His creative mind has helped to bring Lizzie to life with a strong personality. He suggested writing the book in journal form, thus opening opportunities to expand on her strengths and weaknesses. I thank you for believing in me, no matter how difficult I could be at times.

To my family for their support. Garry, my husband of forty-three years, who has tolerated my whims without complaint. My three adult children, Heather (Randy), Christopher, and Justin. I love you with all my heart. My two magnificent grandsons, Riley and Aiden never lose sight of your dreams. Your dreams are out there waiting for you to make them happen, not you waiting for your aspirations to arrive.

My brother Tom (Nancy) Crawford, Matthew (Allison, Mia, and Matt Jr), Kelly (Randy). My twin brother, Jerry (Linda) Crawford, Russell (Margo and Celosia), and Andrew. I love you all.

The Hoffman family. Larry, thank you for listening to me tell you stories and your support. The nieces and nephews, I love you all. Thank you for letting me be a part of this family.

My support team: Kristen and Gregg Orr for your friendship and support. Jennifer Yard, for your friendship and skill in the

English language. Deb Roberts and Nancie Straughan, Molly Brown, Jon, and Maxine Meyer, for your lifetime friendship. Joan Cox for listening to me say for 20+ years "We could write better than that." Also, for your friendship, excellent coworker, and help in getting me started in genealogy. James Mast, my boss of 26+ years and friend. You had to put up with all my stories. The Parson family for your love and support.

Lastly, Lizzie Hoffman, who without her life, this book would not have been possible. You sacrificed yourself in the name of love. Appreciatively, JK Hoffman

HOFFMAN FAMILY TREE

Johannas Adamus Hoffmann
Born October 13, 1835
Died November 4, 1886
Albuquerque, New Mexico

Mary Josephine Sturn
Born October 14, 1838
Died May 17, 1892
Flagstaff, Arizona

Marriage August 24, 1857, Grand Rapids, Michigan

Children

George Henry Hoffman
Born August 23, 1858, in Lisbon Michigan
Died April 1, 1928, in Flagstaff, Arizona Single, never married
JK Hoffman

Nellie Josephine Hoffman
Born October 4, 1866, in Lisbon, Michigan
Died October 3, 1947, in San Bernardino, California
Married William Joseph Connor 1882 in New Mexico

Bert Monroe Hoffman
"Bertie"
Born February 25, 1868, in Monroe, Michigan
Died April 11, 1949, in Flagstaff, Arizona
Married Nora Fredrick, May 8, 1897, in Flagstaff, Arizona

John Bernard Hoffman
"Johnny, Jack"
Born November 12, 1871, Lisbon Michigan
Died May 7, 1945, Prescott, Arizona Single, never married

Matilda Louisa Hoffman
"Tillie"
Born November 5, 1874, in Lisbon, Michigan
Died December 19, 1938, Grand Canyon, Arizona
Married: Jesse Leo Gregg on November 24, 1892, in Flagstaff, Arizona

Elisabeth May Hoffman
"Lizzie, Liz"
Born September 4, 1876, Union Center, Elk County Kansas
Died September 14, 1911, Flagstaff, Arizona
Married Edwin R. Geddes January 24, 1906, Williams, AZ
Married William "Bill" Shroyer April 7, 1896, Rossland B.C.

The map was drawn by Jacques Laliberte and used with his permission.

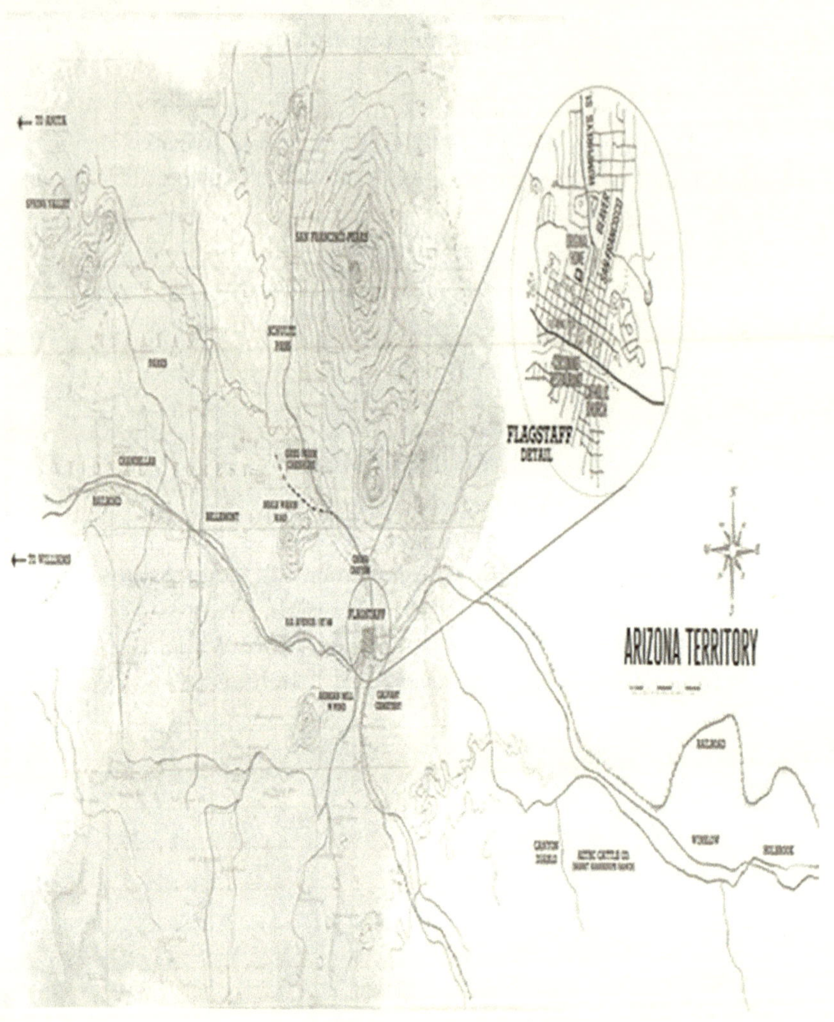

PART I

My Early Life 1886-1896

Photo belongs to Garry
& Judy Hoffman Collection.

CHAPTER ONE

The Birthday Gift

5th September 1886

The fruit from a planted seed, no different from our own lives, will one day reveal if it is bitter or sweet.

I wrote that today in school. Sister Maria says I should think about schoolwork and not my birthday.

My Christian name is Elisabeth Mae Hoffman; my family calls me Lizzie, and today is my tenth birthday. You, dearest journal, are my birthday present, the best gift I have ever received. My initials, EMH branded into the cover of the soft brown leather jacket. You smell and feel so good. There is nothing that smells better than newly tanned leather. I shall call you "LJ" for Lizzie's Journal. I love the way your empty pages jump out at me, just waiting for stories to write.

Daddy gave it to me; well, it was from everyone. He made it, and he knows me so well. He is such an excellent leathersmith. Besides my shoes, this is the first gift he has made for me. My mother and sisters have gotten reticules and my brothers' belts.

I think that Tillie was a little jealous. We had both seen one in the small curio store in Albuquerque and admired it. I never thought that my parents paid any attention to what we looked at in the shop. So, imagine my surprise when I opened you up and to know that my daddy made it, especially for me. You are much better than the one in the store. I shall cherish you always.

I live on a ranch near McCarty's Station in the New Mexico Territory. I used to live in Kansas. That was where I was borned. I have three brothers and two sisters: George, Nellie, Bertie, Johnny, Tillie, and me. They were all borned in Michigan.

Mama said I looked just like a porcelain doll she saw in a store window in Baden, Germany. That is where she and daddy were borned.

They came over on big ships across the ocean. All she remembered was that it smelled of dead fish and dirty bodies. Daddy liked the feel of the boat as it pushed its way through the water, the cold damp air, and the smell of the ocean. He said the movement rocked him to sleep at night, sometimes even knocking him out of bed and onto the floor. I think that I would like to do that someday. I could listen to him tell his stories all day long.

Daddy is the bravest man I know. He often told us the story of when he fought in the Big War between the States. He had to leave mama and George behind in Michigan with family. They lived in Monroe. I know that because that is my brother Bertie's middle name. I am glad that my middle name is Mae and not Union Center or Kansas! That would be appalling to me.

Daddy got his leg hurt very bad when they, and the Johnny Rebels got into a big fight. He has to work even harder with a bum leg. I think he is getting worser. Mama has to help him with lots of chores these days. I do not like to see him like this. It scares me. He says that is why they had all these children, so we can care for them when they get old.

Course, not Bertie or George, they ran off a few years ago, to go cowboying on some big ranch over in Arizona. Well, George did not run off. She sent him away to find Bertie. Bertie got himself kicked out of school for fighting with the Mexicans. The nuns told him not to come back, and he knew that daddy would take him behind the shed and teach him a lesson that he would not forget. Therefore, he jumped a train headed west.

Mama waited for supper on him that night. She and daddy had the worst fight I had ever heard. I listened to her crying all night long. We did not wait for him at suppertime again. She finally got a letter from him. She sent George West to bring him home. He has not come back yet, either. Johnny says it is not fair to him to get all the work. He only went to Catholic school until he finished first grade. He does not like school. Me, I do. Tillie and I go to school.

Mama is thinking about sending us up to the church school in Santa Fe. I will go, but Tillie cries and says she cannot leave Nellie, our oldest sister, alone with the baby. Nellie is married to William Connor. She has been married ever since I can remember. Her little boy, Georgie, is named after our big brother. They live in a house on our ranch. William has a good job working for the railroad. He is a station agent and sells you tickets to ride the train, loads baggage and mail. Mama says my sister is lucky; he is not a farmer or a rancher.

Poor mama, I know she misses her home in Monroe with her family. When she talks about it, she gets rather sad, and she will tell us that it is enough reminiscing for now. It is just her half-brothers and sisters. Her mama died when she was little, so she does not know what it was like to have a mother. Then her papa got hitched again and moved them all to Michigan from Germany. Her stepbrother married daddy's cousin Matilda; that is whom Tillie is named after. As for me, I was named after my daddy's mama, Elisabethea. Except we say Elisabeth here in America.

Tomorrow, we will drive our cattle to market in Belen. Daddy says they will go for a reasonable price and be taken by train to Kansas City. Winter is coming, so we cut the size of the herd down until spring. There will be fewer cattle to feed, and it will save the grasslands from being over beaten. I get to ride along and help herd them. Everyone pitches in and works around here. Someday, I will be as good a rancher as my daddy is now.

Mama says I have to put you away and get to bed since we have a big day ahead of us. I love you, LJ.

Daddy says not to dwell on the past; remember it as a bridge to the future. It is a part of who we are, not what we are.

CHAPTER TWO

Cattle Drive to Belen

4ᵗʰ October 1886

I have missed you, LJ. I have so much to tell you. I wish I were born a boy. Oh, dear, that sounds bad. I mean that I think there should not be such a difference between being a boy or a girl. A girl's life is so dismal; get up, cook, and clean, sew, and cook again. How mundane is that LJ? Tillie thinks it is a beautiful life. She always teases me when I confide in her. I should not ever tell her the truth.

At least, for a few days, I could have an incredible adventure with the best daddy in the world. He understands me. Mama thinks that I am flighty. I am not at all like my two older sisters. She always calls me the baby of the family. I am not a baby. She loves me, but sometimes she does not like me.

My adventure started the day after my birthday. We drove cattle east to Belen. Daddy said that since Bertie and George were not here to help, the women were going to have to go along to work. Finally, I got my chance to herd the cattle. I was so excited.

Mama made the three of us gauchos to wear. Mine is reddish-brown, the color of dirt around here. She said she picked that color for me so that I could get dirty, and she would not have to see it and fuss at me. I wish mama would let me wear them every day. She threatened to throw them away when we got back to the ranch; so, I hid them. Do not tell on me!

I rode the pinto pony. Daddy said he was an excellent steady steed. I like him because he lets me tell him what to do with him. I mean my horse! He is a beautiful brown and white gelding with a long flowing mane that I like to comb. Daddy says to be kind to your horse, and your horse will be good to you. I love that. I have to brush him every night when I take off his saddle. Mama rode a similar horse.

Galloping through the pastures on top of her horse, mama looked so picturesque. She let her black hair loose to let it blow in the wind. I think that she is the most beautiful woman I have ever seen. She was delighted riding alongside daddy. Then, I watched as he carefully helped her down off her horse, and they hugged and kissed each other. I think they forgot that others were around. They never do that in front of us at home.

As night approached, we made camp. I got to help build a fire, prepare dinner, and secure the tents. It takes a lot of work to herd cattle. We sat together around the warm fire; some of us huddled beneath quilts and listened as daddy told us a story about when he was in the Great War and fought for the Union Army. He said he did not care about his leg being all messed up. Is all he cared about was that they won and the slaves freed. He said no man should be treated like that. Every man has a right under God's law to own land and farm for hisself. He said the feud was a brother against brother, all to free the slaves.

As soon as the Army found out he worked with leather, they put him in the saddlery, making the saddles and reins. He told us how many of the men from his company were immigrants Germans, and Poles, mainly, just like him. He explained that they felt a duty to their new country to fight for what was right. They were against slavery. Daddy says that everyone is the same; the color of your skin does not matter. It is your distinguishing characteristic. Everyone has one. It would be difficult if we all looked alike. How could we tell each other apart? He calls it our individuality. I like that word.

That is why I am not like Tillie, and she is not like me. Daddy also says, 'If a man has a deformity, it is a distinguishing characteristic.' We all have them, being God's creatures, and it is what makes us all special. We are all different in our own way, and we should not criticize others. I wish all men were like my daddy. Maybe we would not have a big war. Although, sometimes, you have to stand up and fight for what you believe. My family left their homes in Europe to come to America because they were Prussians and did not want to live under German laws.

Daddy told us that one day there was a massive battle, and even he, who was usually in the back lines, had to fight. For a time, they were outnumbered. The Rebs killed many of their men. Daddy got a bullet in his thigh. He said he was lucky that it missed his big vein in his leg.

He told us that when you were shot there, they are dead pretty quickly. The blood in all your body just gushes out with no stopping it. Tillie got scared and started to cry; daddy quit telling us the story. I was so mad at her, for she always does that. Mama says Tillie's heart is pure, and her thoughts are innocent, we have to respect that part of her nature.

We had a hundred and fifty or more head of cattle to herd. We took the herding dogs with us so's they could help. You would not believe how hard those little dogs worked. They ran after the cattle that wandered off and nipped at their hooves. The cows do not like that, and they try to run away, except that the dogs push them back to the main herd. I think those dogs are smart. A rancher's best friend is his dog.

Sometimes, when the wind is blowing across the open desert, you cannot see because of the little flecks of sand getting in your eyes. I felt inside my ear one day, and it was gritty with sand. Mama shook her head at me when I refused to wash off well at night. It would just come back tomorrow. Tillie used up a bushel full of water, trying to get it all off before she lied down at night. Not I! If I am sleeping on the hard-cold ground anyway, what difference does it make? It is not as if I am crawling into my feather bed.

The moon was big and bright. It was so humongous that it felt like you could almost reach out and touch it. It was the color of fire. Daddy called it a harvest moon. He says that it puts off so much light that you can harvest crops at night and that farmers love the harvest moon. He also told us that he chose to move the cattle during the full moon, and we could keep an eye out for them any cattle thieve. I could barely shut my eyes without opening them back up to keep watch.

Daddy and Johnny, along with some of the hired help, took turns staying up to guard the camp. Tillie said the next morning that she could not sleep for all the mooing and the smell of cattle poop. The chilly morning air made the poop steam as it lay on the cold dirt. Johnny thought he was funny when he brought me a piece of it and said that mama and daddy found me on the Kansas Plains under a cow pie. That is what makes me rotten. I told him that at least I had a warm heart instead of like his being made of ice and snow. I will not let Johnny get the better of me. He and I are too much alike except that I am a girl. If I were a boy, we would be best of friends; instead, I am just a nuisance to him. I will prove to him that I can do anything I set my mind to do.

We had a scare one night when we heard coyotes off in the distance. Daddy says that they can smell us from miles off. They had been following us. Johnny fired shots into the air one night to try to scare them off. That got the cattle and everyone all riled up. Daddy heard one of the dogs barking profusely, so he saddled up to see what the fuss was. We listened to the dog make a blood-curdling cry, then dead silence. Tillie moved so close to me that she was practically lying on me. We stayed there, not making a sound, just listening. It is almost scarier to hear pure silence than a noise. We both jumped when an owl in a nearby juniper tree hooted. Moments went by when we heard the sound of gunfire. There would be no sleep for us that night. I felt I could protect us since Bertie taught me to shoot when I was six years old.

The smell of fresh coffee on the campfire tickled my nose and brought me out of my slumber. I sat up and saw mama doctoring daddy's leg. He held a piece of leather tightly between his teeth. I could feel his pain. As I went towards the campfire, mama told me it might be better if I did not watch. I could see that she was removing cactus needles from what looked like a gaping sore. His pant leg was ripped all the way to the top of his thigh. I told her that I was okay, and would help her. Daddy nodded as he bit down harder on the leather strap. I could hear a popping sound from his jaw as he clenched firmly. He seemed anxious to have them removed quickly because he started coughing. I got scared when I saw that he was coughing up blood.

Mama told me that he always coughed up blood, and she would get the needles out from his old wound as fast as she could. I assumed that he had suffered from the scar on his leg for many years. I have never seen his injury before now. I understood why he would be having a bad day with his leg. Mama always called it gout; but really, it was a festering lesion from the war.

Daddy would have to ride in the wagon with the cook. He still insisted on seeing to it that the cattle be moved into a holding pen while haggling with two men in black velvet jackets and pristine white shirts regarding money. I was watching daddy's face as he bickered with the men. At one point, he turned walking away when one of the men (who had a goatee long enough to appear as though it was connected to his bow tie) called to him to return. LJ, I burst out laughing so hard at the man and his odd whiskers.

Mama scolded me and told me it was not ladylike to laugh robustly. I then had to hold back a chuckle when I looked over at mama, who was covered from head to foot in red dust. Why can't women laugh like a man, LJ?

Daddy explained later that the men had offered him a price under market value for the cattle. Therefore, he walked away from them. He always said to have prices set in your head and not to let anyone take advantage of you; do not ever speak first, do not give an amount. Let the buyer talk and look at them right in the eye. When he turned around and returned to the men, they offered him five cents per head over his price, and he gladly accepted. The deal was finished on daddy's handshake. The cattle would be shipped to the east for slaughter.

Daddy visited the local doctor, so we stayed longer in Belen than we had planned. We telegraphed William at his train station to tell him we were delayed. Mama did not want Nellie to worry. We were an odd group of cowpunchers, which made people gawk at us. Some called us out for being German and too cheap to hire real cowboys. I am an American. We all are, so why would they say that to us?

We bathed in a big copper tub with sweet-smelling lavender soap. Anyhow, that is what 'Miss Know It All,' Tillie said. It cost us five cents each just to wash. I would have just as soon had five cents worth of candy and waited until we got home to bathe, but mama insisted.

Johnny got into a fight with a cowboy who teased him about traveling with a bunch of women. They called him a pussyfoot. I am not sure what that means. I might ask Tillie. He taught that cowboy a lesson!

Sometimes, I rode in the wagon with daddy. We would have long talks about ranching, and he told me that he was proud of me. He assured me that he would teach me how to be a rancher if that were what I wanted. I almost cried because daddy had never told me that before now. He said I would have to learn patience with mama, Nellie, and Tillie. They did not have in them the strength and determination that I did. I was proud of myself. He likened me to Joan of Arc because I am strong-minded and unwavering in my beliefs.

LJ, I think I will go out into this world with a bolder step and my chin a little higher from this day forward.

Life is a new adventure every day that the sun rises. I will make the most of what it offers me.

CHAPTER THREE

Memories

LJ, I cannot stop thinking about the great adventure that I had with daddy out on the trail. I remember when I was young, and I watched from our little window in the kitchen, gazing at the men working on the ranch. It is a good memory because both of my brothers were here, George and Bertie. They were greenhorns just learning the cattle business. In a way, it was my introduction and where I first fell in love with ranching. I pined away at that little window, intent on learning everything I could, right along with the men.

One of the first skills you learn on a ranch was to brand newly purchased cattle. Luckily for daddy, a nearby neighbor was a Caballero, experienced in cattle ranching. Daddy relied upon the kindly Mexican man to teach him the ways of livestock. In time, they became close friends.

Branding was long and hard for everyone, but especially on the cattle. The cows gather so close to one another that they can barely move as they travel through the chute. One by one, each calf or cow was seared with a red-hot branding iron with the ranch's insignia. A brand helps to prevent cattle rustlers from stealing the cattle – though, to be honest; rustling animals was a common practice in the New Mexico Territory, no matter the brand.

I watched anxiously as the iron seared the cows' side. The horrible smell of burning hair and skin permeated the air around the corral. I could tell that Tillie's stomach rolled. Tillie could not tolerate the smell or the bellowing of the pained cows. She slipped away while I sat, mesmerized by the unusual activity. In my mind, I fantasized about being a rancher.

Next, the Caballero performed a roping lesson with such grace and ease that all the men thought it looked easy. I suspected that it would be harder than it seemed. Daddy was the first to try. He tried twirling the rope like the Caballero. After several more lessons on roping, he attempted it one more time. He mounted the horse and chose the calf he would lasso. He decided on a smaller calf, thinking it would be easier than one of the bigger ones. Daddy rode his horse in the direction of the calf, but when he twirled the rope, the horse startled, bucked, and threw him off. You would think that would have been the worst of it, but daddy's boot caught in the stirrup while the horse bolted and ran fearfully around the arena, dragging daddy alongside him. The attached leg was the one already injured during the war. The men carried daddy, not being able to walk, from the arena to the house.

I ran ahead to alert mama that the men were bringing him. She quickly prepared the feather bed for him. Daddy was bedridden for some time while his leg healed. The doctor told daddy that his leg would never be right again. He would have to leave the more difficult ranching jobs to his sons. Daddy was a stubborn man; he vowed to be ranching by the next season.

Of course, by the upcoming season, Bertie had left home, and George was getting ready to find him. Daddy never complained about them being gone. He just said that to become a man, a boy must go out on his own. I guess daddy likens it to him leaving his home in Germany when he was young.

So, looking back, that was my first lesson in roping and branding. Since then, I have had many more. If I could only have a ranch of my own one day, I would be the happiest person alive. Daddy speaks of leaving the ranch to Johnny, but he never mentions giving it to me.

You should not spite a person for doing something you have already done.

CHAPTER FOUR

Loretto School

8th October 1886

LJ, we have had too many chores to do. When I lie down at night to write to you, I fall asleep. Daddy is not well. He has been getting worse since we got home from the cattle drive. Mama has had the doctor out several times. He has a fever and sweats. The doctor told her that daddy had tuberculosis. I do not know what that is, but I am worried about him.

Johnny complained to mama that he needs men to help him out around here. Sometimes she forgets that Johnny is just sixteen. Nellie says that he has not finished growing yet. I know that mama does not want to spend money in the winter on ranch hands.

10th October 1886

Daddy felt better today, so we rode together out in the pastures. I know he is on the mend. Our life will begin to get normal again.

12th October 1886

Mama is so mad at me. Tillie and I got into a big argument today at school. I squirted her with my ink pen all over her frilly white blouse. I do not want daddy to blister me as he does, Johnny. I know I did wrong, but sometimes I just have to stand up to her. She is bossy, and she tells me what to do.

21ˢᵗ October 1886

Mama woke me up early today. She said to me that they were taking me to Santa Fe to visit a school. When I told her, "No, thank you, I will stay at home," she ran out of my room crying. I heard her speak to daddy. She expressed that this was the reason why the nuns must straighten me out. I need discipline. He has allowed me to go astray. It was his fault since he refused to whoop me. He told mama directly that I was of the female nature, and he would never do that to me. They argued for some time, with daddy declaring that he needs me on the ranch. Mama said that it would ruin my chances of having a good life. No man will ever want a woman who can brand cattle better than he can. I should know how to bake pies and cook him dinner. Well, I can do all of that now. Besides, I want to work alongside my husband, not behind him. I love school; therefore, I am not opposed to going away to school…but after daddy is up and around. I do not want to leave him, not now.

Mama and daddy decided that we would travel to Santa Fe and make plans for me to attend the next term. I must admit to you that I was anxious to visit the Chapel of Light and the Nuns of Loretto. Mama told us the story of a mysterious man appearing at the chapel in Santa Fe after the nuns had prayed for help in building a staircase. It hangs in the air with no support. Amazing that he did not use any nails in the building of steps. When he was finished, he mysteriously disappeared without even being paid. It was a miracle from St. Joseph performed for the nuns.

They told me that I would have many girls my age to be with instead of isolated out here on the ranch. Mama says I get bored easily, and in school, I would stay busy.

22nd October 1886

We arrived at the Chapel of Our Lady of Light. It was a beautiful sanctuary. There was the most prominent stained-glass window I have ever seen. Then I saw it for the first time…St. Joseph's stairway. It looked as if it were hanging in midair. Indeed, only a miracle could have built such a beautiful thing. Its beauty mesmerized me. To gaze upon it sent goose pimples up to my arms and a shiver through my body. I believe that it is the most beautiful thing I have ever seen. I have never seen my parents be so humble as they were today.

The school was a bustle of activity with more girls in one place than I have seen during my life. Someone said that close to three hundred girls were going to school here.

The Priest is the only man I have seen today besides daddy. The girls all wear purple uniforms, and all look exactly alike. It is hard to distinguish one girl from the next, unless, of course, your skin is darker or if you have hair that is not the color of the sun.

The nun's and mama decided that I should spend time with the girls in the sewing room. Luckily, she had taught me how to sew, and I felt confident when I sat down with the girls. I could at least act as if I knew what I was doing. Imagine LJ, how stupid I would have looked if I did not know how to sew.

The girls were as curious about me as I was of them. Not all the girls were happy to be there. A small girl sitting alone in the back corner of the room was not having the fun we were. I asked the other girls about her, and they quickly giggled, then explained to me that the devil possessed her.

I was curious because I have never seen anyone who was possessed. The girl appeared to be very lonely. I felt an urge to get closer to her. I could tell that she was embroidering a little scene of a garden. When I could, I spoke to her. I looked right into her eyes, and she looked at me and smiled. I think the other girls were lying to me about her being possessed. Although, a chill ran through my body and the hair on my arms stood straight up when I walked away. She crept up on me from behind and gave me a little carved black horse. Later, daddy told me it was made of onyx. I asked her what its name was, and she rolled her eyes upward as if she were looking up at something. I glanced up and saw nothing there.

She blurted out, "Noble, you shall call him by that name." I noticed that she had a hold of my skirt and was not letting go of it. Then she motioned to me that she wanted to tell me something else. I bent over, and she whispered in my ear to be mindful of the love of my life and a black horse. The combination would be dangerous for me. The two would not get on together. (Says she can see things like that… the future.) I somewhat shrugged it off, thinking that I do not have love in my life or a black horse. The other girls looked as if she had cursed me, and they quickly made their way out of the room.

I had not even noticed that the place was rather dreary and dark. Then I smelled the grey smoke stinging my nose, and a young nun was snuffing out the candles. It was our hint to leave that area of the building.

We followed the nuns into the dormitory. It was a large room with beds placed tightly together. It smelled of cleaning solutions and burnt candles. There were crucifixes nailed against the wall to represent Christ as he was on the cross. It was a massive cold room with windows too high to see outside. Why would anyone want windows that you could not see out? The walls were a yellow color with grey smoke stains running down them. You could see outlines of pictures that had once hung upon the walls, a reminder of lives that had been here before.

The girls shared dressers with only a small area for personal items. Where would I keep you? There is no privacy. I felt like the cattle we loaded into the pens that were being shipped to market. We are to be primed and ready to become a suitable wife for some man or else become a nun. Not me, I will come for an education. That is unless I can talk mama out of this. I will promise her that I will be a good girl. I have some time since I do not return until January.'

Dearest Lord, my fate is in your hands.'

We said our good-byes to the Sisters of Loretto, but I could not dismiss the little girl or her warning to me as I slipped the onyx horse into my coat pocket. I will merely stay away from men, never horses. I am just pulling your leg, LJ.

Mama says that some people have gifts that cannot be explained. Heed the warning but do not dwell on it.

CHAPTER FIVE

Family in Crisis

1st November 1886

Nellie lost the baby. I did not even know that my sister Nellie was with child. Apparently, you do not discuss such matters with someone my age. When I awoke this morning, mama and Tillie were nowhere around.

Johnny came inside with the basket of eggs and told me that I was responsible for breakfast this morning. He barked orders at me on how he wanted his eggs cooked. He acted like he was the boss.

I created such a mess of the kitchen that daddy got Rosita, the ranch foreman's wife, to help me clean up my disaster. I had cracked eggs all over that gave a yellowish color to the red adobe floor. Flour was strewn about, making it appear as if winter had come early. I burned the biscuits so severely that one could not recognize them as such. The odor of burnt bread lingered about the house during the rest of the day.

Rosita appeared, saying that she could smell the burned biscuits all the way down the road. She was yelling at me in Spanish. I understood a word here and there, but I knew that she was very perturbed with me. When she left, there was no sign of my fiasco in the kitchen. Everything was clean and orderly.

Mama and Tillie did not return until later in the evening. Rosita appeared at the back door with warm tortillas and beans for our supper. I enjoyed every bite of someone else's cooking.

When mama returned home later, she looked tired and worn. I had never thought about her age before, but tonight she appeared older. A strand of gray hair emerged from underneath her scarf, and I would swear she had more wrinkles on her face. Her voice crackled as she announced to us that Nellie was in good health, but the baby boy was dead. The birthing was a difficult one. They sent William to fetch the doctor, but he did not arrive in time to save the baby. LJ, having a baby sounds like the scariest thing to me.

Tillie said, rather nonchalantly, that the next baby would be healthy. I could see it in Tillie's face that she considered it all part of a woman's life. "Those things happen," were her exact words. Her attitude surprised me. Undoubtedly, this was not the Tillie I knew. She cried over a bird that died when it hit the window.

I seem to get more confused every day. I think I know someone or something, and then I do not. Are nuns like me? Are they just women who will not marry and have babies? Am I to be a nun?

4th November 1886

I am too grief-stricken, LJ, to write in you. A great tragedy has struck our family. Until tomorrow, my friend.

5th November 1886

I have not stopped crying since yesterday. My dearest daddy has died.

The angels came for him yesterday. Daddy got up and went out to the barn as usual. We, women, were indoors working. There had been snow early in the morning that had surprised us all. Winter was coming prematurely this year. I suppose when daddy saw the snow, he felt he needed to bring the cattle to a nearby pasture. It was something he and Johnny had discussed earlier in the week. There is always so much to do to prepare a ranch for winter.

Earlier, mama sent us down to Nellie's with a pie and a treat for little Georgie. I came back to the house only to find mama in the barn flailing around her arms and in hysteria. She was trying to saddle her horse with no luck. She kept saying that daddy was gone. I immediately saw that his horse and his saddle were not there. I told mama that he must have gone out riding. Now, he has not gone alone since his injury in September. Why, LJ, would he have gone out today with the snow upon the ground?

Johnny, having heard the commotion in the barn, came in to see what was going on. He immediately saddled his and mama's horse and told me to stay home in case daddy returns.

Of course, I ran down the road to Nellie's house as soon as they were out of sight. I had to tell them what was happening. My sisters would kill me if I did not.

I found William at home, and he immediately saddled up his horse. We grabbed little Georgie and hurried back to the house. Everyone agreed all would be okay, and daddy would show up to the house unscathed. Even with that agreement, no one sauntered. Something felt different.

We waited anxiously inside the house, trying not to make each other nervous. That proved to be difficult. Every noise made us jump and look out the wind-pitted window. Finally, a rider appeared. It was Johnny. He was visibly shaken as he spoke the words, "Daddy is dead." He told us they followed his tracks; he explained how they found him lying in the snow. There was blood everywhere around him.

Dead, departed, deceased, passed on. My body felt numb. I tried to cry, but I kept thinking that I had lost the most important person in my life. I am a hollow shell. Empty. What will happen to me, to us, our family? Mama is not strong enough to care for a ranch and a family. Tillie stood motionless. I went over to her, and we comforted each other.

We watched as a slow parade of horses and riders made their way to our house, except for one horse that had no visible rider. Daddy's lifeless body was draped over his saddle, and a blanket placed over him. I had seen dead men on the back of horses before, but they were nameless to me, not my daddy.

Mama came in looking as if she had seen God almighty himself.

She hugged each one of us and quietly went to her room.

I hold on to you dearly, LJ, knowing that you are the last gift I shall ever receive from daddy. His love for me will always be present, as long as I have you. Now, I can cry.

6th November 1886

Mama, her eyes red and puffy, came out of her room today to greet the mourners who went to the house to pay their respects to daddy. His body lay inside a casket in the middle of the parlor. Daddy had touched the lives of many of the people who lived beside us.

Our house feels cold and empty. I tiptoed toward the sound of whispers, hoping that a miracle had happened, and daddy would be in the kitchen, enjoying his morning coffee with mama. I quietly screamed at God for not answering my prayer.

We sat like statues in the parlor. Everyone was dressed in black. Mama said we could not open the window curtains, something about daddy's soul escaping. They do not tell me anything.

Bertie and George came in on the train from Winslow and not with the usual "welcome home" greeting from family. Someone said to George that this was our first death. George replied that it was the first of many to come. I think of the black onyx horse and the little girl, an omen. Did she bring this on us? Did she curse us? Is it possible that a young girl could have such powers?

I will get rid of the horse. I have to. Please, no more death.

9th November 1886

We left our ranch this morning on the train. We were a small procession headed to Albuquerque. It was a somber group. The mortician came with us. He made my skin crawl. He was a slightly built man with a skinny face and large ears. He had so few whiskers that someone (not me) could count them. He smelled of formaldehyde. Anyway, that is what Johnny said.

When we arrived, there was a wagon waiting for us. The wagon carrying daddy's casket was decorated with black sateen material. So was our carriage. We were taken over to a hotel. I wonder where they took daddy?

10th November 1886

The November day was blustery and cold. Clouds were rushing by as if they were in a hurry to be passed such sadness. The parish of San Felipe de Neri was where we held the funeral service. We sat in the front row, unfamiliar for us since we were usually late for church. The walls of the chapel felt as if they were coming in at me. It was as if the Priest was addressing only me, preaching to me in chants of righteousness and Godliness.

My head was aching, and my throat was as arid as the desert. I felt lightheaded as we made our way by the casket for the last goodbye. I was scared, but Tillie took my hand and walked with me. I watched as mama bent down, kissed him on the forehead, and told him that she loved him. I felt honored to have witnessed the true love between a man and a woman. I felt a love for my mother that I had never felt before now. A connection was there between us…being the loss of this man.

Outside, I gazed at the clouds, and I know I could see him on a gallant horse waving to me as he rode off towards heaven. Nellie scolded me and told me not to say that around mama.

Our slow procession to the grave in the cold air made it possible for me to 'accidentally' drop the onyx horse from my pocket as the wind picked up the hem of my skirt. I could think of no better place for it to live than in a cemetery. I am convinced that it caused the two deaths in my family this month.

Daddy was laid to rest in the cemetery in Albuquerque. The Priest called him Corporal Adam Hoffman. I like that. It makes him sound very important. I grieved until I could not weep over him anymore. Mama says it makes you feel better if you can.

As we began readying ourselves for the train ride home, my legs were like mush, and I recall George telling me to hang on to him. My limp body was like a drenched rag doll. How could I be sweating so badly on such a cold day? Then came the shivers.

I cannot recollect the ride home. I heard mama say that she had never seen anybody as sick as I had been. Then someone said, "Ssshhh- Don't let her hear you."

After many days of family fussing over me, I began to feel myself again. Mama said I scared the bejeebers out of her. She said she was afraid that she would lose me too. Even Rosita came with a special soup just for me.

15th November 1886

I am stuck in bed. At least I have you. Mama says that I need to rest and get my strength back. My sisters are worrywarts over me. I have never had this much attention in my whole life. Everyone, even Tillie asks me what I need. The other day I told her I just wanted to talk as we used to, and she sat down on my bed and proceeded to tell me everything that had happened since the funeral. We sat together and cried, consoling each other's pain. Sister's through thick and thin.

16th November 1886

George and Bertie went back to Winslow. George was all puffed up like a frog because he is so vital now to mama. He is currently the oldest male in our family. Mama called him the 'Patriarch' of our family. It must be something special because he took it on as if it was an outstanding job. He and mama spent the last few days going through daddy's papers and talking among themselves. Bertie was included some, but none of the rest of us. Nellie says that whatever happens, we will still be a family. I started to protest to her when she explained that until mama and George finished with the business of daddies will, we would all be waiting for news.

"Mama will tell us when there is something definite to divulge. The doctor will be by later to check in on your recovery. Until then stay in bed." I think Nellie needs to have me be her charge. I think that helps her forget about the lost baby.

20th November 1886

I am bored silly. The doctor said I must rest for a few more days, and then I am to take it easy. He told the family that I was blessed; there were a few families who were not so fortunate. He said I was an active, healthy girl to begin with, and that made it harder for the fever to take hold.

Johnny came in and told me he had a surprise for me. I was so excited. He hid his hands behind his back, and he asked me to pick, I blurted out, right! He opened his hand as he brought it from behind his back. I did not know whether to scream or cry. There in his hand was the onyx horse.

"You must have dropped this at the cemetery. I was going to give it back to you, and then you got sick." He could tell by the look upon my face that I was not excited to reunite with the horse. "Is there something you don't like about this horse?"

I said, in a panicked voice "Like? How can you like something that is possessed? I think the little girl at the school put a curse on us through the horse."

Johnny did not believe in curses or possessed toys. He offered to take the horse to the Priest for a cleansing. Trust him and that it would be a long time before death came back to haunt us. It will be a good lesson for me on trust if he is successful. Besides, it is Johnny, and he loves me. He is the one man left on this earth that I can trust the most.

George and Bertie loved me, but to them, I am a nuisance. George told me that he was through raising other people's offspring when Nellie had little Georgie. He did not care if he was his namesake or not. Grumpy George, set in his ways! He was only taking care of himself from this day forward.

"Mind you, and I don't love you any less; it's just that you are now grown-up enough to take care of yourself. So, don't come running to me if you get yourself in any trouble."

Then there is Bertie. Mama said he is a thinker. He likes to get into fights, almost as much as Johnny does. When I think about my brothers - since I never have in the past before now - they are all out of the same mold. They are intelligent, loners, hard workers, stubborn, independent, quiet, and reliable men. Mama says she has never seen men who can spend a day working so strenuous and then spend the night drinking and fighting even harder. She says that she thinks they do it every day. I miss them. Why do they have to live so far away from us?

10th December 1886

LJ, my mama, has been so busy going back and forth to Albuquerque. She and Johnny are occupied, finishing daddy's business. Funny to think that your affairs go on long after you are gone. Mama apologized to Tillie and me saying she will have more time for us when she gets this wrapped up. I hope I am not sent away to school. She did say, "Not this term. I need to have you close to me." LJ, can you imagine that? She needs me. Every time I bring it up, she asks me to have patience with her right now. She cannot make more than a few decisions every day.

A telegraph came today from George. Tillie had to sign her name and give the man money. I thought we could open it right up and read it.

"What if it is important?" I asked her.

She laughed at me and said in a very sarcastic tone, "It's a telegraph, and all telegraphs are important, silly child." Then she stuck it inside her pinafore as if I would steal it. I did not talk to her for the rest of the afternoon.

Mama returned home and seemed rather excited to receive the telegraph. Tillie seemed to be in on the secret. I was treated the way I had always been, since before daddy died. It is so confusing to me that one day I am treated like an adult and the next like a child.

Make up your mind, for Pete's sake!

28th December 1886

They finally told me, LJ, that we were moving from here to a town called Bellemont, Arizona. George lives there now, and it is just a few miles west of Flagstaff. Except this time, instead of by wagon, we shall load everything we own onto a boxcar and travel by train. I am so anxious. Mama said she told daddy she would never move again unless it was by train. She was not betraying her vow to him.

Mama told us the story of the move from Michigan to Kansas. She was pregnant with me. She said she was so sick and miserable that she could not even hold food down. The ruts were bad along the trail that it jarred the wagon back and forth. She said she would walk along beside the wagon whenever she could but that there were still Indians waiting to attack them at any moment. She feared for her children and family. She knew I would be strong to have survived inside her through all of that. Not to mention, I survived life on the Kansas Plains as an infant. It seemed as if mama was proud of me. That makes me happy.

I do remember moving by covered wagon from Kansas to New Mexico. I did a lot of walking and sleeping. Sometimes we would get into the worst wind and rainstorms you can imagine. We called them cyclones or twisters in Kansas. The desert has smaller ones called dust devils. I hope Bellemont and Flagstaff do not have tornadoes! George says he has not been in a twister here yet, but that anything is possible.

I hope I can be brave, moving west. I found out that Nellie would not be traveling with us. William must stay here for his job right now, but they will try to get him transferred west. Mama says that my being at the school would cause Nellie nothing but worry. She does not need to be worrying about me. It will be hard enough for her without us there.

I will not have time to write to you until next year. I will keep you safe, LJ. 'Adios Amigos' as they say here in New Mexico. Oh yeah, I forgot; Tillie found the onyx horse in a back corner of the Pantry. I cannot seem to get rid of it. I will just give in and accept it.

I will try to pay closer attention to the good around me rather than give in to evil.

CHAPTER SIX

Move West

21ˢᵗ January 1887

LJ, I have so much to tell you. Mama gave her permission that I could bring one thing with me on our trip; I chose you. For a few days, we are finished packing. We packed everything in straw and wooden crates. Then we will have to unpack. No one treated me like a child when it came to hard work. I do not think a man could pack a house on his own. Well, maybe if he had no woman around to pack for him.

Mama was concerned about her grandmother's dishes from Germany. I cannot tell you how many times now, I have heard the story of the move to America. I could close my eyes and see the beautiful green grass hills with the brook running in front of the little ivy-covered stone cottage where her grandmother lived. The baby lambs were grazing on the wet grass after a spring rain. Her grandmother raised her since birth, her mother having died in childbirth. She would have stayed there forever if her father had not come for her one day to take her to America. Her grandmother begged her father not to take her with him. Mama was fourteen when he took her away, never to see her beloved grandmother again. Grandmother gave her favorite dishes to mama to remember her by. Mama said she loved her grandmother very much and would never forget her.

She met daddy after she arrived in Michigan. He was a shoe cobbler apprentice, and she was a scullery maid to a prominent family there. No one in the household ever wondered why she was always the one to volunteer to take the shoes to the cobbler for repair. Then one day, she entered the shop. She loved the little bell that rang, and the thick smell of leather. A young boy asked her if he could help her. "I am accustomed to Adam, the apprentice. I wish to see him."

The boy told her how Adam had finished his apprenticeship and was leaving for Germany immediately. She left the cobblers in shock and disbelief. How could he go without telling her? I just love this part of the story! He sent her a letter saying to her how much he loved her and that one day he would return to America for her. He did return four years later, with enough money to open his own shop.

They were married in a beautiful church (St Mark's Cathedral in Grand Rapids, Michigan, on August 24, 1857). I have goosebumps, don't you, LJ? Maybe, I am a romantic at heart, after all. Tomboys can enjoy a good love story, too. Even if Tillie tells me that I will be alone and miserable for all my life.

We are staying here in Albuquerque, leaving our ranch behind. Mama had business to finish. We are thrilled and feel very special to be able to stay in such a beautiful hotel. I think that she wants us to enjoy ourselves. I am, that is for sure.

I surprised Tillie when I told her that I wanted to dance in the beautiful room of the hotel here in Albuquerque. The highly polished oak floors called out to me. 'Dance, Lizzie, dance,' I could hear my feet saying to me. I convinced Tillie to dance around the room with its green satin curtains and a fireplace, so big that my entire family could crawl inside of it. Silly, of course, there was a fire going. Land sakes, it is January.

Mama coaxed us out of bed with her speaking in German. 'Schnell, Schnell,' she ordered. 'Komen out of bed.' We giggled when she combined the two languages. Daddy forbade her to speak in German. "English is our new language," he would say when she slipped.

The big feather bed with the warm comforter did not make it easy to arise. The sunlight danced on the red Fleur-de-leis velvet wallpaper. There was a train coming that would deliver us to our new home, and here we stayed in bed. Tillie and I laughed as we tickled each other's feet to wake us up. I think this is the most fun that she and I have had together.

Johnny was the one acting out. He was mad at mama for moving and selling the ranch. He said it was not fair to sell it out from under him. Daddy had promised that one day it would be his. George was the one who made all the decisions now. Mama just went along with whatever he told her was the right thing to do. I had not seen Johnny this riled up since the day the nuns removed him from first grade. They told him never to return. He did not ever go back to school. I guess she did not want to ask him to stay behind because she was afraid he would do just that. She gave him no opportunity.

That is when I realized that he and I had more in common than I thought stubbornness. I would pretend that I was the one who needed him to go more than anyone else. He was like daddy in that way and could not tell me no.

I began by crying every time he said that he would just run away (he knew how much I bawled when Bertie ran off, and that I could weep a river if I set my mind to it.). He would begin to say something, and I would run off blubbering. In turn, I upset everyone else. Then George saw me turn off the weeping at the drop of a hat and confronted me. I thought for sure that I was in deep trouble. He was grateful to me for the distraction. I did something right! George approved of his baby sister.

We marched out of the hotel and down the street to the cemetery. We could not leave Albuquerque without saying good-bye to daddy. That was the hardest part of our day. I shed real tears at that time. George had to pry mama away from his grave.

We trudged through the snow to the little train station. I felt we were special since we had a whole boxcar of our belongings with us. George said he could use the wooden crates later to build furniture for us.

The small potbelly stove in the corner of the room was the most popular place to wait out of the cold. The wind was whipping around the building as if it were trying to find its way inside.

Johnny was quiet, with his arms crossed, in a way that said, "Leave me alone." I knew I had to do something, especially when the conductor announced that the train was arriving from Tucumcari. Johnny went further back in the corner to hide in the shadows. The family, all but gone from the warmth to the room, proceeded to follow the conductor's orders. Johnny hid behind the stove. I snuck over, sat down beside him, and continued to talk.

"You ain't gonna cry, now are you?" he said.

"Not if you come and race me to a seat. The first one there gets the window seat." As we were running out of the door, George came in and said it would be a few minutes. He came in to warm up. We proceeded to go outside, still wanting our window seat. Johnny decided to sit down on the rope barricade. As he did, he swung backward and landed with his rump right onto the platform floor. George said to him, "Are you practicing your rope tricks for the rodeo?" Then he looked down at Johnny in his shiny new cowboy boots and said, "Never mind the rope, feet where are you taking him? Your feet are much bigger than mine. If you keep growing, we will have an awful time fitting you in clothes. The circus might want you."

George has the kind of sense of humor that only George appreciates, sometimes thinking that he is so funny. I am learning this about my oldest brother since being home with us for a while now. He can be somewhat bothersome. LJ, why do you think George ain't married yet? I wonder whether he will ever be.

I bet you are wondering who got the window seat, LJ. Me! I was so fast. I would go crazy if I could not see out the window. Mama says I have ants in my pants and cannot sit still.

George laughed as he boarded the train. "It's going to be a long day." He snuggled himself into a seat, placed his cowboy hat down over his face, and prepared for a long nap. I noticed that he would glance from under the brim of his hat to check on mama.

I watched mama place her bag under the wooden seat and sit down. She let out a sigh and was exhausted already. Mama adjusted her heavy velvet skirt and felt where a pocket had been sewn into the lining to hide money. She sat quietly as the train made its way west. I noticed a tear rolling out of her eye, glide down her cheek and, come to rest on her hand. Rubbing off the tear with her handkerchief, then she gently placed it over her heart. She crossed herself as the clickety-clack of the wheels on the train continued. I knew she was praying for us all.

I watched out of the train window as the landscape changed. We passed our old town. I waved good-bye as if someone would see me.

West of our town lay areas of black volcanic rock lay strewn across the land. It looked to me as if someone had thrown them about haphazardly. I shut my eyes and imagined trying to travel through it in a covered wagon.

"Impossible," I thought. The unfortunate horses and mules would lose their shoes; the cattle would stand still forever in one place, not moving. Everyone knew that cows were stupid animals.

At Fort Wingate, several cavalrymen boarded. I assumed they were officers, apparently, with their navy-blue uniforms and gold trim. The men looked sharp as they embarked upon the train.

As one of the officers sat down next to George, he explained that they would be going as far as Gallup. Gallup was the next town west of Fort Wingate. George looked happy to have someone to talk with, especially since George had always wanted to join the Calvary. He asked the officer many questions about his life in service.

The train was traveling at a reasonable speed when suddenly a loud squeal of the brakes shook everyone on the train. We were all trying hard not to fall off the seats. The train came to an abrupt stop. Luckily for me, LJ, I could grab a hand bar. However, you went flying through the air along with my pencil. I cannot lose you.

Mama asked one of the soldiers if he knew why we stopped. He told her in a deep voice, "Don't worry ma'am. It is a regular occurrence out here," the soldier said nonchalantly. I am sure he did not want to upset the other passengers. I saw him slowly lower his hand to keep it near his revolver.

Out the window, I saw several men on horseback. I could not see their faces because they wore bandanas. Only their eyes were visible. I jumped up and yelled, "Train Robbers! I see them." Tillie began to cry, holding tightly on to mama and hiding her eyes.

It was so exciting, LJ, when the soldiers told everyone to settle down and be quiet. "If this is a robbery, just give them what they want… jewelry, money whatever they ask for," one soldier said. "We will protect you. That is our job. Just don't provoke them."

I panicked because I remembered my ring. I was wearing the little silver and turquoise ring that daddy had given me last Christmas. Tears came to my eyes as I imagined having to surrender my ring to a stranger. Quickly, I took the ring off my finger and slid the ring into an opening of the wooden seat. I promptly crossed myself and said a prayer that they would not find where I had hidden it. Mama always told me not to waste my prayers on nonsense; 'God was too busy for that.' I thought about it and decided that this was no-nonsense. God would understand. What do you think, LJ? I found my gloves and quickly put them on. I could feel the indentation where the ring had been on my finger. LJ, my finger must be getting fat because the ring feels tight on my finger now. Does that happen?

Johnny was enthusiastic finally. He was bored until now. "Bandits!" He teased, trying to upset us.

We did not move, and finally, one of the soldiers stepped out of the train car to investigate. When he came back on, we asked, "What is it? What's wrong?"

As it turned out, it was cowboys from a nearby ranch removing perished cattle from the track hit by a previous train. They were discussing with the engineer about receiving compensation for the deceased animals. The railroad paid the ranchers for each dead livestock hit by the trains. One of the soldiers told George that the ranchers made more money from the railroad than by selling the cattle at the market.

There were the people on board from the East who did not know why the men wore bandanas. I could not believe it. The soldier said, "Well, it is pretty darned cold out there, and they protect their faces from frostbite." I was about to laugh. Of course, Tillie gave me [that] look, like do not do it. Then everything calmed down, and we soon got to Gallup. The soldiers got off, and new people got on.

Everybody quickly agreed that we were glad to have had the soldiers on board, anyway.

Mama gathered us together for lunch from the basket she had the hotel made up for our journey. We ate bread and dried meat along with some apples. As a surprise, the cook gave us some cookies. Yum.

It was siesta time! You know, afternoon nap time. I am too wound up to nap, so I began looking out of the window once more at the colorful boulders and rock formations' west of Gallup. Using my imagination, I could envision the rocks looking like weird animals.

Looking south, I could see the faint outline of mountains: peculiar country, LJ.

We stopped in Winslow, and the conductor announced that people were welcome to get out and stretch their legs. We would be at a standstill for half an hour or more while the boxcars were unloaded and loaded once again. I hope they leave our boxcar on the train. I was glad to get off for a while.

We first saw the local Hopi Indians gathered at the train depot with their jewelry, baskets, and pottery for sale. George told us they were Hopi Indians who live out on the mesas in pueblos. He pointed to the flat top looking mountains in the distance, and he explained they called them table mesas. They do look like tables sitting way off. They did not even look real, with the grey sandy haze that filled the sky to the north. I asked him if one day we could visit the Hopis. "You have to be invited to visit the Hopi's." He then proceeded to tell us that it was "their home, and like anyone's home, you need an invitation to visit. They are very private people, rich in tradition and ceremonies." It would be an exciting place to visit one day. It was like when we were invited to attend the Pueblo Indians in Santa Fe.

I did notice similarities between the two tribes of Indians. I was not afraid of them, even though there were many stories of white people abducted by Indians.

A Hopi woman, dressed in a colorful blanket, was making their traditional piki on a hot stone. The bread, which was prepared with ground corn, was a blueish-grey and spread on the heated rock very thinly. The women rolled the cooked mush very tightly together. The blue bread flaked off as we proceeded to eat it. We enjoyed the flaky piki and wanted more. The little Hopi woman laughed at us, as George paid the woman. Odd, how you can make someone understand you, even when you do not speak the same language.

Tillie asked George if Flagstaff looked like Winslow. George laughed and pointed west toward the vast snow-covered mountain range.

"No, we live at the bottom of that big mountain," he said, pointing directly west. "We have ponderosa pine trees, snow, and water."

"We have trees?" He said, "Yes, we have large ponderosa pine trees. The largest ponderosa pines forest in the world is in Northern Arizona," We looked towards the mountain with its white peaks of snow and became somewhat anxious to be home. We both giggled and whispered that George was funny. You ask him a question, and he gives you a long slow answer.

The mountain looked so majestic and beautiful. We heard the train whistle and knew it was time to board the train for home. Flagstaff would be our final stop for today. I guess we might go to Bellemont tomorrow.

It was sure more comfortable to move by train than wagons!

Home is where your family is… not the four walls.

CHAPTER SEVEN

New Lives

2nd February 1887

I am so excited. I love our new town. Mama decided right away that she did not want to live out in the country again. She insisted that her girls needed a real community to live in. She thinks that I will reap the benefits socially. LJ, I have never seen her so emphatic about where she will live.

Poor George, I think he was somewhat dumbfounded. He had grand plans of buying a couple of hundred acres, and we would become farmers again. Mama put her foot down so fast. She said she had spent all of those years on a farm in Kansas because that is what daddy wanted.

Did George remember why we left there? The massive grasshopper infestations, fires, freezes, cyclones, heavy rain, and flooding, just to mention a few of our disasters. So, before the boxcar could be unloaded in Bellemont, it went back to Flagstaff. The poor railroad men said, "Are you sure, Ma'am?" She said, "Yes, I am."

I was not sure what city life would be like, but Tillie was delighted. So, we got us some rooms in the boarding house until mama could buy land and have a home built. Johnny stayed in Bellemont with George.

Mama put us in school and not a church school but a regular public school. It was the first time a Hoffman was in public school.

No uniforms or nuns, actual real teachers! They are young pretty women who are eager to teach the youth of the territory.

6th February 1887

I am so happy about going to school. I have friends who are girls. Mary Elisabeth, Cynthia, and Cecelia are my best friends. We all live uptown above the railroad tracks. Many kids came from Milltown. They live down there if their daddies worked for the Ayres Lumber Mill. It is not that we do not like those kids; it is that we go home in a different direction. Now the boys on both sides are always fighting. The mill kids say that they are gutsier than the store-bought kids. That is what they call us. Most of the dad's work in the saloons, stores, etc.

Oh LJ, I forgot to tell you, I learned that today – etc. – it is an abbreviation for other things that you do not want to add but are there. You might hear me say many new things with this modern teaching. Every day, I wake up full of excitement.

Everybody is new. A few have been here since the town started, but more of us have only recently arrived. It is just peachy. I am about the only one who is from as close as New Mexico. Most are from the East or Midwest. My friends say that since I have lived in the West so long that I am not as new as they are. Isn't that funny, LJ? Here I thought I was the latest. The girls cannot believe I drove cattle to market.

Tomorrow I am going down to the millpond to go ice-skating. Mama is going to go along. First, we have to go to Mr. Brannen's store and purchase skates. Toodles! (that means good-bye).

7th February 1887

LJ, ice skating is so much fun. A crowd of us all held hands and skated. Even mama bought herself a pair of skates. She used to ice skate in Germany and Michigan. She looked so beautiful on the ice. I think she was the prettiest woman on the rink. I could hear other women gaggling over how she glides on the ice.

One woman said, "I wish she could teach me." She did not even fall once. I am proud of her. I fell many times on my rump. It is sore today.

We are going to church for the first time. There is no Catholic Church here. I thought they were everywhere. We will go to someone's house, and there will be a traveling Padre saying a mass. My friends will be there. Mama says that a church can be everywhere. We only go to church once a month, so we will make do with that. Other churches are being built around the town. One day, we will have our own. Everything is so different here… even mama.

It is almost bedtime, but I just had to share with you how enjoyable our day we had been. Since it is only us womenfolk, the people hosting the service today asked us to stay for Sunday dinner, including the Padre. I have never had a meal with a man of God before. I was so nervous. Mama said to mind my etiquette (that means manners). Since she has always told me that I do not have any, how could I mind them? I walked off very sad and afraid of my etiquette. Tillie came up to me and asked me what was wrong. When I told her, she laughed at me and explained that it was a figure of speech that mama uses. She told me just to watch her and do whatever she did.

So, I did. When Tillie kicked my shoe under the table as grace was being said, I kicked the man's shoe next to me. Apparently, he thought I was cantankerous, and he said: "Excuse me, why did you just kick me?" I tried explaining that Tillie had told me to do exactly as she did.

He did not think it funny, and he asked that I be taken to the kitchen. The Mrs. took me to the kitchen, and I explained the whole story to her. She giggled but told me that it must stay between the two of us.

Obviously, she does not think highly of the man at the table. She mumbled something as she was leaving as if she would have liked to be the one to kick him. She took mama aside later and told her the story, so mama did not whoop me when we got home. We will practice the art of manners more often. Tillie apologized to me for starting it. She explained to me that it was a way to get my attention. Sometimes I am scatterbrained.

14th February 1887

On my first Valentine's Day, I got a valentine from a boy at school. He said he loved me. He asked me for a kiss, so I punched him in the eye. Tillie will not stop teasing me. Maybe I do not like Valentine's Day.

16th February 1887

What is it with boys? I thought a punch in the eye would send him packing, but now he thinks we are boyfriend and girlfriend. OOhh! What am I to do now? Margaret W. likes him, and at the moment, she is mad at me. Mama says he will get over it if I do not pay any attention to him.

LJ, Tillie, and I were downtown today when we witnessed the scariest accident we have ever seen. Poor Mrs. Crawley turned the wagon over right in the middle of Railroad Avenue! The horse reared up on its back legs when somebody shot off a pistol. Every reasonably intelligent person knows that animals do not like the sound of a gunshot. We immediately ran home to tell mama what had happened because mama has met her. Mama does not know very many people yet. She insisted on knowing if she was okay.

"I think she was hurt pretty bad," Tillie said, concerned; Tillie knew how many children Mrs. Crawley had, and she began to worry about who would care for the children.

Dr. Brannen came right out of his store and started tending to her when we ran off to tell mama. Somebody said that she had blood all over her. I then began to describe in detail what the scene looked like downtown. Mama frowned in my direction, making me stop in mid-sentence.

"Now, girls, make sure your facts are straight before you go telling that story. Rumors in a town like this are bad. Gossiping is when you begin telling stories that you overhear," lectured mama. "We will say a prayer for her today at supper, and I shall go out later to check on her."

"Yes, Mama." We both said at once, as we were running out the front door and down the street towards the town again before she could stop us. Of course, mama had to yell at us to not be late for supper. We would have to be doing something pretty special to miss supper. We always wave at her to signal that we heard her, and we understand. I wonder if all kids do that, or if it is just us? Maybe city kids do not have to, but out on a ranch, it is pretty essential.

Tillie and I paid no attention to the ominous black clouds that were building towards the west of town. A wind picked up that sent our skirts twirling about in the air as we ran back towards the town. We were set on finding out news about Mrs. Crawley. Tillie was worried about all the children she had and if she should tend to them. Tillie is just that way. I have heard mama call her a mother hen. She calls me a bull in a china shop.

When we were inside the store, we heard someone say that it was starting to snow. To us, a little snow was nothing to worry about, so we continued to stay around. I could spend all day reading the little penny books that Dr. Brannen carries in the drugstore. I have found a little corner at the back of the store where I can sit and read. He says he keeps them stocked just for me. Isn't that a thoughtful man, LJ?

I was telling you about the storm that was coming into town. Oops, foolish me. By the time we were ready to head home, there must have been a good three or four inches of snow. We did not have a coat, gloves, or hat with us. It was spring when we left and winter when we went home. Silly weather, we reached the porch looking like snowmen. My nose was so red that I did not need a carrot.

When we went inside, we found mama looking through an old trunk. She was so busy unpacking the trunk that even she had not noticed the snow coming down. We, of course, were lectured on always going out prepared for severe weather when you live in a mountain town.

"I hope you two will learn to take your coats and gloves with you when you go out," She laughed as she watched us huddled beside the warm fire.

We both spied the dolls sitting in the rocking chair.

"Oh, Mama, we forgot about our dolls. Where did you find them?"

"In that old trunk," She said as she continued to unpack. "That trunk came with my family and me from Germany. It has been in our family for a long time."

Mama proceeded to go into the kitchen to make dinner. She made enough food for sharing with the Crawley family.

Mama got on her coat, hat and left to go to Mrs. Crawley's to deliver food and help in any way she could.

It is late LJ, and mama is still not at home. Tillie keeps saying that she will go over to Mrs. Crawley's if I want her to go looking for her. Mama would not like for either of us to be out on a night like this. I am anxious about her, but I do not wish for either of us to get in trouble.

Mama got home after we were asleep.

17th February 1887

We have lots of snow. Hooray. I want to go outside and play in it after I finish my chores. I do not have to wash windows today since the weather is terrible.

I am so excited, LJ, that I can hardly stand it. We got invited to our first party. Her name is Elizabeth, and I think she is sweet. But what will I wear, and will I be pretty? Mama makes nice clothes. I hope mine is red. With my black hair, I think I look good in red.

We are going to town today to buy fabric. Doc Brannen got in a new shipment of fabric just the other day. At least, that is what it said in the newspaper. Imagine, it was brought from Chicago.

Doc Brannen, as I have learned, is the town doctor, store owner, postman, fireman, and a genuinely good person. He will help out anybody that needs help. What a nice man.

Mama has been so busy sewing our dresses. They are pretty. I cannot wait to see what the other girls cwear.

Elizabeth's party was on Friday afternoon. The house was at the top of Gold Avenue, one of the main roads that ran north and south into town. The hill was steeper than it looked. The house was made of malapis stone with a big, nice front porch. All the young women looked lovely in their dresses; Tillie and I looked just as beautiful as the other girls did. In a very formal fashion, the guests ate tea and cakes. There were games and singing which everyone enjoyed.

The next day, we were pleasantly surprised to find an article concerning the guest list in the "Coconino Sun" newspaper. We wore our dresses to the church on Sunday. This particular month, the congregation was meeting at Hawk's Hall downtown. The church leaders of Flagstaff are raising money to build a new church. The Catholic Diocese of Phoenix had promised them a priest after they made a church.

"I will donate land for the church to be constructed," Dr. Brannen announced to a room full of parishioners. "I have a piece of property south of the railroad tracks that the church may have."

Dr. Brannen received a very hearty round of applause for being so generous. The discussion soon turned to how to raise the money for construction. Everyone offered suggestions and was genuinely excited to help.

Tillie and I were just as excited as the adults were. Naturally, the Babbitt's and the Riordan's would be significant contributors for supplies. Rumors flew that the Riordan's were purchasing the Ayers' sawmill shortly. That was only a rumor, and the town would have to wait and see what would happen.

Back home we went, both of us trying to visualize what the new church would look like when it is finished. We had never been in on the building of a new church before. We both eagerly awaited the new adventure.

6th March 1887

It was a beautiful day outside today. The old-timers say that we have had a mild winter. When the girls and I walked home from school today, we noticed that the boys ran off in a different direction. I was so curious as to where they were off to that I told the girls; I was going to follow them.

Would you believe that I had to teach the girls how to track someone? I thought that was a natural act. First off, I had to tell them to be very quiet. My brothers taught me well.

Then we stashed our satchels on a dry stump. They were scared to leave them, but I told them it would be fine. We had to hurry at first to tail the boys. They got away from us. We went up a wash that led from downtown up to the North. It took us to the original flagpole, and I learned that was the reason they called it Flagstaff. The first people here put up a timber pole and hung a flag on it. Anyway, as we snuck behind them, we realized that they were sneaking up on something too. Well, it turned out to be two different things. The Chinese had a camp out there, and so did the Gypsies.

I spotted the Gypsy wagons first. They were painted in bright colors. I remember seeing them when I was young and moving to New Mexico. We were going to camp near a river, and daddy said no because of them. Mama was all disappointed because she wanted to do laundry.

Anyway, there are Gypsies out here. We sat and watched awhile, but nothing was going on. As we were deciding among ourselves as to what to do next, the boys went running past us. They looked as if they had seen a ghost or something. They were wrought with fright that they looked right at us and just kept on going. We left the way we came in down through the canyon.

Mary Beth says her daddy calls it China Canyon since the Chinese have taken it over. You know that a Chinese person cannot be seen on the streets of the town. It is illegal. It does not sound right to me. Don't the Chinese count as people, too? Daddy would say that is why he fought in the war. I cannot wait for summer to go exploring. That is if mama does not find out.

Easter, 1887

We are going to Church today. Mama is happy. Her boys, as she calls them, will be coming in from the ranch today. Is all we have done is cooked and cleaned to prepare for them. We do not see them much this time of the year as the ranchers were getting new herds off the train, which seems like every day. Tillie, who does not want to get any part of her dirty, refuses to go down to the stockyards with me. Mama says it is not any place for young women. Hogwash! I grew up on a ranch. Daddy taught me how to herd cattle when I was six years old. Tillie says it smelled terrible. I like it.

The whole town reeks of animals and fresh-cut timber.

Off to church. Later, LJ

*****

Oh, LJ, something deliciously incredible happened to me today. I met a very handsome man. He called me Liz. Well, he also called me Cyclone; me and him being from Kansas. He said I had as much energy as a Kansas cyclone. Anyway, LJ, I was shocked when he called me Liz. Mama introduced me as Lizzie, and it was as if he never heard her say that. He said, "How do you do, Liz." I stood there, speechless. Imagine me, without a word to say! Then he took my hand and gently shook it. My hand was as limp as the dishrag as I had been hiding it behind my back. I felt like there was a butterfly in my stomach, and my heartbeat so fast I thought for sure that he could see it. Did he sense it also? Is this what love feels like to girls?

I have never had anyone who made me feel this way before.

I love Ed! I want to write his name on everything I see.

His name is Ed Geddes. As I said, he was from Kansas too. Just up the road a piece from where we lived. His smile is so divine, with two sizeable dimples on his freshly shaven face. He smelled of new leather, soap, and cigars. His face tanned from the sun. I am in heaven.

My brothers brought him to the house to have Easter supper with us. He is a cowboy, a real man. Of course, he spent most of his time out on the porch with my brothers. They stopped by Brannen's store and purchased cigars from Cuba. I could hear them talking about the cigars as if they were something special. Almost as if they were discussing a woman. I laughed to myself.

Mama told him not to pay me no mind if I started talking too much. She explained to him that it was just the way I am. He said to her that it was okay, he had baby sisters back home, and he missed them. Did he just call me a baby? I am devastated, humiliated, and broken-hearted.

Mama enslaved me in the kitchen to help her and Tillie. My mind wandered as I was setting the table. Tillie teased me about what I might be thinking. How did she know? I purposely sat as far away from him as I could while we ate.

I asked mama as we were drying the dishes, what she considered aged. I mean, George is old. He is thirty, and Bertie is twenty. I wonder how old is Ed? He is probably older than Johnny, who is sixteen.

Earlier, I found a small black-and-white kitten out in the back yard. I carried the cat inside the house with me. Mama's rules… no cat in the house. I knew she would not scold me in front of the company, so I broke the rules. Kitty got scared when George sneezed (anyone gets worried when George sneezes!) and ran off. After our pie, and as the men were leaving, Ed pulled the kitten from under his coat and returned her to me. I could feel her sharp little claws piercing my arm as I held her close to me. The deeper they went into my arm, the harder it was for me to maintain my composure. I thanked him for finding her for me. He asked me what I called her, and I shouted out rather loudly… "Boots," I said. "Her name is Boots," I stuttered.

We said our goodnights, and Johnny scowled at me. It was as if he knew what I was feeling. I then felt self-conscious. Was my face turning red? Oh no! Not in front of Johnny! He will never let me live it down. The incessant teasing over this day will haunt me forever with him. Is all he needs is a little ammunition, and my life is over. Mama will get wind of it, and I will have no choice but to become a nun, draped in a black-and-white habit with my eyes looking at the floor for the rest of my days. Mama threatens me with that every time I do something wrong. I cannot tell Tillie how I feel because she will not keep a secret from mama or Nellie. I am doomed for eternity. I can only say, LJ, I love Ed Geddes. Never shall there ever be another man for me. On my honor, I tell you this now.

Mama is coming up the stairs. She thinks that she is quiet, but I can hear her shoes hitting the wooden stairs. I have to hide you quickly, LJ, before you will be taken away from me forever. I cannot risk that.

I pretended to be asleep when she opened the door to gaze in on me. The candlelight flickered softly in my room before she told me to go to sleep. She then blew out my candle. How did she know that I was awake? How do mothers know these things? Does she have a crystal ball like the gypsies in the camp outside of town? Can she read my future? If only she could, I should ask her if Ed were my intended.

An idea has come to me, LJ. I shall not write it on paper yet. No one is to find out my plan, especially Tillie. She acts as if she knows my most profound thoughts, but I know better than to confide in her. She is a goody-two-shoes. She never does anything wrong. Except, I know that she has a massive crush on Jesse Gregg. I see the way she oodles over him when she thinks no one's looking. Nevertheless, I have seen it. It is our secret. Why else would she go to every baseball game we have? It is not that she loves the game that much. Tomorrow after school, I have work to do. Goodnight LJ

Is this how God feels when he says he loves us? Does he get all tingly inside?

CHAPTER EIGHT

Gypsy Camp

11ᵗʰ April 1887

I could barely sit still in school today. I had to make up an excuse to my friends as to why I could not walk home with them. Okay, so it is a white lie. I will confess to the Padre later. For now, I could not worry about the girls and their safety; I had a mission. I had to ask a soothsayer. I had to know if Ed was in my future. Was he connected to the black horse? Was he a danger to me? I had to find out.

I waited behind at school and made my way up to China Canyon. The snow on the mountain was melting, so there was water in the usually dry riverbed. It made it harder to get around. Once, I got my shoes wet. From then on, my feet were so cold. I was going to visit the woman who told fortunes from my hand. I had to know if there was any hope for Ed and me. I was prepared for her to say no and to drop that notion from my head right then. I wanted to know my future and clear my head about the premonition with the young girl at the Loretto School. That still haunts me at times.

I never told you, LJ, that a few weeks back, I had a bad dream about that. There was a black horse that I loved more than anything else in the whole world. Whenever I tried to ride him, he was so wild that he would knock me to the ground, and this man was yelling at me and beating the horse. I was afraid the man would kill him because of me. It scared me so badly that I woke with night sweats. I remember trying to scream at the man and make him go away. Maybe the seer can help me with that dream and the prediction of the girl at Loretto. Perhaps she can see what the girl witnessed, too, and keep me safe. I hope I can see her. Please, God, do not let anybody find out I went over there.

I reached the Chinese camp and scurried past them as fast as I could. My legs were shaking so badly that I could barely walk. I hid behind a large pine tree and tried to figure out which colored wagon I needed. After a short time, I noticed a regular man come out of one of the coaches. He was placing his hat back on and straightening out his clothing as if he were getting dressed all over again. They do not make you get naked to have your fortune told, do they?

I thought that leaving sounded as if it were a good idea. Then I saw a young pretty Gypsy girl come out of the wagon and hand money to an older man. They seemed to be having words, like an argument or something.

I turned, hoping to skedaddle back home fast. I was not so lucky. As I turned around, someone grabbed my arm. The man accused me of spying on them. I quickly tried to explain that I just wanted a fortuneteller. The man laughed and told me that I had to have money for that.

"We make our living telling fortunes; we do not just give that away to little girls."

He held my arm so tight, and I was begging him to let me go. I said I was sorry for being there and that I would never come again. The loud talking brought others out of their wagons, descending on me in imposing numbers. They were everywhere. I was surrounded. My heart was beating so fast I thought it would jump out of my body: women, men, children, and scrawny dogs all around me. I glanced around, hoping to find a spot that I could get through and escape. What have you gotten yourself into this time? Mama's words "If you look for trouble, Lizzie, you will find it," just kept running through my head.

Two of the men and one woman seemed to be discussing my fate. I said every prayer I ever knew. Do you think Gypsy's are

Catholic? Why are you worrying about that now? Sometimes LJ, I cannot explain my brain.

The woman came up to me and told the other man to let me go. She could see that he hurt my arm.

"You fool," she told the young man. "You will bring us trouble." She was not speaking to me. Was that good or bad? I just knew that he was in as much trouble as I was.

Then she turned towards me and asked me, "What do we do with you now? What is your name?"

I blurted out, "Matilda. My name is Matilda." Yes, I told another lie. Why did I use Tillie's name? Poor, sweet, Tillie.

Then she asked, "Why do you lie to me? I can see things."

That was my opportunity to blurt out that I wanted my fortune told, and I would never say to anyone what I saw or heard today. Please, please.

"Leave me something of yours, say that pretty scarf around your head. I like it. Come back tomorrow with ten cents and I will read your fortune, and if you tell or bring anyone with you, then I shall keep your scarf and maybe tell someone you were here today. Understand, Matilda? My name is Madame Zander."

"Yes, I understand I said as I tore off my scarf. "Tomorrow, ten cents." The hordes of people scattered as she motioned on her hand for them to leave. I raced as fast I could run, except this time, I went by way of the wagon road that led north of town. I had never been this way before, but I knew if I went south, I would end up near home.

As soon as I walked in the door, Tillie noticed I was not wearing my scarf, and I looked frazzled. "Where were you? We have looked everywhere for you."

I blurt out yet another lie, "At the stockyards watching the cowpunchers rope the cattle for branding." When mama was about to get mad, Tillie spoke up and said that she forgot to look there. She saw me there last week. Yes, of course, I was there the prior week and then again today. My scarf blew off in the wind. Mama said she believed me and my explanation. She told me from this day forward, try to make it home earlier.

Oh LJ, I do not have ten cents. Maybe I could borrow some from Tillie without her knowing, and I promise to replace it as soon as I can? If we had a Priest to confess to, I would be in the confessional all day.

Wish me luck tomorrow! Of course, I am going back. They will not hurt me. Besides, I need my scarf. That is evidence against me.

8th April 1887

Men, omens, and premonitions should not be worth either my time or effort. What a time of it these last two days. Maybe, when I turn eleven, I will not be in as much trouble as I am now. I have a few months to go before that happens, and at this point, I just hope I am alive.

Want to hear about my day, LJ? Okay, so I went to school, and I could barely make it through the day. I thought that maybe everyone knew what I did yesterday. Did the boys follow me and bear witness to my entrapment? If so, where were my brave cowboys to save the little gal? Cowards!

I traveled North, following the wagon trail. There was less water in the stream today. As I grew closer, I heard the sound of someone approaching. I stood still, frozen in place. I could turn and run, or I could face them. I had come this far, so it was now or never. Reaching into my pocket, I felt for the coins. The cold metal indicated to me that they were safe in my pocket.

Then, I saw the men; there were at least two of them, one on either side of me. My heart raced as I bravely moved toward the first man I saw. Stuttering, I blurt out that I was here to see Madam... Madam, what? I just stood there, as my mind was blank. I could not even remember her name. He motioned for me to follow him. Campfires with pots above the flame were cooking food. There were pungent odors that my nose had ever smelled before. Women stared at me as if they had never seen anyone like me intruding upon their territory.

Cautiously, I followed him, making our way around several wagons until we got to the largest of the brightly colored ones. I observed that it had fewer cooking utensils attached to the outside. Nervously, I climbed the steps behind him, running my head into the middle of his back, not seeing that he had stopped. He turned around and held out his hand; it was the cleanest man's hands I had ever seen. I dropped the two coins into them. Okay, so I practically threw them at him. They missed his palm and fell to the platform at the top of the stairs. One turned on its side and rolled off and onto the ground. I mumbled, sorry. We then made our way back down the steps and retrieved the coin.

Once again, we ascended the steps; he opened the door and motioned for me to enter. I made my way into the dark interior, and all I could see was an eerie shadow of flickering candlelight. I thought I was alone, and then I saw her seated at a table. As my eyes adjusted, I saw that the candles were in every nook and cranny. Beautiful scarves were hanging from the walls of the wagon. There it was, my scarf hanging in plain sight for all to view.

Then I spotted a parrot sitting on a shelf in between the scarves. It was as if the bird was not real as it sat very stoically with the eyes fixated on me. The only part of the parrot that moved was his head turning on occasion.

"What is it that you want from me today?" a voice said.

I thought she knew. Did she forget who I was already?

"Fortune," I blurted out. "Tell me, my fortune. Read my palm."

"Sit there, girl she commanded me and motioned for my hands to be placed down flat on the table. She studied both palms for what seemed like an eternity. Then she took hold of them and held them in her hands. Her eyes were fixated on mine as if she were reaching deep into my soul. My mind raced, waiting for her to tell me what she had seen. Time seemed immobile as I sat stationary in front of her. What is it? What does she see?

I reached for Noble deep in the folds of my skirts and held him gently, wondering what this woman knew about him.

Nervously, I sat waiting for my fortune to be revealed. Suddenly, Madam Xander stated that I must leave immediately.

"There are issues in your future that even I will not reveal to a young girl like yourself. Return when you are older, and I shall give you a reading."

"Is it bad?" I stuttered, begged, and asked her why? Suddenly, I noticed that the man was back at the opening of the wagon, motioning for me to leave. Then I pulled the black horse out of my pocket to show her. I knew I would regret not revealing it to her if I went now.

Studying the horse, she answered, "I can feel that there is a foreboding danger for you later in life with a man and a black horse. This man is someone whom you will love with all your heart and soul." She moved backward as if trying to get away from it.

My eyes burst open, and I felt Noble bucking against my leg! No! – that is just my heart. She knows!

Did she see what my face hid? Did it tell what I was hiding from her?

"Leave, child, you are young, live every day to the fullest, as if it were your last. You are too young to understand life, much less death. Do not dwell on death; it is what we all do, even me."

I ran out of the wagon and down the road towards home as fast as I could run. As I neared the town, Tillie came out from behind a tree. "I caught you," she said. "Were you at the Gypsy camp? It is that silly horse is not it and what the girl said to you. You are obsessed with it."

"How did you know? You do not have a spell cast on you. I am scared, and I needed to talk to someone. Daddy is not here, and the rest of you all laughed and made fun of me. I can't help it if I was born last."

Oh LJ, I just kept sobbing – no, for real this time. Cross my heart and... oh, forget it.

"I read your diary," Tillie blurted out. "I saw what you wrote," I told her I did not care; I had bigger problems than that. "My fortune was so bad that I even scared a Gypsy!"

Poor Tillie got so frightened for me that she promised not to tell mama. At least, this time anyway. We locked arms around each other's waist and walked home slowly, not uttering another word.

LJ, even though I do not want to, I must hide you away from prying eyes.

You and I are not safe.

Goodnight, and by the way, I love you, LJ.

In the words of a fortuneteller, make every day count as if it were your last.

CHAPTER NINE

The Shootout

3rd June 1887

Oh, LJ, I have missed you so much. I have hidden you away for such a long time. I do not know where to start catching you up. I love my new life in Flagstaff.

First, let me tell you that we are finally in our new house. The men in town were helping George build the house. It is just now finished. It smells so good, like a pine forest. It is made of big timbers. I have my own room with a window upstairs. I can see the beautiful mountain without going outside. Mama said she spared no expense. She wants a beautiful, comfortable home to live out her days.

School is out now, and all the girls and I got autograph books from Dr. Brannen's store. We passed them around to all of our friends, who wrote poems in them. Back East, it is all the rage. Everyone does it. Dr. Brannen had to special order them because he said he had never heard of it before now. It is so we can look back years henceforth and remember each other.

I did not miss a day of school, and so I got a new chalk tablet as a reward. The Principal said I was a good student. I will miss school.

10ᵗʰ June 1887

I am helping mama with her garden. I would rather be outside working than inside. Tillie helps us, but she does not like to get dirty. I want chickens and rabbits, just as we had in New Mexico. Oh, maybe a baby calf, also.

15ᵗʰ June 1887

Johnny surprised us today. He had to come into town for supplies, and he stopped by to see us. He is herding sheep. Most of the sheepherders are Basque. Luckily, Johnny knows a few Spanish words, so he can communicate with them. He says it is okay, but he prefers cattle. It is hot and dry on the mountain. We need rain. I sure do miss him, LJ.

He says that when you are on the mountain and the moon is full like it is tonight, there is no prettier sight than the forest. The breeze makes the Aspen leaves rustle. He says you can lay there, and it is as if they are singing. The air is crisp and clean. How I wish I could be up there with on that mountain curled up in a bedroll.

If I shared that with my girlfriends, they would think I was mad. I will keep those thoughts to myself, or else I shall find myself abandoned by them. These Eastern girls are different. At least, mama is happy. There seems to be no more talk of sending me away to school.

I am going to tell you a secret, LJ. I made a scarecrow for the garden just so mama would bring out the old boy's clothes. I am supposed to meet my friend on top of the water tower tonight since the moon is full. He says it is beautiful. Yes, it was the boy who punched me in the eye. Remember, I punched him back. We are now friends. I shall say no more of this in fear of getting caught.

27ᵗʰ June 1887

The big celebration is coming up on the Fourth of July. The town is full of cowboys. I will keep my eyes open wide in hopes of seeing Ed. I am going to go down to the stockyards this afternoon and watch the barrel racing. Some of the boys in town have been practicing lassoing. I might watch them for a bit. They have an old cow skull that they attached to a stump. It is out by the Gulch near China Canyon. Do not worry, LJ; the Gypsies have moved on. Wish me luck showing those boys up on lassoing.

1st July 1887

Wow, I showed those boys! I walked up to them and acted girlie. You know, "Hi boys, are you practicing for the rodeo? Golly, that sure looks like fun. May I try?" Of course, each boy gave me his rope.

"I can't use more than one at a time, can I?" Boy, they are gullible. I gathered the rope in my hands the way the Caballeros showed my dad the first time I was watching him learn to rope. I imagined and practiced roping the cow by myself. Anyway, I got the rope twirling around in the air at a good speed and flung the rope toward the skull. On my first try, I lassoed it, and then, the second and third time, the same thing. The boys were most unhappy with me. I thanked them for letting me lasso and asked them if we could do it again sometime. I know that will not happen again, and I know my secret is safe with them. What would they say, "That Lizzie is sure a good roper?" I hardly think so, don't you?

I went along with mama and Tillie to watch some of the rodeos. I did not see Ed or any of my brothers today. Maybe, tomorrow. The rumor is still going around that the Riordan's are buying the Ayers Sawmill. It seems like it might be right.

4th July 1887

I saw him! Ed was in town. We were at the rodeo, and they called out his name to be the next contestant. My heart started pounding so loud. He was bull riding! Well, at least for a second, then the beast bucked him off, and he went down hard. His leather chaps were dusty and dirty. He had a difficult time getting up, and the other cowboys were getting nervous for him. The bull was still loose in the arena. I yelled at him to hurry and get up. Mama and my friends looked over at me as though I was crazy. The announcer said,

"Let us give a hand to the Kansas tenderfoot. Better luck next year."

I explained to the girls that this was the gentleman who found my kitten for me at Easter. I told them I would introduce them to him. Of course, I did not explain to them how I feel about him, silly.

I found him after the rodeo was over. Mama told me not to hang around the corral too long (she knew how much I love being around the cattle and horses). We found him standing with a group of young men. Being afraid he would not recognize me, I began to introduce myself as Johnny and Bertie's youngest sister.

I almost forgot to tell you about the parade. There were bands and wagons covered with decorations in red, white, and blue. The Calvary from Fort Wingate even marched in our ceremony. Yes, I looked for the men on the train but could not recognize any of them. Their band is playing tonight at the barn dance. I hope mama lets me go. The local prostitutes even walked in the parade. The men all whistled at the scantily clothed women. Men from the cattle companies like the Aztec rode their horses, and some did rope tricks. My brothers were not in the parade.

Mama says I can go for a short time to the dance with her. She does not want to go alone. Tillie and I shall escort her. After all, she is a woman in mourning.

6th July 1887

The barn dance was so much fun. The band from Fort Wingate was terrific. Mama danced several times with a man named Bill Shroyer. He is new in town. He was a miner in the mountains of Colorado looking for gold when he heard that there was a discovery around here. The man seems kind enough. She protested that she was a widow, and he told her that he understood and still managed to get her on the dance floor. She said she would confess at church next time the Padre came to town. Tillie was beside herself because she is a goody-two-shoes.

Johnny showed up to the dance, having had too much liquor. I had never seen him that way before. He left after finding out mama was there. He saw her dancing with Bill, and boy was he ever mad at her. He said some awful things to her and caused everybody to look at her. I thought Mr. Shroyer was going to have it out with him right there in the dance hall. Tillie went away crying, saying she could never hold her head up in this town again. Why? It was not she that made a scene. Me, I do not care what people think. Ed came into the hall and saw what was going on and managed to get Johnny out the side door and out of trouble.

Well, at least for a while anyway. He managed to get himself thrown in jail later that night for disrupting the peace. Bertie came bringing him home the next day to our house to sleep it off. Mama was very mad at Johnny. He did not even remember the fight with Mr. Shroyer.

Ed stopped by later that day to ride with Johnny back to the north pasture. He said hello to me, but that was all. I could tell that his cockles were still up at me. Oh well, I could help him if he simmered down and listened to me.

2nd August 1887

The summer rains are here in full force now. I have been sneaking out after chores to meet the boys at China Canyon. They have all been practicing shooting. There is talk that Buffalo Bill Cody will be here in a couple of days. No, not for a show, dang blasted. He is coming with a group of men to go hunting at the Grand Canyon. They say he will stop for a couple of days. The boys hope that there will be some sort of competition in town to show Mr. Cody what good shooters we have here in Flagstaff.

Oh, LJ, do you know what I hope for? I hope mama lets me show him how good I am. Why I can hit every tin can and bottle, I aim at! The boys miss every other one they shoot. It gets their dander up every time I show them up. I hear that Mr. Cody is friends with Annie Oakley. Now, there is a good shooter. I would rather have her coming to town than him, but that is our secret. She is my idol. There is a real woman for you.

I want to be just as courageous and bold as she is.

4ᵗʰ August 1887

He is here. Mr. Cody arrived on the train today. I went down there to welcome him to our beautiful city. We went all out to receive him with open arms. They set up a platform, and the Mayor gave a speech. Then they announced that one performance would be given this evening, weather permitting, to the townsfolk. Nothing was said about the competition, but I will go prepared. I have my ways. I won the bet with the boys, so they owe me. Not only do they owe me, but also, they have to say that I am the best shot in town. Wish me luck.

Evening

I did it, LJ! He did have a shooting match for all the young men in town. Therefore, I had to cheat a little. The boys loaned me a pair of jeans and boots. I tucked my hair up under my hat and fooled everybody, or so I thought.

I entered the competition as Bernard. That is what gave me away. I used my uncle's name and Johnny's middle name. Tillie ratted on me to mama, but after it was over. It was worth it. I would take a thrashing if that were my punishment to do it all over again.

The boys knew they did not stand a chance with me. I felt sorry for them. However, a gal has to do what a gal has to do to prove herself.

They used a real target with a bullseye. I had to quiet myself down before it was my turn, or else, I would be shaking so hard my shot would not come close. I took in a deep breath, steadied my arm as I lifted the shotgun, lined up the bulls' eye with my eye, and shot. I was scared to look, but the crowd cwent wild, so I presumed I hit what I was aiming at.

I made one mistake. It was a doozy. I immediately took my hat off to thank the crowd when my hair came down. Oh no! Everybody was quiet as Mr. Cody himself walked up to me and took his hat off to me.

"I must say, young lady; you are very talented with that weapon. Men, when she gets older, you had better watch your step around her. She has some talent." A roar of laughter went out in the crowd. I was so mad I could have screamed from the rooftops. That is all I got was a hat off and a laugh from the man who knows Miss Annie Oakley. He then went on to explain how difficult it would be for the men of this town to lose to a woman.

"The rule of this match was open to "Boys only! Sorry, Miss." Then he grabbed me by the shoulders and hugged me. I felt uncomfortable and small, never having received a hug from a man his size, even if it was Buffalo Bill. He did not embrace the boys.

Out of desperation to be acknowledged for my accomplishment, I shouted out, "Lizzie Hoffman, my name is Lizzie Hoffman."

He gave me a consolation prize. It was an autographed picture of himself and Annie Oakley. I did not get the twenty-five-dollar first prize. That went to my friend George.

Oh, and people did tell me that they were impressed with my shooting. Ed was there and said to me that I did a remarkable job for a girl. Is my heart part of someone else's body because my body could have punched him right in the eye for that remark, and the other part of me could have hugged and kissed him.

I will dream of being like Annie Oakley every night. Now there is a real woman. I aspire to be just like her.

5th September 1887

Today is my eleventh birthday. Everyone pitched in and got me a pony. I cannot ride it yet because my brothers have to break it in. That could take forever. I want to be excited. What good does it do me if I cannot ride him yet? I will not tell them that, though. I ride too well for a pony.

Daddy would have said to me, 'Lizzie, be true to yourself. You are the only one who matters to you.' I will, daddy.

CHAPTER TEN

Mr. Shroyer and Mama

23rd September 1887

School started, LJ. I am so sorry I have not written in you. Consequently, much was going on in the church, school, and chores. We have ninety children in our school. That is a big school. Our new teacher is Miss Weatherford. She comes from Weatherford, Texas. She is stunning, and she dresses awful nice. Listen to me, LJ, talking about fashion. I hear that Miss Annie Oakley makes a really elegant lady and a sharpshooter. If she can, then so can I.

Mama is somewhat proud of me, I think. I know she wrote to her half-brother Bernard and told him about me. When he wrote back, I asked her what he said about me, and she took the letter and squeezed it in her hand, then said, "Hello, he said hello. It does not matter what others think."

Well, LJ, I could tell that he said a lot more than that, especially since she had a tear in her eye. I wiped it off her cheek and said to her that I loved her. Sometimes, you would think that her brother was like Prince Phillip. Hoity-toity. He believes that the west is a wild and unruly place to raise children.

We learn geography in school. I just love studying maps and see new places in the world. I want to travel and see the world. I guess that I am like my daddy; I have itchy feet to go.

Miss Weatherford and Miss Coffins are always telling me that I can do anything I want. Maybe even change the world. They have helped me feel better about myself because I am different from most girls.

Then at church, we are raising money for a church building. We will have a bazaar next month. If we build it, the church will let us have our own Padre here all the time. Everyone wants that. There are enough sinners around for confession all day and night. Mama says that she has never seen so many sins take place in plain daylight.

My brothers came the other day and built us an animal pen and started a barn. I got to help dig the fence posts. Bertie showed me how then went inside to have coffee with mama. That is good because she is not called on much. Since she was visiting, I got to work outside with George and Johnny. I hope I get to have a horse along with my pony. I miss riding.

Mama and the boys talked about building another house. Mama thinks that maybe she can get Nellie over here to live. Mama and Nellie are more like friends than mother and daughter. She says it is because of all those long, lonely nights on the Plains. You learn to rely on each other more than city life. I think Tillie is jealous of how she feels about Nellie. That may be why she tries so hard with mama. She and Tillie can get work taking care of the sick and indigent. That way, she can think of other things besides daddy.

Mama scolded Bertie and Johnny for drinking and carousing around the saloons. She said they should spend their time looking for good women and get themselves married, George, also. Taint right for men to be alone. She just wants more babies.

She has also heard talk of the Pleasant Valley war over to the east. It is a war between the sheepherders and the ranchers over land. They were both cattle ranchers except that the Tewksburys has supported the sheepherders. The Grahams and the Tewksburys kill each other all the time. Each family saying, they have rights to the grazing land. Johnny says he is going to quit working sheep and become a ranch hand with Bertie. Johnny says they both just like to fight. He can get him on with the Aztec Cattle Company. That way, if the dispute comes over our way, Johnny will be on the right side. I wonder how Ed feels about that since he was working sheep.

The boys told mama she could do as the women in Holbrook and Winslow do to warn the men if there was a Tewksbury in town. The women will hang their tablecloths inside out to dry, and that tells them to be wary. Johnny does not like the Tewksburys because he has heard they are part Indian. George and Bertie have heard that too. I spoke up and said that daddy did not teach them to judge a person by the color of their skin.

The men left with a stern warning from mama not to go looking for trouble.

15th October 1887

LJ, we had a very successful church bazaar. We raised over eight hundred dollars, and Dr. Brannen donated land south of the tracks for the church. I have missed not having a real church to go to on Sunday mornings and get-togethers. I know; God is everywhere, but it sure seems better in a church than somebody's house.

I got to bring a rabbit home. It is so cute. The cat, Boots, does not know what to do with it. I do not want him to hurt the little thing. Mama says not to name it because we will eat him one day, and that makes it harder.

She forgets that I am not like Tillie. I understand how these things work.

16th October 1887

Good news, my sister Nellie is moving here. Mama got a letter from her saying that William got the transfer he asked for. He will not be a station agent, though he will work in the railroad yard. We all agree that it will be better than having them away from us. I guess she was right in having that new house started. It will be fun, but then I will have two mothers. Tillie says that Nellie is too busy with Georgie being five years old now that things will be different.

Mama told me that she and I will take the train in a few days over to Albuquerque to help Nellie pack up for the move. How exciting! Tillie has to stay here and watch over the place. I heard mama say she will stay with the neighbor. Besides, Tillie could not leave Jesse. Two little love birds doing you know what….k-i-s-s-i-n-g! Yuck!

28th October 1887

Tillie is mad at me. Let me say, first off, that she has a boyfriend, and I have known about him for some time now. She, however, did not know that I knew. His name is Jesse Gregg. He is older than she is, so she did not meet him at school. I heard she met him through one of her friends. He seems nice enough. Why is she mad? Well, I caught them kissing out behind the barn. Not just a little peck, either. It was a momentous mouth slobbering kiss. I was not spying. Well, maybe I hung around a bit too long watching them.

I guess they heard me with all the leaves and all. She yelled at me in front of Jesse. I hardly know the man, and she is yelling at me. She sounds just like mama. She will make a good mother one of these days. She looked at me straight in the eyes and said if I wrote about in it my journal that she would burn you to a crisp. How mean is that? I have to hide you very well and not just anywhere. We have to share a room now that mama has taken on the indigent.

She will not threaten me. She would not dare to harm you. She knows that you are my best friend in the whole world, and you know all my secrets.

Just to be safe, I know the perfect place for you.

*****

30th October 1887

LJ, we have been so busy with Nellie and her family, helping her unpack and entertaining Georgie for her. She says that it helps her having us nearby. She and mama are always together. Nellie is lucky. Tillie is not jealous, but I am. I guess it is because I do not get on with her the way those two get on. It seems as if I am always in the way or cannot do things as well as they can. I am not even allowed to have a hissy fit.

Christmas, 1887

I trudged out to the barn in the snow to feed Moonbeam, the pony. I had to find you. Today I felt lonely, and I missed daddy.

We have a big tree inside the house with candles on it, and we strung popcorn and placed pieces of fruit for decoration.

Mama has invited Mr. Shroyer to come for Christmas dinner. We have a goose. George will be here today. William has to work in the train yard. Apparently, George and Mr. Shroyer are the same age and are friends. Of course, she used the excuse that George needed someone to talk man things with instead of sitting around with us women all day. I have no doubt he appreciates it.

I hope Mr. Shroyer does not expect George to do the talking because George hardly says anything to anyone unless it is necessary. He is a man of few words.

They are calling me inside. I can never be alone. Merry Christmas, LJ.

New Year's Eve, 1887

What a great year. We are going to the New Year's Eve gala at Hawk's Hall. I helped the women decorate. I think it is the prettiest place I have seen. It smells so good with the fresh pine boughs that adorn the walls and tables. The women loaned their beautiful silver bowls and excellent service. I had to be careful because the pine sap on my hand would make my finger stick to the silver. Some rather forceful woman came up, yanked it out of my hand, and said that children should not be allowed in here. I ignored her and went on about my business. A man walked up to me and said, "Ain't you the little gal who shot so good for Bill Cody." I said yes, and then he quickly told me to pay that woman no mind.

"She is just a cranky old biddy." Later, I found out that it was the man's wife. Happy New Year, LJ.

Be thankful for your family and friends, not only for the holidays but all year long, even your big sisters.

Young Lizzie

The photo belongs to Garry & Judy Hoffman Collection.

CHAPTER ELEVEN

Becoming a Young Lady

2nd January 1888

The dance was so much fun even though I had to go upstairs with the children. Georgie and I were the only ones not downstairs. Tillie was allowed to be down all night. It is not fair. We did get to have a few treats and hot-spiced cider to drink. Then we laid down on our blankets and went to sleep. I just want to be grown up.

We have had so much snow. I guess last year was unusual by not having much. I am excited to take the first sleigh ride that I can remember. We had a sleigh in Kansas, but I was too young to have any memories of it. Besides, this ride will be with a group of young folks. Tillie and Jesse are going along. We are going to go over the hill to see where the Greenlaw sawmill is being built. That should be fun as I have never been out that direction before.

4th January 1888

We enjoyed our sleigh ride. We talked them into taking us out at night. That was even better, but it was so cold. We sang songs, and when we got home, we had hot cocoa.

We just got new neighbors across the street, Mrs. Miller and her husband. He works for the railroad and is gone all the time. Mama told her not to worry because they can become friends. I think it is funny to hear her talk about friends. I cannot remember her having many friends before we moved here.

19th January 1888

I wish the weather was better, so I could go out more. Everybody is in a hurry to get inside out of the cold. There are too many people getting frostbite and losing fingers and toes. The newspaper says some people have died from the cold. They call it exposure. At least, the ice-skating rink at Millpond will open soon.

21st January 1888

LJ, I heard the sound of crying early this morning. It was Nellie. William was working, loading, and unloading train cars. He was using a hoist, and the machine smashed William's hand. Word traveled fast to Nellie and us. Nellie and mama rushed to William's side.

"Looks like your husband was pretty lucky, ma'am," said Dr. Brannen. "It could've been a lot worse. He could have lost his whole hand. I see these types of accidents in this town a lot with the railroad and the mill. It sure seems like somebody's hurt almost every day."

Doc told him that he would be out of work for a while. It will take time to heal," Doc was empathetic, knowing that a man with a family cannot do without work. "Didn't you say you'd worked as a station agent for the railroad?"

William answered yes, and the Doc said, "Maybe I can talk to them and see if we can get you back on as a station agent." He would sure be appreciative of anything he could do. Doc Brannen is so considerate nice that way.

Doc told Nellie to go home and have him take it easy with that hand. He said for her to put some clean snow in a bowl and have William put his hand in it and to use an icicle wrapped up in cloth. Very clever. That should keep the swelling down. He has to go back next week to redo the bandages.

Poor William is so distraught. He says that if he goes back to work as a station agent, he will receive a transfer from Flagstaff. We do not need a station agent. He knows that Nellie loves living here as much as he does and that it will break her heart to move away from her mother. He is a good man. Nellie is lucky to be married to him. Little Georgie would miss the attention from us too.

Oh LJ, even though I was jealous of Nellie and mama, it makes me sad to think that they may have to leave.

Do you think, LJ, that Ed is a caring man like William? I hope so.

1ˢᵗ February 1888

Everyone around here is in such a foul mood that mama suggested that we all go to the ice rink today. Little Georgie was so cute all bundled up in warm clothes. Nellie was beside herself with worry that he would catch pneumonia. We got him skates from Salzman's store. They are these tiny little things. Of course, mine is not much more significant. I have a small foot for my age.

I like it when Georgie wants to be with me. He calls me Izzie because he cannot say L's and holds on to me for dear life but wants to skate faster. Then he wants me to carry him. Tillie is too busy gliding with Jesse, anyway.

10ᵗʰ February 1888

William is sad. He blames himself for the accident. I like William and it has been good for us to have a man around close. Around here, there is not much work for a man with a mangled hand. He will take a job out west in a town called Hackberry. It is small, not much there except for the mining and saloons. He will not go until summertime, so we have a little more time with them.

4ᵗʰ March 1888

Today, Mama announced that she was having our picture taken down at Mr. Fetter's photo studio. She wanted Nellie to have an excellent portrait of us when she moved. She told us to look our best.

I wore one of my favorite dresses. The jacket had a velvet trim on the front. The white button-over collar made the coat look dressy. My long black hair tucked neatly behind my ears; my short bangs curled using small strips of cloth. We felt very special having our picture taken. Mama was very proud of us. She thought that both of us looked very beautiful. Even little Georgie had his picture taken.

3rd April 1888

George came into town. He spent the winter down south being the cook for an outfit with a big herd of cattle. He was very talkative and told me this story of what life was like out on the trail.

George was the cook now because he had received too many injuries to continue being in the saddle and herding cattle all day. He had gladly taken over as the cook, especially since the old cook was going blind and could not see what he was doing. "Cookie," as the elderly man was called, was mixing up sugar for salt. The beans were inadvertently seasoned with sugar, and it was not acceptable to the ranch hands. Cookie would always get mad and cuss the men out for complaining and would retaliate by burning the biscuits or the cobbler. The men, in turn, would begin to laugh, taunting Cookie even more.

Often, George explained, the men would play pranks on Cookie. Even going so far as to replace some of the coffee with dirt. Cookie always went to bed before everyone else was up early to begin breakfast, and had his coffee first. When he took a swig of coffee, he knew immediately what the men had done. He got so mad he refused to cook for the men all day. The men made their meal of jerky and old bread. He said it served them right.

Therefore, as George told me, the men were glad when he became the cook, and Cookie became the helper. He was not a rambunctious cowboy like his youngest brother and other cowboys. Often quiet and a loner, so, when George drinks, he prefers to be alone rather than in a saloon. Too many times, he had been with a group of cowboys who would drink and then get into the most tremendous fight with each other that would carry on until daylight.

I could sit and listen to his stories all day. Anyway, George was going to go back out to his farm in Bellemont and give up cowboying. He would try his luck at farming, having had the background for it since our family had a farm in Kansas, and he helped father with it. On his farm, he could even have a few cattle and pigs if he wanted to.

For the first time in George's life, I think that he is pleased. I hope he gets his wish. I wish he could find some kind of woman, like our mama, to make him happy. He is already old at thirty.

29th August 1888

LJ, summer has flown by. We are going to have a fall harvest festival with a bazaar and a dance. I cannot wait. It should be so much fun. Tillie and I volunteered to help post flyers around town advertising the event.

1st September 1888

The weather was great for the big affair. You should have seen it; sellers arranged the produce in methodical designs on the back of wagons. There was fruit from all over, such as apples, pears, melons, peaches, and cherries from Oak Creek. Other items included vegetables like corn, squash, potatoes, and pumpkins. Women brought quilts and other handmade items, including jams and jellies.

We decided to make some crafts to sell. You know me; my work was far less superior to Tillie's. She is an exceptional seamstress with many ideas. We took the scraps of mother's material and transformed it into beautiful doll clothes and hats. Some of the girls made aprons.

The day was a success. The committee planned a barn dance and dinner for the last evening after the event. Everyone got in on the act and dressed in western clothing. My dress was red, paisley with a white pinafore over the top. The skirt swirled when I went around and because of all the petticoats underneath. Mama had made sure that I would feel feminine. The local town band got in on the festivities and played music at the dance.

Guess who came to the dance? Ed. My eye caught him just entering the barn. He looked sharp, wearing a plaid shirt and vest with a fancy wool jacket. His boots were new and shiny. I could tell that he had gone out that day to purchase the outfit. Then I suddenly realized that I was not the only female in the barn who had noticed him enter. It seemed as if every single woman's eyes lingered on Ed. Jealousy immediately befell me. He is mine, I thought to myself. I knew him first.

Ed saw me from across the room and waved at me. My heart leaped as I waved back at him. That was when I noticed the women were glaring at me. I was suddenly very excited that he was walking over towards me.

"May I have this dance with you, my little Cyclone?" Ed asked calling me by his endearing nickname.

I was blushing as I answered him, "Why, I would be delighted, Mr. Geddes."

Ed, being a good six feet tall, towered above me. His towering masculine features stood out in the crowd. I, being just over five feet tall, must have looked little dancing with him. I sure felt short, anyway. His hand in mine seemed big and robust. For a man who worked hard, they were softer than I had imagined they would be. He smelled so clean as if he had just gotten out of his bath. I could have let him lead me around the dance floor all night.

He must have felt the tap on his shoulder. When he turned around, there was a boy from school who very apparently had a crush on me, and asked if he could cut in. Ed, being a gentleman, graciously stepped back and let the young man dance with me. Other teenage men soon followed until I insisted on sending one to get me a glass of punch. I do not know about you, but I think that a rule should be made that another man cannot just cut in like that. It is so rude. I know you agree with me.

I took the opportunity to look for Ed. I scanned the room and could not see him. I approached mama, who was sitting with a group of people, to ask if she had seen him. She introduced me to the people sitting around the table. I ended up sitting there for the next hour watching everyone else have all the fun. I just wanted to tell Mr.

Geddes goodnight and to thank him for dancing with me; I said to her.

The nosiest town biddy said to me, "He left with a red-haired woman on his arm."

"Gone? Do you think he is coming back tonight?" My remark sent the group of women cackling. I knew that my inexperience with men was what the women were laughing about, not the fact that Ed left for another woman. They were laughing at me. I was so mad at the woman for her enjoyment over Ed departing with a woman that my face turned red. She thought that I was embarrassed about my seeking the attention of a man. Little did she know that I was mad as a hornet at her. Mama must have known because she excused herself for the night, and we left the gala. Again, my young age hindered my social life.

As for Ed, I was intelligent enough to know that I had no claims on the man or who he chooses to be with; not yet anyway. My hopes and dreams are to be with that cowboy when I get older. Right now, I must wait for my time.

Of course, I received a lecture from mama about manners in public and respecting my elders. It could have been that I [accidentally] spilled my punch on her as I was leaving the table. Children can be so clumsy.

13th September 1888

Mama saw a small article in the newspaper about Johnny. Tillie and I get our names in the paper for things around town but never Johnny. It said he was following a calf east of Flagstaff where steep canyons, formed by flooding over hundreds of years, would appear without warning. Canyon Diablo was an unusually entrenched canyon. I know there was a story of the railroad building the bridge across the ravine and how dangerous it was to construct.

As the trail descended, small pebbles caused the horse's hooves to slip. Johnny fell off the horse, and it went over the edge, leaving Johnny hanging, for dear life, onto a shrub brush on the side of the cliff. With the help of other cowboys, Johnny could climb back up and out of the canyon. As men would, Johnny received a harder teasing than he did a fall. The horse, not as lucky as Johnny, had to be shot due to a broken leg. I am glad that Johnny was not hurt, but sadly, the horse had to be put down for humane reasons. It is what happens out on the range. All the men say that you toughen up to death faster, being out on the range than city life. I have to practice being strong when I become a rancher.

Oh, LJ, did I tell you that I have decided to be the first woman rancher around these parts? I will accomplish that one day; just you watch and see.

Christmas, 1888

Nellie and Georgie are here with us. It makes it so festive. The men came in from down south where they were wintering the cattle. I just love to hear them tell their stories and dream it is I out there. I said to them, "I'm going to have five hundred head of cattle. My ranch will be the largest spread in all the territory," They all laughed and chided me about all the pretty clothes I wear.

"Aren't you afraid of getting them muddy?" they teased.

I told them that I would not be worried about a little mud; besides, I would buy myself a pair of jeans to wear. Then Bertie said, "You can put one of those fancy peacock feathers in your cowboy hat."

George, sitting back on two legs of the chair, just shook his head and said nothing. He loves me and knows that I am just stubborn enough to show them all up. He never doubts my ability to run a ranch or to do anything else I set my mind to.

"You two better watch out," George spoke up for me and said, "You'll be running cattle for her."

Then, mama called me into the kitchen and added, "You better come learn to cook so you can feed all those men." I told her, "I don't like to cook; I'll have a maid and a cook." She told me we did not have a maid so go get the table set.

Another year is over. I love you, LJ.

Dream as if you can fly over the mountain and watch what you can accomplish when you set your mind to it.

CHAPTER TWELVE

New Freedoms

14th June 1889

Poor Nellie, she has had to move yet again. I do not think that I told you that she had a baby girl. We were so busy taking care of her and then the baby that I have had no time to write in you, LJ. She named her Nellie after herself. Isn't that funny? It confuses us. Mama will say to go and check on Nellie, and we say that she is right here.

"No," she says, "baby Nellie." We could call the baby Nell.

Anyway, back to Nellie's move. She is living out in the desert in a town called Yucca. William is the station agent there. At least they can live above the train station. We have planned a trip to go out there this fall after the summer heat is gone. I have not seen cacti since we lived in New Mexico. Nellie says that there are different types out there. There is one that is called Joshua, and it is about the only kind of trees they have. They also have Yucca. She says that she misses the pine trees and the fresh air. It is hot there in the summer. The baby has a rash, so mama told her to burn flour and put it on the outbreak. She wrote back and said that it worked very well.

22 November 1889

LJ, I got to take a trip without my mama to the Grand Canyon. A group from our parish organized a trip to the Grand Canyon. Mama reluctantly gave her consent for us to go, with the understanding that we should stay with our chaperone at all times. We eagerly boarded the train in Flagstaff and rode west to Williams. It was a short train ride to Williams, where a stagecoach driver met us. He then took us on our journey to the Canyon. John Hance has built a small hotel on the Canyon rim. We know Mr. Hance, as he is a regular visitor to Flagstaff. The accommodations were up to date, making the stay very comfortable.

You should have seen Tillie. The Canyon immediately put a spell on her. We have never experienced anything like it before. She could not pull herself away from the edge of the canyon. I have not seen her get so excited over anything like that. She kept saying how she wished that Jesse were here to see it with her. For a while, I thought I would be returning alone. She did not want to leave.

The food in the hotel was pleasing. All of it was fresh game cooked perfectly.

When we returned to Williams, local hunters were coming back from a turkey shoot. Among the men was Ed, who rode into town with several turkeys that he had shot. I was so surprised to see him. It had been a long time since he had been at any events in Flagstaff. The men spread all the turkeys out on the ground so the local photographer could take pictures of them. It was quite a display of turkeys and hunters.

My heart started pounding as if it was going to go right through the top of my head. I wondered if it was visible underneath my clothes. I immediately struck up a conversation with Ed. He is living on a ranch near Williams. He was as surprised as we were when he saw us standing among the crowd. He quickly offered to have a turkey bagged for us to take home to our mother for Thanksgiving dinner.

"You will join us, won't you, Mr. Geddes?" we both said in unison. "Mama would be quite disappointed if you didn't come for dinner," I added as if Ed needed any convincing.

"Tell your mama I will arrive at three pm," Ed said as he handed the bagged turkey to us. "I can hunt the birds, but your mama sure does a better job at cooking than I do." I laughed and said we would be happy to have him visit.

You should have seen the look on mama's face when we came in the door with a turkey in our hands. LJ, at least she was pleased with both the turkey and the guest.

Thanksgiving, 1889

I had an extra two days off school for the holiday. We have snow early. The lumber mill shut down for the winter leaving the pond to freeze, which makes me happy. People say that the weather is surely crazy around here.

Mr. Geddes and my brothers arrived for the festive meal. They were happy to see their friend and talk old times.

"I hope you boys can stay the night with us." Mama offered the men as they were just taking the first bite of the bird.

"We had planned on staying, Mama, that is if you don't mind us going downtown this evening for a spell," Johnny spoke up fast; he was asking to be polite more than he was asking for permission.

"You boys don't need my permission to go, just don't go getting yourselves in any trouble. The Sheriff is getting tired of all the rowdiness at night." She managed to get a warning about the Sheriff and his arresting the drunks disturbing the peace with fighting.

The men went out on the porch after dinner. The women cleaned up as usual. I was not happy that I was in the kitchen doing dishes while the men were relaxing and enjoying a cigar. I enjoyed the smell of the tobacco and wondered what it tasted like. Water slopped onto the wooden floor, just as I imagined the thought of actually smoking the cigar. I was jealous of the freedom of what being a man offered.

"Careful, Lizzie," mama said as you could hear the tiredness in her voice, "that is the good china, brought all the way from Michigan."

I told her in a cranky voice, "I know, you tell us that story every time we use them," I snapped back at her, "I wish I had been born a boy. Boys get to have all the fun while women just spend their lives working." I threw down the dishtowel and stormed off, leaving the work for her and Tillie. I figured for sure that I was in big trouble.

Apparently, mama shook her head and told Tillie that they would leave the dishes for tomorrow.

She came to me and said that she understood my frustration. She was just like me as a young woman. Her mother had died giving birth to her, and her father had remarried soon after. It was insisted on, is the oldest of her half-siblings, to perform the household chores. Then she was sent out to work in the household of another family. She did not want to see her girls doing what she had to do. She married a good man. Patience and prayer are goals to live your life by, she told me. Mama was smart.

Tillie had a hard time understanding mama's reasons for letting me get away without helping. Tillie was born doing what she was supposed to do. She had a kind of knack for it. Her intuition told her what was right and wrong. Not I; I do something and think afterward if it was correct. I will ask God in my prayers tonight to help me be more patient with myself.

Ed left the next day. He did tell me how pretty I was for a cyclone. Then he called me Liz again, not Lizzie. I had to stop for a minute, LJ, and think about that one. I like it. However, I shall insist that he is the only one allowed to call me Liz. It sounds worldlier than Lizzie does. Do not you tell anyone, but I found a butt of his cigar, and I smoked it. Not bad.

Often, we see differences first before we see how alike we really are.

CHAPTER THIRTEEN

Fire

17th May 1892

I miss the days when I could take the time to write in you. I stay so busy; the days just slip away. Tillie is connected to Jesse like glue. All my friends say I should be seeing someone special by now like them. I am having the best time without all the drama of a relationship. Tillie cannot do anything until she talks to Jesse. I do not have to get anyone's permission… except for mama. As long as I finish my chores, have a chaperone, and be home by ten, I can do what I want. These days it is riding my horse. I can always find someone to ride with me. Even Tillie likes to ride. It is like an adventure every day. There are so many trails to ride. We live in a beautiful place.

The days are warming up nicely with the nights being cold. Mama was anxious to get the garden started as usual. She planted cabbages, lettuce, carrots, and began her beans. She hoped we would not get a grasshopper invasion like the one in Kansas that killed all of our crops.

The men are working out on various ranches in the area. We have not seen them for several weeks. Mama seems to miss them more than ever. The spring cattle move is in full operation. Every available hand is needed to move them from their winter grazing out west of town to the peaks. She knows they will show up one of these days and expect a good home-cooked meal. Poor mama. She has seemed so lonely lately, with all of us busy.

She misses daddy still. She has been caring for John Hovey's little boy, Eddy, for several weeks now while John worked out of town on the railroad. Odd, it is just he and Eddy; the mother is not around. Mama says it is not polite to pry. If John offers a reason, then that is okay, but do not go sticking your nose where it does not belong. The work suits her. She can still care for the sick and elderly, as she has been doing for some time. We all enjoy the little boy. He is mischievous. He is the same age as little Nell. That is why mama loves having him here.

We gathered him up and took him to town in the buggy. Mama needed sewing supplies from Brannen's store. Of course, I have a hat that I want and will show her when we are downtown. I think I will take you with us so that if it takes too long, I can sit in the buggy and write in you. I get bored shopping and have so much to tell you.

*****

Shopping went as I thought. I only like it if I get something new. Mama said, "Not today, Lizzie!" Then I said, "My friends all get a new hat when they want it. They have pretty clothes bought from New York and Paris. When I grow up, I will make sure I marry someone rich," I pouted.

"You mean you won't marry a dirty cowboy like Ed Geddes," said Tillie teasing me. Then I said, "I never said I would marry Ed Geddes. Ed cleans up well. Besides, Jesse Gregg gets himself dirty too. Now, leave me alone," I said as I ran out of the store.

Mama said she would drop us off at our friend's house, so I will leave you here and get you later. We are going to the church tonight for a rehearsal for the spring play. Of course, she asked if we had an escort to church. Tillie told her that Jesse would be there. Mama likes him, so all is well.

Love you, LJ.

17th June 1892

I found you today, LJ. Just where I had left you before the world turned upside down on me. I do not honestly know if I can write about that night yet or not, but I will try my hardest, lest I forget any of the crucial details. I worry about this because I am not myself. Everyday tasks are as difficult for me as new ones. I know this because I experience brand new and challenging things every day. Even my prayers, whom I know by heart, have difficulty coming. I question my belief in you, God that you can be so cruel.

This account of the Seventeenth of May 1892 is not for the faint of heart. If you cry at a show at the Opera House, then beware. I have warned you. Least of all, have your hankie ready in your hand to wipe the tears, because I guarantee that this story will make even the harshest person cry.

Let me start by saying that I am now an orphan. There was no sickness or indication on that day that I would be placed in this position so rapidly. Not knowing that we would not meet again on this earth, I had no chance to kiss my mother good-bye.

My fault that our last hug was hurried, as I was but a child thinking only of myself and the fun that I should have that day. Was I selfish? Could I have changed the ending had I been home? On the other hand, would I have been a victim too? I ask myself these questions daily, hourly, and by the minute. To die so cruel a death is unimaginable. I am told that time heals all pain. I know this to be true from the loss of my father. However, at this point, my sorrow is so profound that I cannot seem to find my way out of the dark abyss. Some people call her a hero, and others blame her as if the gusty wind were her doing. I shall let you have your own opinion. I call her a hero. The wind started blowing very hard when we were at our friend Edith's house. The typical spring wind that seemed to come from out of nowhere arrived that day without warning. The gusts were blowing loose pickets off fences, and you had to close your eyes when you walked out in it for fear of getting dirt in your eyes. Your walk was as if you were on a drunken path, blowing you off your feet.

The streets were full of piles of pine needles swept into the corners of buildings along with all the garbage that was around.

I went with my group of friends to the church below the railroad tracks. We prepared for a long evening of rehearsal for a biblical play for the children of the church. Baskets of food were made and taken so that we would not have to be bothered by going home for supper. Supper…a mundane daily ritual required by loving parents. It is a time for the family to gather and connect to discuss our day. A custom that I now pine for.

The evening seemed to move along rapidly. Jesse was there only to spend time with Tillie, as the two could not be separated from each other for extended periods. Jesse was an educated cowboy. He had morals and standards. He stepped outside to roll a cigarette. He thought he smelled smoke in the air. Someone's fireplace, he thought to himself. He looked at his watch at Nine O'clock. Then he heard the sound of a gunshot. Immediately, two more shots into the air. Three bullets in a row indicate FIRE! He, being a volunteer firefighter, knew he must leave and help. He ran inside and began yelling "fire," to the other men. They immediately departed to go assist. The more men on a fire line, the faster it could be extinguished. On a night like this with the wind, that would be near impossible. No one wanted the fire to spread to homes or businesses.

We were cleaning up the rectory when he reappeared. The look on his face was sheer desperation.

"House fire, over by you. It looks like a bad one," he managed to blurt out. We grew excited but not fearful because everything like that happens to someone else, not you. Although genuinely concerned for our neighbors, the thought never crossed our minds that it was our house.

We hurriedly began making our way home across the tracks and up to Humphreys Street. I cannot remember the instant that Tillie and I both realized that it was our house, but we both began running as fast as we could go. There were so many people gathered that it was difficult to make our way through the crowds. I fell on my face, landing on a wooden sidewalk. Someone helped me up and realized who I was, thus clearing the way for me. I could taste the blood running into my mouth. I was numb. For the first time in a long time, I did not care what I looked like to others; I just needed to be with my mother and console her.

As we approached the house, the smoke thickened, and it burned my throat and eyes. I could barely see. My ears, however, were excellent, and I could hear sobs coming from women and men talking about how they have never witnessed anything as gruesome as this. Then they saw Tillie and me approaching the house. Mrs. Miller was the first to grab us and keep us back. I was protesting, telling her that I just wanted to help mama. She grabbed me by the arm and pulled me close to her. She whispered in my ear that the angels took mama and little Eddy. She told me that she and Eddy were gone. They were safe in heaven.

"Safe," I snarled. How dare you call mama safe if she is dead?" I regret what I said to her now. I was mad. Mad at the awful wind for making the fire worse, mad at myself for leaving her alone and angry at God for taking her from us. I got away from her and ran toward the front door. Is all that was left was a doorframe. To think that we teased George so badly for making the strongest, thickest, doorframe imaginable. Now, it was about all that was left of the house itself.

There on the red Moenkopi steps into the house lay mama. In her arms clutched tight were the charred remains of baby Eddy Hovey.

As I started towards mama, to go to her, hug her one last time. Shock and disbelief hit me as she was unrecognizable. She had been burned so severely that there was nothing left of her face or hands. Then the smell hit my nostrils. Burnt flesh and hair, a repugnant odor. An odor that etches itself into your memory so that every time you think about it, your brain produces the smell inside your nose.

I sank to the ground; my feet and legs lost all control. I passed out cold. I remember the feel of freezing water being splashed on my face, and although conscious again, I felt as though I was not in my own body.

I do remember the men having to go back to the house where a tree combusted into flame, and they doused it out. The tree was on the lot that Nellie once lived in. Nellie, our poor Nellie, I thought how lost she would be without her.

I have a memory of mama being placed inside the hearse and me crying. I watched as it drove away until it was out of sight.

I watched the angels take her, my father standing near – precious souls together, so tender and so dear.

CHAPTER FOURTEEN

Coming to Terms with Life

23 June 1892

LJ, Tillie does not understand my needs and desire to know details. She feels that I am too young to understand death and fears that I will be bitter with God. I hope that I can make her know that I need to know what happened. Shielding me from the truth was far more harmful to me. I chose to pay Mrs. Miller a visit. She did not seem surprised by my appearance at her door. She gave me a full account of all she remembered of that day. She knew that my mind would never quiet down unless I had all the facts. I will fill in with things that I remember of that night.

She began by telling me that she and Eddy had an enjoyable evening before he fell asleep playing with wooden blocks on the floor. She said to her that Eddy had a tantrum while we were going to our friends. He cried out that he wanted to go with Izzie. He too, like Georgie, could not say his 'L's' so it came out with just the 'I,' which she enjoyed hearing. Mama expressed to her that she was indeed missing all of her children that night. Mrs. Miller had to stop at that moment and wipe the tears from her eyes. I forced my tears back, knowing that if I did not, we could not go on with our talk.

Mama told her how Eddy had played with his toys on the floor until falling asleep. She picked him up and put him to bed. His bed consisted of a short feather mattress and quilts on the floor in the living room. On a small table sat a kerosene lamp. She took advantage of Eddy's sleeping and began her sewing. Mrs. Miller came to the door to visit. They talked sewing as usual, and mama went with her across the street to help her fit the dress she was making on a form. She left the doors open, one in the back of the house, and the other was the front door. The winds were gusting quite strong. She even discussed with Mrs. Miller about blowing out the lamp. She talked herself out of it, knowing if Eddy awakened in the darkness, he might be scared. Consequently, she left it on the table.

Mrs. Miller began to sob so intensely that we had to suspend the conversation while she recovered. LJ, it is the most challenging task for both of us to discuss the events of that fateful night. I have to be strong and make it through this ordeal. I could not live my life if I did not have every detail. That is where my brothers, sisters, and I differ. Where they would rather not know right now, I must have all the details.

Mrs. Miller returned with tea for both of us. She began by saying that both she and mama saw flames shooting out of the front door about the same time. Terror shot into both. She ran frantically from the house and across the street with Mrs. Miller following close behind. It was impossible to enter the front door, so she ran around to the back door. Mrs. Miller went to summon the other neighbors at the time someone shot the alert of three bullets into the air.

My mind stopped at that point, and I froze. Mrs. Miller could see that I was distraught. I had the memory of being inside the church when Jesse ran to announce the alert. From that moment on, the account became very real for me. I could place myself from then on at what I was doing while my poor mama fought for both her and Eddy's life.

The same questions of 'what if' raced back through my head. "What if I had been there? Would a door have been closed so that the wind could not whip through the house and knock the lamp over? Could I have saved myself and them?" I would never have an answer, only questions.

For my sanity, I knew that I must stop the questions. Then an idea was brought to my attention. One of the men, first on the scene thought that maybe the boy himself had taken the lamp off the table and dropped it, causing the blaze. Again, no answers, just an idea. Mrs. Miller and I discussed how cruel some people could be with their judgments. As I have told you, some blame mama for being irresponsible and leaving the boy alone. They say her death was a blessing, or she should have been tried for murder. I know my mother, and she was never one to be irresponsible. I also know that she would have chosen death herself because she could not have ever forgiven herself for Eddy's death. Suddenly, it was as if I could see it all now, as if mama were speaking to me, explaining it all to me.

A sense of peace came over me, and I was no longer bitter at God. I understood. She chose death herself when she realized that her charge was deceased.

We continued our discussion with a full sense of realization. Mama gave her life to try to save Eddy. She paid the price with her life without any selfish thought.

Mama managed to make it out of the front door with Eddy in her arms. Engulfed in flames, her skirt burned like a torch. She collapsed onto the rock porch, cremated by the fire and intense heat just moments before I appeared.

Oh LJ, I thank the Lord for exceptional people like Mrs. Miller. She and I developed a unique bond. She understands me as well as any living person. She had witnessed events that I was thankful I had not. She told me how brave I was to endure the story. I insisted that it was not bravery at all. The truth is stronger than all of us, and with that knowledge, I could move on with my life. She treated me with maturity, and in return, I am choosing adulthood instead of a young waif.

She then told of how Mr. Geddes had appeared almost immediately. He picked me up off the cold, wet ground after I collapsed. Ed demanded water, which was used to wipe my face. He was not the one who threw it upon me. He ordered someone to get a blanket for me, which he wrapped me in and carried me away from the ruins of the house. He told people that he was the closest thing to kin, whom I have right now.

Jesse took control of Tillie. It was not until Doc Brannen came around that either man gave up his job. She expressed that the men regarded their roles most seriously and would not let anyone help.

Dr. Brannen and Sandy Donohue were severely burned fighting the fire. Doc insisted that Tillie and I be taken to his house to recover. Ed stayed with us to see to it that we were made comfortable. He assured us that he would see to it that our brothers were notified out on the range, and Doc sent a telegraph to Nellie, who was living in Yuma at the time. He told everyone how our family had taken him in when he was new to town.

It comforted me to know that Ed cared for me during the night. I was not alone or abandoned. I know that Ed and I will be connected forever in life through this tragedy. He mourned beside us, sharing our pain.

Boots finally made an appearance several days later. She was covered in soot and looked scrawny. Mrs. Miller took her in and cared for her, bathing her, and gave her all the cream she could drink. She and Mr. Miller kept watching for our cow, who had wandered off during the chaotic scene. As I was leaving her house, I asked if she could continue to watch Boots and the cow for us, as we were not sure yet of where we would end up living. She agreed and kissed me on the cheek. I returned the kiss and hugged her tightly.

Angels come to us, often disguised as humans. We are grateful to have them in our presence

CHAPTER FIFTEEN

After a Funeral, Life Must Go On

20th June 1892

I will pick up here, with my story. The men came from three various directions: all working in varied areas within the territory. George arrived first since he was at Bellemont. By the time I saw him, his clothes and face were covered in soot from being at the house. He gave us a stern warning not to go there. He looked at me straight on with a firm "I mean it, Lizzie."

I could not stay away. The family gathered when everyone arrived in town to plan the services. Well, not me, as I was thought to be too frail. It allowed me to sneak over to the house. My legs were trembling as I stood in the muddy soot-covered yard, blackened timbers strewed around haphazardly and soaking wet so that they could not reignite. The smell gagged me as I made my way up to the sandstone steps to the charred doorframe. How lonely it looked, standing there all alone with no house to surround it. I cautiously entered, making my way through remnants of furniture and logs.

There was no roof, or second story left. I stood where I thought little Eddy's bed would have been. I was right because there in the ash was the tip of the cross from mama's crucifix, which she had it hanging on the wall. Though most of it melted, and you could no longer see that it was Jesus. I knew that it was still her most prized possession. I tucked it into the pocket of my borrowed dress and devised a plan.

I then went in the buggy where I had placed you just hours prior. To my great relief, you were okay, LJ. No harm came to you. I held you in my arms and dropped to the ground sobbing. That is where my family found me. I was getting a lecture from everyone when George finally came to my rescue. "With much thought, I think it is time to stop treating Lizzie as a small child and realize she is now a grown woman." It was as if the patriarch of the family had granted my freedom to me.

Nellie secured rooms for us at the boarding house on Gold Street. An outpouring of clothes came to us, donated by local families. We planned for the funeral. When I asked where mama's body was now, they looked at me oddly and replied that she was at the mortician.

Mr. Egbert, the mortician, was an odd being. To a child, almost scary if you let your imaginations go wild. She would be transported to the church tomorrow. I panicked and excused myself. I had a job to do.

I grabbed the crucifix from under the mattress where I had hidden it. Stuffing it into my pocket, I ran down the street to the funeral parlor. The mortician's family lived above it in a house. I rang the bell, and Mrs. Egbert appeared. She was a small woman with rather plain features. I told her that I must speak with her husband right now.

She said, "Yes Tillie, I know who you are, and you have my condolences on the loss of your mother." I said that I was Lizzie and not Tillie but saw that it made no difference when she finally introduced me to her husband. I gave up on that and decided to focus on why I had come.

"I need to place this cross in her hands over her heart." He mumbled that she was already placed in the casket and that I should have brought it by earlier. The Mrs. was the one who convinced him to take the cross and do as I ask. I had a few coins that I had found in the ashes of the house, and I paid him with those.

Because the man made my skin crawl, I decided to trust in the fact that he would do as I asked instead of demanding to place it there myself. I quickly thanked them and ran off out the door and back down the street.

I was happy with myself that I was brave and did not turn and run away before finishing my job. I decided to keep my outing to myself. No one but mama, the mortician, and I need to know about the crucifix.

Judge me not by how I die, judge me by how many lives I touched while I was alive.

CHAPTER SIXTEEN

Visiting Michigan

2nd July 1892

LJ, we gave mama a lovely service. Mary Josephine Sturn Hoffman interred in the new cemetery south of town. It is called Calvary Cemetery, but to non-Catholics, it is known as the Catholic cemetery. As you come in the gate, the cemetery faces north towards the majestic San Francisco Peaks. It is a peaceful place in a clearing surrounded by tall, beautiful ponderosa pine trees south of town. The burial plot itself faces east.

The Priest gave a lovely sermon at the funeral. Mama was a devout Catholic her whole life. Faith was the center of her existence. She would have been pleased with the mass.

I spoke to the undertaker before the funeral, and he assured me that the crucifix was with her. I smiled, hiding my face under the black lace mantilla, knowing that mama would be pleased.

Ed attended the funeral. When he arrived, the family asked him to sit with us. He was pleased to be regarded so highly, and to us, it felt natural to include him. The church was crowded with mourners. The town came out in full force to support the family and mourn the passing of a beautiful woman.

*****

Nellie was beside herself, knowing there were many things to take care of for the family. First on her priority list was Tillie and me. Where would we go? She suggested we go back to Michigan to live with relatives. It would be good for us. It would be a civilized place for us to recover from our loss. She would have to write to Uncle Bernard Sturn. He was the patriarch of the family on Mama's side. Uncle Bernard was never happy about the family's move west.

"Savages!" he said to my father when he was told about the move to Kansas. Nellie knew that daddy would object, and mama would be pleased. Upon everyone's agreement, she wrote to our uncle.

Dearest Uncle Bernard,

It is with great sadness that I inform you of the death of your half-sister, my mother.

Writing that line was one of the hardest things she had ever done. The words seemed to linger on the page. It sounded so final, saying it like that. The pen did not want to move on the page. Determined to finish the letter, she proceeded. She told him all that had happened and that she was only living in a small railroad house in Yuma. She would soon be moving, but for now, she had no room for the two young women.

We would not be asking you to take the girls for long, just time enough for their brothers and me to figure out where they will live. We also thought a change would do them both well. If, by chance, you cannot possibly take them both at this time, then perhaps the youngest one, Elisabeth. Elisabeth is sixteen and requires guidance.

We would considerably appreciate any help you could give us on this matter. Please respond with alacrity. Your loving niece,

Mrs. William Connor

With the letter completed and a heavy heart, Nellie told us that she sent the correspondence out. She certainly did not want to send us away to Michigan; however, it seemed like the best thing to do at the time.

A telegraph arrived a short time later from Uncle Bernard insisting that we come to stay for as long as we would like. He offered his condolences to the family after the death of his sister. He expressed how all the family was in mourning. He would provide financial support if needed but also stated to bear in mind how he would be helping the two youngest girls.

Nellie promptly replied to him with the date and time for the trip. George would accompany us to Monroe and would only be staying a few days to visit family before returning home. George had grown up knowing the Michigan family, so he was quite comfortable in escorting us to the Midwest.

Tillie, upon hearing the plan, protested immediately. She and Jesse were in love and had secretly made plans to marry in the short time since Mama's death. She could not possibly leave her beloved at this time; especially, to go to an unfamiliar place. It was just out of the question.

However, the siblings had other ideas regarding our traveling to Michigan. They needed to know that our care was being met; mama would have wanted us to go. Besides, watching after two young women happened to be too much for their own busy lives. Settling the estate would require much of their time. Luckily, she had purchased fire insurance on the house after the town had several fires.

Tillie resigned herself to the idea. Nellie convinced her that leaving always makes returning home enjoyable. Jesse was still cooperative and understanding. I am excited to travel and meet a new family.

7th July 1892

We wasted no time in preparation for the trip. As Tillie, George, and I boarded the train and headed east, we waved good-bye to family and friends; even Ed came to see us off. I was pleased that he had been there to see me off and to say good-bye. I ran to the back of the train watching the beautiful mountain range disappear into the far distance. I quietly crossed myself and said a prayer for a safe journey and a rapid return home.

July to October 1892

We had just taken the longest train ride of our life. The Michigan family welcomed us with warmth and understanding. When we disembarked the train, we became grown women. The trip away will be beneficial.

Monroe, Michigan, was a city with a refined social life. The homes were big and beautiful Victorian style with pristine lawns surrounded by fences. Inside each garden were areas of gorgeous flowerbeds, all manicured by groundskeepers.

We were taught proper etiquette, learned many new modern dances, and bought beautiful clothes for us. The Sturns saw to it that we were always busy. The family told us stories of our mother and father that we had never heard before. They even took us to Grand Rapids and showed us the exquisite Episcopalian church where our parents were married. Tillie silently wished that she and Jesse could be married in the gorgeous church.

Time passed quickly, with each day, bringing a new surprise.

October 1892

Summer was over, and fall was in the air. Tillie and I grew homesick for our town high in the mountains. The trees were in full color but lacked the beautiful sound of the breeze through a grove of Aspen's on the mountain we called home.

Uncle asked me one day to describe the beautiful mountain that I talked about so much. I first described the rise from desert to plateau and told him how in the middle of all of this, standing tall and majestic, are the San Francisco Peaks, silently watching over the land. I said to him that the Navajo and Hopi tribes considered her very special, being home to the sacred beings. Then I explained to him how it had formed from a massive volcanic eruption, making several small mountains around her as if they were her children. I sketched him which he liked very much.

The time came to return to Flagstaff. I was as apprehensive coming back as I was leaving, LJ. It is the funniest thing to think about being anxious about coming home.

The train pulled into the Flagstaff station just before Halloween. We traveled the return trip home by ourselves. Again, I kept a keen watch for the first glimpse of my mountain.

"Tillie, I see them," I cried, "Our mountains are over there."

Tillie chuckled at me and said, "Did you think that the mountains would disappear without you here to watch over them?"

We found the family anxiously waiting for us as we disembarked the train. Nellie and the two children had come from Yucca, Arizona, where they were now living. We quickly accounted for everyone, including Jesse.

However, Ed was not present.

"Where is Ed?" I questioned, all in a dither due to his absence.

"Why would Mr. Geddes be here to greet you?" retorted Nellie in a motherly fashion. "Is there something you should tell me about the two of you?"

"No," said I forlornly, not wanting to discuss the matter any further with Nellie.

"Later, you and I can discuss that," expounded Nellie as we walked toward the brand new nine-passenger buggy driven by Bert. Bert had gone into business for himself as a drayman while we were away. He was no longer a cowboy. We would witness many changes that the family had made during our absence.

We exchanged many stories in the days to come. Many questions about the Michigan family and their lives were discussed. We educated the family on the proper way to conduct ourselves. Of course, the men wanted nothing to do with that triviality.

You know LJ; I suddenly understand George. Knowing now that he spent much of his early life in the Midwest, where experiences were different. Cut from a distinct cloth, as they say. His early life was so different from ours. He was raised in Monroe in a very disciplined household. He is often the only male in a house full of women. He was just a boy and luckily could not go off to war as the older ones had to. Maybe that is why he seems to be a loner. Their lives are so structured.

We ate every meal at a sizeable well-placed table of fine German china and silver place settings. The family is of a higher society than we would ever be. I liken them to the Babbitt's and the Riordan's. George was well suited for his life. I noticed him immediately feeling at ease with the men and their daily routine. He seemed so different than the George we knew. I now understand his being unable to live how he was raised. Had we not gone back and witnessed it ourselves, I would have never known. He has sacrificed his way of life for this family.

2nd November 1892

The local men in town erected a new house for us, just down the street from the old one. The women in town decorated the house with a female touch. Mrs. Miller was waiting anxiously with Boots and the cow for me.

Tillie and Jesse spared no time in announcing their marriage. Jesse had purchased land and had begun building a home for the two of them. It was three miles north of town with a gorgeous view of the mountain. Although the family acted surprised, most had suspected that a union would take place in the future, just not as soon as November.

Honestly, though, I will be relieved when they are married. Poor Tillie is beside herself with worry feeling it is improper to marry so quickly. She should not care what others think. I do not care.

As usual, the dilemma came as to what to do about me. I see no problem, LJ, at all in my living in the new house. I could cook and take care of my brothers just fine. They know my dislike for the domestic side and balk at that idea of me being responsible for the home. They announced there were many good eateries in town that they could get food at and that it would taste like food, they teased. Usually, I would have pouted and runoff; however, I was now a refined woman, and I would not act in my old way.

As for the moment, LJ, the family has chosen to not conclude until after Tillie and Jesse's wedding day. Bert, as he prefers to be called. Tillie and I will live in the new house. George will remain in Bellemont on his farm.

9th November 1892

My dear LJ, Nellie, and Tillie tell me that they suspect there is something wrong with me. Ha, ha, I know what you are thinking. I am not crazy. I mean with my woman parts. They are concerned because my "flow" is so irregular. Apparently, I should be plagued with that bothersome nuisance once a month. I barely have had one since mama died. Nellie says she worries that one day when I marry and want to have children, I may not be able to have any. They are both quite concerned for me, but I am not. Maybe it is my youth, and I am as naïve as they claim. Time will tell.

Wedding plans are coming along for Tillie. She spends most of her time out at the cabin site. Now that the snow has happened, it is good that it is nearly complete. I rode out with her in the buggy the other day to watch its progression. I share in her excitement. She will make Jesse the perfect wife.

24th November 1892

Oh LJ, you should have seen her; Tillie made a beautiful bride. With respect to the family still being in mourning for mama, it was a small affair performed in the Episcopalian Church on Leroux Street with a few friends and family attending. Tillie has converted to Episcopalian, of course, denying the fact that it had anything to do with the beautiful Episcopal Church in Michigan that we had visited.

Tillie and Jesse will live in their new home north of town immediately following the wedding. The cabin is small now, but it will do nicely. Tillie has insisted on a honeymoon for a few nights at the Grand Canyon.

20th December 1892

Exciting news, LJ, Nellie is expecting another baby. Mama would have been so delighted. The railroad has transferred William back to Yucca. Poor Nellie can never make a permanent home anywhere. At least, she is closer to us.

Just as one flower dies, new life appears within the circle of life.

CHAPTER SEVENTEEN

Horny Toads and Yucca

Spring 1893

LJ, they want to discuss my future. I thought we were long past that dilemma. Nellie is pregnant, and she needs help with the children in Yucca. Yucca is a small train stop west of Hackberry and Kingman. It is named for the tall tree-like plants that grow in the desert. I understand that there are mountains in the far distance. Summer is hot and dry and when the wind blows - which it blows all the time - feels like a blast of hot air.

Everyone agrees that in the winter in Flagstaff, the hot air would feel good.

My dilemma is, how do I say no to my dear sister?

16th April 1893

LJ, it is against my wishes that I have found myself moving to the middle of nowhere.

"How is it possible to go from having an active social life in Michigan to nothing but Joshua trees and rattlesnakes in the desert?" I despondently ask myself repeatedly, LJ. You will be with me. Imagine me of all people, a nursemaid to three children. It is not what I have envisioned for myself.

16th May 1893

Nellie gave birth to a baby boy. William insisted that he be named Emmett William. Emmett had been born with a birth defect, which would require special care. The doctors said it is a condition called Spinal Bifida. He has a hole in the bottom of his spine. The doctors do not give him many years to live, so his birth has been a significant concern for all the family. I thought to myself, if only mama had been alive, she would have eagerly helped Nellie care for the baby. I had another thought: I would be afraid to have children.

"What if I gave birth to a baby who was not right?" I was not as brave as Nellie and Tillie. Yes, LJ, I forgot to tell you that Tillie is expecting a baby. Childbirth is not for the faint of heart, especially me. Motherhood is a demanding sacrifice, and I do not relish the idea. No children for me. If I married Ed, I would inform him right away. He would just have to accept that from me, and besides, maybe, I cannot have children. God knows what he is doing.

23rd June 1893

LJ, I think I am going crazy in this place. I have never been as hot as I have been here. It is miserable. Even the nights do not cool down. If there is a breeze, it is hot air and does not help the way you feel. It makes sleeping very uncomfortable. I hear people talk about sleeping naked, and I understand why they would.

I knew that Yucca consisted of a train station, eating establishment, barber, saloons, bath shop, and post office. There are burros, rattlesnakes, tarantulas, scorpions in abundance there. Not to mention prospectors headed for the hills in search of gold. I would trade places with them in a minute. I can feel the gold pan in my hands.

Nellie is having a difficult time raising small children here. Since the death of our mother and Tillie's marriage, Nellie is experiencing difficulty getting by. She has been sad, crying episodes. Poor William cannot manage work, children, and a wife who suffers from mental sickness.

Nellie and William have been talking of sending Georgie to the boarding school in Santa Fe. William felt that I am not to be trusted with the children. He accuses me of my mind traveling off on tangents.

"Lizzie would take the children off into the desert and follow a horny toad to its hole and watch for it to appear the next day," William exclaimed to Nellie. "No, we can't have her taking care of Georgie, Nell, and the baby."

I heard Nellie stick up for me and say, "William, you can't say that about Lizzie."

"Georgie will go to St. Michael's, a boy's Catholic School in Santa Fe," he said, having earlier made the decision; he quickly enrolled him in school. Nellie told me her protests did no good as William had his mind previously made up.

Nellie is a woman who does what her husband says. LJ, between you and me, I am not the least bit disappointed to be returning home to Flagstaff. Nellie will take the children to Flagstaff for the summer then travel with him (George) to school in the fall, at the expense of twenty dollars per month to go to school. William has a good job, but twenty dollars a month is a hefty sum. However, the railroad covered traveling expenses for employees and family members.

I could not help but think of the little girl I once met at the Loretto School. I have not seen the black onyx horse since the house fire. I wonder if it survived. Is it buried in the ashes of our past life?

******

1ˢᵗ July 1893

LJ, every day that I am home, I am grateful. I love the mountains, trees, and my life. I do not know how Nellie copes out there in the desert.

I volunteered to take the children shopping downtown. We purchased clothes and school supplies for Georgie. The school had sent a list of items that he would need. It was hard to know who enjoyed it the most, the children or me.

I made sure to pick up composition paper and ink, including instructions to write home often - his mama would be lonely with him away. Little Nell said, "Mama will be too busy with baby Emmett to miss him." Truth from a small child.

I took the children by the ice cream parlor for a soda. I can be the auntie very easily. I love to indulge the children in simple pleasures.

4th July 1893

My friends and I are planning on what to wear to a dance at Hawk's Hall. I really have missed those carefree days and going to the local events. I am ready for the world.

I saw Johnny walking up the street. I quickly cautioned him about all the children at Tillie's house. I explained where I was going, and he was immediately interested in the dance. The girls in town all love him. He is tall, good-looking, and loves to dance and party, not to mention drinking.

He told me that he would be at the dance. I knew that he would drink too much and fight. Johnny always gets in fights, celebration or not.

5th July 1893

Oh LJ, the dance was so much fun. Ed showed up alone for once, and he said he barely recognized me. I am almost seventeen. It has been a year since I have seen him. He looks and smells so good. I think we danced every waltz. I like the slow dances when we are close to each other. No, LJ, it is my secret if he kissed me. I am not one to kiss and tell; even you, my dearest journal.

I returned home late to find the house quiet. The children were sleeping, but Nellie and Tillie were up talking, which did not include me. I said my goodnights and came to bed. I miss Tillie going with me to the dances. Possibly, other than you, of course, LJ, Tillie was my best friend. I say, "was" because she is now a housewife. She hardly remembers our life before she married Jesse.

Bert and George had to go down to the sheriff's office to bail Johnny out of jail for fighting. It sounded to me like Johnny started the altercation. I heard Bert say that the Judge is strict. Bert should know; he gets in his share of fights. Tillie and Nellie agreed that if he found a good woman and settled down that a wife could put a stop to that nonsense. Bert and George rolled their eyes and pretended to agree with them.

5th September 1893

Today is my birthday, and I am seventeen years old, which makes me contemplate where I am in life. Nowhere! I am wedged in between childhood and adulthood. What is worse is that I cannot get over this feeling of being an orphan. No one else feels this way. Neither Johnny nor Bert shares this opinion with me. They say only babies can be orphans. I disagree. They are men and would not even contemplate discussing the idea with me. I feel that my loneliness in this matter complicates my dilemma.

If I had an opportunity to do whatever I would like today, I would ride my horse as far away as I could or maybe- that is it, travel. See new lands that I can only gaze at in books or at the picture show. Paris, London, or perhaps even Australia.

With all the commotion going on in this house, no one can get any sleep. Bert went to sleep out in the barn. He can sleep just about any place.

7th September 1893

My goodness, it took everyone to get Nellie and Georgie to the train. Nellie is leaving baby Emmett and Nell here with Tillie and will pick them up on her way home to Yucca. Little Nell was missing her mama before she ever started her trip. Georgie was the man of the family when his dad was not around. He had to show little Nell how brave he was, even though, inside, he was nervous. I had a longing to go with them. I could feel the itch to do something different still building inside me.

13th September 1893

Today, I confessed to the family about mama's crucifix. I know I cannot keep a secret for very long. It was Nellie's fault because she brought us each one back from Santa Fe.

"It's just like the one mama had," Tillie said, trying to hold the tears back. "We never found mamas, did we?"

I could not hold it in, so I confessed to the family about what I had done with the crucifix. Tears were flowing down my face as I told them the story of the undertaker and the cross. All the family thought that it was right what I did with it. As usual, George stuck up for me, "That is where it belongs."

"It didn't protect mama, did it?" Johnny barked.

"Yes, it did. Now we all have one to protect us," Nellie exclaimed.

Johnny could not be stern for too long and said, "Lizzie better take mine. She is going to need two if she hangs around Ed Geddes." Everyone, excluding me, was trying hard not to laugh, but I could not help but chuckle. I am confident that a man to care for me was what they had all secretly been praying for.

11th October 1893

I have started to work at Doc Brannen's store. It gives me extra money to save. George gives me an allowance from mama's money, but it is not much. I am holding cash back for traveling. I have all the clothes and bonnets I will ever need.

29th December 1893

Tillie gave birth to a baby girl. Doc Brannen delivered her with no complications. Thank the Lord; both mother and baby are excellent. Of course, it is snowing quite hard outside. Nellie came for

Christmas with her children and stayed to help Tillie. She will be an excellent mother. The family keeps growing.

If offered a choice, would you really want to change lives with someone?

CHAPTER EIGHTEEN

A Chance Meeting

6th June 1894

I attended mass today for the first time in months. Friends made me feel guilty for being absent for so long. I guess I am melancholy today. A group from church is planning an outing to the Mormon Dairy west of town. It is not an adventure that I ever thought about. I mean, I am certain it will be fun, and I shall definitely attend, but shouldn't I be experiencing more excitement being young and single? Some are convinced that I shall become an old maid. Phooey on them. I know who I want, and I shall wait.

After church, I felt like being alone, so I walked south down towards Milltown. It was a beautiful late spring day. The days are hot, but there was a cool breeze. Spring was not yet ready to give into summer. I have seen it snow in June.

Wrapped up in thought, I did not notice that someone was walking behind me. A slight pull on my hat bow startled me and brought me out of my daydream.

"Hey, gorgeous," Ed said as I turned around. "Where are you off to this beautiful day?"

"Walking, silly, can't you tell?" I teased. Could he hear my heart pounding with excitement? I wondered?

"Want a friend, or do you want to be alone?" He knew that when you needed to be by yourself, there was nothing to do except being unaccompanied.

"Walk with me," I demanded.

"I was looking for you. I saw your family in town, and you weren't with them," Ed said inquisitively.

"Yeah, I had enough of the family for one day. I might walk down to the cemetery and visit mama's grave," I said quietly. It is nice to have mama buried in Flagstaff instead of Albuquerque like my father. He is too far away.

It was so scary LJ; we were walking and visiting when suddenly a pack of dogs came running toward us. Ed was ready to grab his gun to scare them away when I practically jumped into his arms. He said he wanted to lecture me about gun safety, but the dogs were closing in on us. He shot towards them but did not harm them. The dog packs in town are becoming a real problem for people.

I just held on tightly to his neck as the dogs ran off. I was not as scared as I let on. I think Ed enjoyed me in his arms, for he did not let go of me. When he put me down, he blurted out for me to be his date for the Military Ball next month.

"Oh good," I said, talking aloud. "I already have a date for the dance on Saturday night at Hawk's Hall. However, I will attend the Military ball with you," I said curtly. I did not want him to know that I lusted over him and would prefer to go with him instead of Bill Shroyer. Actually, Mr. Shroyer had stopped by the house when Nellie was in town and asked me to go to the dance with him in front of her. She immediately insisted that I should go with him. Yes, I am calling him Bill from this day forward. William seems so stuffy. No, I will not call him Billie. That seems far too immature for him. Even though my family uses the "i.e." for most of us. Just as I would not call Ed, Eddie.

"There is a dance on Saturday?" he questioned me. "Who is the lucky guy?"

I explained that Bill was a friend of ours, and I was sure that he had met him before and just did not remember.

"You mean that man who claims to be a gold miner and is twice your age?" Retorted Ed, jealously.

"You are twelve years older than me, Ed Geddes," I snapped. "You are jealous."

"Absolutely, I don't want any other man dancing with you," he said honestly.

Can you imagine; I did not have a reply to that? Ed had never once spoken that way to me. I was on cloud nine as we walked down towards the cemetery. Ed left me alone to sit by my mother's grave. I wanted so much for mama to be there right now so that I could ask her advice on men. Bill asked me first, and I would honor that, I thought, but if Ed just happened to be at the dance and asked me… I would have to be polite and dance with him too. Problem solved.

"Ed, I have an idea," I shouted hurriedly. "If you show up and ask me to dance, I will dance with you."

"Why, Miss Hoffman, is this your first kiss from a man?" he said as he kissed me again.

My mind was racing, and my heart pounding. I started to remind Ed that he had kissed me once long ago, but he stopped me from saying anything. I did not want this moment to end. I had always loved him, but I never knew that he felt the same. He removed his coat and placed it on the ground for me. We stayed locked in each other's arms in the warmth of the sun for the remainder of the day. No, LJ, remember I do not kiss and tell.

The sun was setting in the sky when we realized we should begin walking back to town. I knew that my family would be getting worried since I had been gone all day. However, when Ed asked me to go to dinner with him, I did not hesitate.

We entered the restaurant together as people turned to stare. Gasps could be heard when they realized that it was me with a man. I greeted people I knew with an air of importance. Secrets in this town were in the paper the next day, anyway, so why not make the most of it. Gossip, they could. I could not be prouder.

Headline: *The town tomboy had a man on her arm last night.*

I was halfway through a massive steak that Ed had ordered for me when Bert and George walked into the restaurant. They had been searching for me for close to two hours. While they were looking for me, they ran into someone who had just left the restaurant and told them where I was. There was anger in their faces.

You know me, LJ; I never like to see my brothers get mad at me. Usually, I would have tears come to my eyes, and that would stop them in their tracks. Not this time, I thought to myself. I was a woman now; Ed told me so himself. I would defend myself; not show Ed, I was a baby.

However, Ed had other ideas. Not wanting to insult my brothers, he insisted that he had been nothing but chivalrous towards me. Ed told them where the two of us had walked and that we were both hungry when we reached downtown. George requested Ed to ask for permission next time he takes his sister on a walk. Ed quickly agreed.

Humiliated by the talk between my brothers and Ed, I sat and fumed. The men did not even acknowledge that I was sitting there. How could he kiss me one minute and then act as if I were not present the next? Without the men noticing, I quietly removed myself from the restaurant.

Ed Geddes would have to bow down to me and beg me for forgiveness before I would kiss that man again.

I was told that my sisters would be speaking to me about that later. I pray that later will never come.

Am I indeed a jealous woman or just pig-headed?

CHAPTER NINETEEN

17th March 1895

I have the undivided attention of two men. I desire nothing more because both men lavish me with gifts. Ed and Bill compete to be the number-one man in my heart. It is almost comedic, LJ. I can be shopping with them, and I pick a trinket or hat up to inspect, but what it is purchased for me immediately. I have taken to placing my arms behind my back and not letting on that I like something. I enjoy the affection from both, although my heart is set on Ed. If forced to choose today, it would be him.

We shall see how the Saint Patrick's Day dance works out since both will attend. I will have a man on both arms. It should give the town gossips a story to tell tomorrow. Luckily, both men are courteous to each other when they are both with me. I said to them, I would not tolerate fist fighting around me. If they wish to have an altercation, they must do it when I am not present. I will just read about it in the newspaper. Neither man wants to throw the first punch. My friends say that I am a vixen. What do you think? I suppose that I am not the first woman to have two suitors, nor will I be the last.

Nellie, Nell, and little Emmett visited for a few days. Nellie and I have become closer. She offered me advice on Ed and Bill. I confessed to Nellie that I loved Ed but knew that he was not one to settle down. He was a loner- a trait of most cattlemen. Ed wanted more than anything to have his own ranch. I share his desire for ranching. He only comes to Flagstaff on occasion from Williams. I never know where he is working.

As for Bill, he has traveled. He has a significant trip planned to search for gold. He has dreams of traveling to the Southern Hemisphere. How could I not want to do that? My only complaint is that Bill treats me with the utmost respect. Sounds silly? I know. I feel like he is my guardian. He self-appointed himself to that position since my mother died. He will only kiss me on the cheek and is never anything but courteous. I feel like he is there at times with Ed and me to prevent us from being alone. LJ, is Bill trying to be my father, my guardian, or my beau? I will not let myself think about it because it is disturbing to me.

3rd May 1895

I attended the Gala with Bill. Ed did not make an appearance. When Ed appeared at my house a few days later, he gave me a piece of his mind. He informed me that I owed him alone time then he apologized with a very passionate kiss.

We tried our luck at riding bicycles. This newfound way of getting where you need to be is ducky. It is like riding a horse except that you are on two wheels. A big man, such as Ed, does look a bit comical since he zigzags back and forth on it while cussing all the way up the hill. I am more refined than he is on a bicycle. I first rode in Michigan, where it was all the rage.

We followed the game trail up the mesa. I love the view from up there. The wind came up and almost blew our food basket away. We used the wind as our excuse to cuddle up snug. Ed's hands were rough and weatherworn with calluses on the palm of his hands. I pretended to be a palm reader. I traced my finger slowly around his hand. Our eyes met, fixated on each other. Slowly, I told him he was a man who worked hard. I then said I saw him on his own ranch. He asked if I was on the ranch. That question surprised me, LJ. I was flustered. I did not want to seem easy; I told him that travel was in my fortune. He seemed disappointed with my answer. We made up for it later.

4th May 1895

I awakened from a nightmare last night. I was on a black horse; Ed and I were quarreling with each other. The horse reared and came down on top of Ed. Panicked- I awoke to the reminder of the little girl at the Loretto School and the black onyx horse she once gave me. I felt relieved after I had my wits about me to realize that I had never found the black horse after the fire. Surely, LJ, I am beyond its curse.

1st June 1895

LJ, I have been seeing Ed more than I have been seeing Bill; he goes off mining around the Grand Canyon. He is talking about going to South Africa to mine for gold. There have been some significant strikes down there. It sounds so exciting. He jokingly invited me to go along with him. At least, he said he was joking. One can never tell with him. He has a very dry sense of humor, and sometimes I cannot know when he is joking and when he is earnest. At least, when Ed drinks too much, and Bill is there, he can handle his drunkenness better than I can.

The other night at the dance, Ed dressed as a stylish cowboy, and I came as a saloon girl. Ed even won first prize for his costume. Of course, is all Bill has to do is read the newspaper and find out about us. Flagstaff is so much fun. There is always something to do. The circus came to town. We attended arm in arm.

I loved the elephants. Magnificent creatures, I thought. I pictured Ed and me riding down Railroad Avenue on the elephants' backs, waving to the crowd of people below.

11th July 1895

I am so angry with Ed. Is all I will say for now is that we got into a nasty dispute the other night. He acted out of control with his drunkenness. He scared me so badly that I do not care if I see him for a long time. You know, he has an unscrupulous side to him when he drinks. He reminds me of Johnny. I love that man so much when he is sober.

2nd August 1895

Bill had missed us at a few events and came calling on me to find out why the absences. Was I well, had he been hurt? No one seemed to know. I told Bill that Ed and I had gotten into an argument a few weeks prior. He left town angry and drunk after shooting off his gun inside my house. I was so mad at him that I did not care if I saw him again or not. My brothers would not stand for him repeating that another time. I assumed that they had found him and taught him a thing or two.

Bill, feeling sorry for me, asked me to the International Order of Odd Fellows dance, of which he was a member. I graciously accepted his offer. I felt no guilt since I had not heard from Ed since the gun incident. Would he show up at the dance I wondered? I hate the fact that men have freedoms that women do not. Am I supposed to sit around and wait for him?

11th August 1895

Bill arrived punctually to escort me to the dance. He was dressed in what looked to be a brand-new suit right off of Mr. Salzman's clothing rack. I smiled and thought to myself that he was trying hard to impress me. He looked very handsome, but he is not as handsome as Ed. I scolded myself for comparing every man to him. Bill reminds me of George, and that is possibly why I feel so comfortable around him.

Mr. Taylor's new restaurant had a dance hall on the top story, which was where the dinner was held. They served fresh clams and mussels that had arrived that day by train from Los Angeles. Fresh beef and lamb supplied from the local ranches and fresh fruit and vegetables from Oak Creek is always a favorite of mine.

Bill escorted me back home in the early-morning hours with a polite kiss on the lips. I thanked him for a marvelous evening. I would head right to bed. I dreamed of dancing with Ed…What am I to do, LJ? It seems that I have myself in a fix. My desire to socialize makes it hard for me to sit at home and pine for Ed.

4ᵗʰ September 1895

I have not heard one word from our Mr. Geddes. I am worried that I have cast him off. I cannot reach him; he is the one to contact me. I feel that I am going crazy with worry. I will be nineteen tomorrow. I really am a spinster.

I continue to see Bill socially. We have much in common with each other. He wishes to be an adventurous world traveler, and I am desperately longing to see the world. Flagstaff is growing too big, time to get away from civilization.

"I'll take care of you, Elisabeth. I mean, come with me when I go away." It was hard to not seriously consider an offer from Bill. The relationship is making a change towards something more serious. Should I tell Ed just how much I love him before committing any further with Bill? I am at a loss as to what to do next. Ed comes first in my heart. Will I have regrets if I do not approach Ed?

15ᵗʰ October 1895

No sign of Ed in town. I have heard that he is living in Williams now and cowboying around there. Bert delivers salt to the ranchers out there and says he will watch for him. What have I done?

Christmas, 1895

Bill returned from the Grand Canyon last week. He gave me a beautiful filigree necklace for Christmas. I gave him gold cufflinks and joked that he did not have to travel to South Africa to find gold. Bert did not see Ed personally in Williams but did ask around, and people said he lived there in the winter months. I am still in a state of hesitation with Bill. He seems to be very serious about me going with him, although I do not wish to marry him or anyone else right now.

I can only see myself married to Ed.

1st January 1896

Ed appeared at the New Year's Eve Ball and had several ladies on his arm. If I did not know better, I would think his entourage was a group of ladies he paid to be with him. He seemed to be going out of his way to make me jealous. Could that be? I was not going to make a fool out of myself in front of friends and family. Therefore, I missed my opportunity to confront him. He was gone before anything could be said.

Bill could see that I was hurt over Ed's behavior. I, sort of, pouted the rest of the evening, and then he and I had words. Apparently, I ignored him when Ed was with us and was upset. He then suddenly told me that our relationship was over. I was too young, and he did not have any desire to be a nursemaid to a little girl. I am nineteen years old. He continued with a few other hurtful things, and I excused myself and went home. What an awful night. I hope the rest of the year gets better, or I am in for it. Looking back on today, Bill's behavior was so unlike him. Is this his way of letting go?

A New Year is a fresh start in life. Let us choose wisely.

CHAPTER TWENTY

The Final Straw

14ᵗʰ February 1896

The faint sound of someone knocking on my front door brought me out of peaceful slumber. It was late evening, LJ, and I thought I dreamt of it. The banging grew louder, and I rose out of bed. While I was putting on my lace robe, and I heard the clock in the parlor strike midnight. I assumed it was one of my brothers desiring a place to sleep after a night at the saloons. I unlocked the skeleton key that I always left inside the knob. The hat, height, and smell I knew to be Johnny. He was drunk. It was not until he grabbed me by the waist and kissed me that I realized it was Ed. Angrily, I pushed him away. He got up and stumbled to a chair. He almost missed the chair and would have ended up on the floor had he not caught himself. I laughed aloud.

You should have heard me cuss that man out; I said words even I did not know I knew. Then we sat quietly for some time. I made him coffee to try to sober him up a bit. He kept repeating that he needed to speak to me. He had something to tell me. I left it at that, not wanting a proposal from a man who was still too drunk to stand. It could wait.

We moved to the settee, and he laid his head on my chest. My nightshirt and lace gown were not much coverage. He kissed me and fondled my breasts. We spent the rest of the night together. I gave myself to him thinking he would propose. Oh, LJ, I am a fool for him. Never in a million years would I allow Bill to touch me the way he did.

How many months had it been since I had laid eyes on him? Six, eight, or maybe longer?

"Why is Ed here?" they both demanded. "Don't lie to us Lizzie, his horse is tied up out front. Do you want to be known as Ed's whore? The whole town knows by now. He is a married man now, or were you not aware of that? If he lied to you, we would kill him right now."

My brothers were as mad as hornets. I had never seen them so angry. My heart sank to the bottom of my stomach. Married? The son-of-a-bitch never told me he was married. I stopped cold. It was my fault. I prevented him from telling me when he first arrived. My naivety did it to me again.

I yelled at them, "You knew he was married, and you never told me?" Tears started to run down my face. "I didn't know. How could I have known?" My family all must have heard rumors of his marriage and decided to protect me from the news. Hysteria began to engulf me. I could not stop wailing.

Suddenly, Ed appeared with his gun at his side. He seemed to know precisely why Bert and Johnny were there.

I slapped him across the face. My palm stung, and he just stood there. There was no reaction from him as to my assault on him.

"Slap me back, cry, yell, scream anything but just don't stand there looking at me," I yelled. Time stood still as I stood there. Finally, Johnnie escorted me back into the house.

"Sorry Lizzie, I thought you knew. I thought that was why you were seeing that Shroyer fellow. I intended to come over last night, but I was too drunk. I would have told you sooner, had I have known you didn't know."

"No, Johnnie, it is my entire fault. I thought it was you at the door last night. I let him inside, drunk. He wanted to tell me something, and I would not let him. I thought he was here to propose to me. I did not want to have him ask me when he was drunk, and

I wanted him to stay with me. I am a whore. Do not blame Ed. Just let him go."

I finally convinced Johnnie to go outside and inform Ed to remove himself from my property. I asked him not to contact me again. Bert came inside, and I told him my story. Although not happy with me, they also said they understood. We discussed waiting a few days to divulge it to Tillie. They thought it a good idea to tell Jesse, and he could maybe keep Tillie from hearing the gossip. I would keep a low profile inside my house. For a time, I would not make a public appearance. I was very capable of that.

Now that I am alone, my thoughts are racing. I should leave Flagstaff for a time. I have money put back. I could travel… yes, LJ, that is it… travel. If I could convince Bill to take me with him to South Africa, that would be my ticket out of here. No, I would not marry him. A whore does not have to marry. I have to hurry to find him. He will leave the day-after-tomorrow on the train to Los Angeles. I will just happen to be on that train myself. Once we are traveling, he would not tell me no, nor would he abandon me.

I have much to prepare before then. What would I do without you, LJ?

24th February 1896 Midnight

I hate you, Ed Geddes!!! I hate you. I hope I never will see you again in my life! I cannot sleep. I will be glad to be gone from here. I am plagued with that nightmare.

As with all of us, there comes the point during our lives that we must leave our childish desires and thoughts behind. We are either ready to grow up or are forced into doing so. I am at that point, LJ. I had unhappiness and pain, but overall, my childhood was excellent in this mountain town. There are many memories. Where my life will take me from here, no one knows.

Plans made under duress should not be acted upon until one has had sufficient time to think them through.

WHAT HAPPENED TO US GOING TO SOUTH AFRICA? 1896-1903

The photo belongs to Garry & Judy Hoffman Collection.

CHAPTER TWENTY-ONE

Next Train to Los Angeles

25th February 1896

LJ, I will write down as much as I can on my adventure. Having made my decision to follow Bill south, I sat on a long narrow bench at the train station to wait and board the train. I was deep in self-pity when Bill approached me quietly. In the noisy train station, that was not a difficult task. He took a seat beside me. I sat on the bench, furthest back to be alone to hide and think.

I know that we will go to Los Angeles and leave on a ship to the Southern Hemisphere. I am very excited. I would never have been bold enough to do this without the recent turmoil with Ed.

My mind is going in many directions. I am angry and hurt. Ed has deceived me, and no man will ever do that to me again. It is over, finished! Never can I go back to him! I have never experienced such humiliation in my life. All I can think of is leaving.

"Oh Bill, you startled me; I didn't hear you sit down."

"Why are you hiding back here? Are you meeting someone?" Bill asked me.

"No, I am taking you up on your offer to travel with you."

"I? Travel with me? I remember saying that to you one evening; however, I spoke without thinking you would ever take me seriously. When I set out, even I do not know where I am going. I go in the direction that life leads me. I do not take other people with me, especially women. I am as much of a loner as your brother, George." Bill's voice was getting nervous as he tried to talk me out of what he thought was a hair-brained idea. He told me that reasoning with me should be an easy undertaking, as he could never see me leaving my family behind because I am far too close to them to run away.

Boldly, I said to him, "I won't change my mind; if that is what you are thinking. My mind is made up; you will not have to look after me. I can take care of myself. You can't stop me from riding this train."

He told me that he would not be responsible for me, should I decide to be stubborn.

Obviously, LJ, he does not know me! I could feel the tension coming from Bill. Poor man, I thought to myself. You could tell he was stunned and did not know what to do with me. I would just have to take over and be the boss. I was very good at telling men what to do. I had a way with them that made some men surrender to me. At least, that is what Tillie always tells me.

Time was running out for Bill to convince me to return home. The train was just pulling into the station.

"Let's get on board; it's too noisy here," I said as I got up and began to walk to the train. Bill obeyed as if he were a young boy following his mother. I smiled to myself and thought that this would be easy.

As the train pulled away from the station, I ran down to the back of the caboose to watch my mountain slip slowly off from me. The mountain is such a beautiful sight. I will engrave the picture in my mind forever. Will I ever see my mountain again?

We traveled west at a steady pace. When passing the towns of Williams, Ash Fork, and Seligman, the conductor would call out the names of the settlements just before arriving at them. He was giving the people getting off the train enough time to be ready to disembark. Each time Bill glanced over at me; it was as if he were hoping I would disembark.

Soon the train was passing Hackberry. I knew this town. Nellie and William once lived here. Looking out the train window, the community appeared to be deserted. A once-thriving silver-mining community was now a ghost town. I was astonished at how quickly a town could come and go in a matter of five years.

We stopped in Kingman; a small thriving town built by the railroad. Each stop we came to, Bill looked at me as if he expected me to go running out of the train in fear of my new adventure. This just caused me to dig my heels in deeper. When the train pulled into Yucca, Nellie, was waiting. An urgent telegraph arrived from Tillie telling Nellie to check the train for me. Sure enough, I was on board. I lowered the window and yelled at my sister, "See you in a few years!" I had never spoken to my big sister like that before. I will make it up to her next time I see her. I will make it up to everyone in my family when I strike gold.

I am a grown woman, and they all know there is no stopping me once I make up my mind. At least none of them; there was only one man [Ed] on this earth who could have brought me back, but no more. Did he know? Would my family tell him that I was gone?

The train was back on its way towards Needles and beyond. I settled in my seat. From here on out, I would see a country that I have never seen before. My adventure was officially starting.

"Bill, what do you suppose it is like in South Africa?"

"Hot, wet, snakes and crazy miners; It ain't a place for a young woman like you," he said with sternness in his voice. "If your daddy were alive, he'd turn you over his knee and spank you. It is what I should do, but I will not harm a lady. He'd probably shoot me for not stopping you from getting on board this dang train."

"Oh, now Bill, don't speak like that," I begged him. "Sounds like you are having second thoughts about me coming with you."

"Second thoughts? Now just you wait a darn moment miss. Let us clear the air right now. I did not invite or encourage you to come with me," he said emphatically. "I am too old to be a nursemaid to a flighty young girl. Don't you go forgetting that either? You are on your own. Right now, I am as angry as a bull with a rider."

"Fine with me," I said, not letting him see that my feelings were hurt.

"I can take care of myself!"

The train is coming to a stop in Needles, California. I will pick up my small piece of baggage and exit the train. I will not speak to Bill again.

26th February 1896

I had two men fighting over me, LJ. I know I should be paying closer attention to my surroundings, but I did have to laugh. Anyway, a man waiting at the station immediately came up to me and asked if I was going to the hotel?

"Why, yes, sir," I answered in a flirty voice.

"I can take your bag across the street for you," he said. Then before I knew it, Bill came up from behind me and grabbed me by the arm.

"Honey," Bill said in a delightful voice, "I asked you to wait for me." Off we went, with me trying hard to get away.

"That man could have stolen your bag back there and robbed you of all your money. Be careful from this day forward," he lectured. With that, I broke down into tears; the unique whimpering that would make a man do anything for me. I was sobbing so hard that everyone could hear me. My tears chastened Bill. He led me to a bench in front of the hotel.

"Where did that come from?" he asked me, feeling confused about my behavior.

"I cannot go back home. Ed has shamed me forever." Then LJ, I proceeded to tell him the truth as to why I was leaving town. You could see the anger in his eyes. If Ed had been here, I know that Bill would have liked to set him straight; to put it nicely.

"I will get you a room for the night, and then you will be headed back home tomorrow on the train going to the East," he said smugly, thinking that he could reason with me. He prided himself not to worry about things because life takes care of everything.

I slept very well that night in my bed at the hotel.

The next morning, I seated myself down on the bench and proceeded to wait for the train going west. Bill arrived and mentioned to me that I would be going home today. I politely smiled at him and said nothing. I was going along with him, and I would be fine. I boarded the train and sat down next to an older woman. The rest of the train ride was agreeable as I visited with her during our journey to Los Angeles.

I disembarked the train, and I wished my fellow passenger good-bye. As I walked past Bill, I did not make eye contact with him. However, I said, "Come on, Bill, we need to find a hotel and make arrangements for our travel."

I was dismayed at the weather in Los Angeles. The temperature for late February was warm with a light breeze. You could feel the moisture in the air. The landscape was green, with flowers growing all around. There were carts of fruits and vegetables lined up along the street. All of this fresh food in February, I had never seen the likes of it in my life.

My Spanish was limited to a few words, and I could converse with the locals at the street markets. Luckily, I knew the words to many foods. I asked the woman for Pan de Molde and Vino Tinto; bread and red wine.

I could feel Bill watching my every move. Was he observing my actions to see how I handled myself in the unfamiliar territory? If he needed to see how strong I was, I would show him.

We came to a Spanish style hotel. The building was made of adobe. Of course, my time in New Mexico made me very familiar with adobe; the earthen clay mixed with straw and then sun-dried made a sturdy brick, which was naturally warm in winter and cool in summer.

"We'll stay here," I informed him.

"We need dos rooms for several nights," I said to the clerk behind the desk.

"Excellent, Senora."

"No, it is Senorita, por favor." The clerk excused himself for his mistake. Imagine him thinking I was married, LJ.

The room was large, with elegant Spanish furnishings. I had immediately sunk myself into a leather chair, brightly painted with a parrot and greenery on it. Before I knew it, I found myself awakened by the smell of cooking consuming my room. I was hungry.

Leaving my room, I could smell the sweet gardenias, their aroma almost intoxicating. I made my way down onto the plaza, where, in the middle, stood an ornate fountain flowing with bubbling water. Never before had I seen so much water. Water, or the lack of it, had plagued my family forever.

I must have caught the eyes of several young men in the courtyard because of all the catcalls coming from them. I blushed and found a small table. Suddenly, the waiter started bringing me glasses of Sangria.

"I did not order these," I told him.

"They are a gift from your admirers."

I was about to pick up one of the glasses of fruity wine when I discovered that the men had surrounded me. My nerve was weakening as I watched as they handed me pesos. Shock ran through my body as I realized they thought I was a *prostituta*. I stood up to leave and realized that they had other ideas. A young man pointed to a hallway and grabbed my arm. They began pulling at me. I was trying to explain that I was not a prostitute. The more I fought, the closer the men crowded around me. There was no escape. I began resisting them harder and harder. I would not succumb to this treatment. Halfway down the dark hallway, I heard gunfire and orders shouted from the policía. The crowd soon scattered in every direction. Bill and the policía were all that remained in the plaza.

"Elisabeth, are you hurt?" cried out a distressed Bill.

"No, just a bit shook up."

"Let us call that your second lesson in dealing with men of the world. You are not allowed out, unaccompanied. You have much to learn about how to conduct yourself away from home. I may not always be there to rescue you. I feel that the sooner our plans are made, the better. Unless you are now ready to return home? I shall arrange for that immediately. I will even escort you."

"Absolutely not! Did you have something to do with this? Did you set me up to test me? You are right. I made a mistake, and I will be much more careful in the future. I think that I should carry a small pistol. Tomorrow you and I shall go and purchase one for me." The next day, I found a nice little pistol that I could place in a pocket

I had created in my skirt. I carry the gun with me wherever I go now. Of course, when Bill asked me if I could shoot it, I said proudly, "If Annie Oakley can do it, then so can I." That seemed to break the tension that had been building between the two of us.

Live your beliefs in what is right; be strong, keep your chin up high, and your eyes wide open. Do not settle for less than you are worth to yourself.

CHAPTER TWENTY-TWO

What Direction are we Going?

1st March 1896

Apparently, LJ, I do not understand men. I have been busy learning all I can about South Africa for our upcoming adventure. Just today, I overheard Bill tell a friend of his that he is going to British Columbia. When I confronted him about it, he told me not to worry - that he was looking at other options for us. I think he is planning a charade for me. You know, tell me one thing, and then he will go to another. I am feeling somewhat alone and not trusting him. I will try to weasel more out of him later.

2nd March 1896

I told Bill precisely what my suspicions were and that I want the truth from him. We do not exactly talk much. I seem to do the majority of the conversing. He did not deny talking about going to British Columbia. He explained to me that he had news of a find up there and was waiting for more information from his friend. He had mined in that area before with little luck and wants to be sure that his information was correct. I feel as if I am wasting time and money just sitting here in Los Angeles. However, it turns out; I shall either be hot in the jungle or freezing in Canada.

3rd March 1896

A telegraph arrived for him today. He seemed happy and told me to buy warm clothes. I assume that means we are headed north. He is testing me again to see how far I will travel with him. As I understand it, he is a good man, and I have no reason not to trust him wholeheartedly.

4th March 1896

Bill and I have booked passage on a ship headed to Seattle, Washington. From there, he said, we would purchase some necessary items for our trip.

I sent a letter home to the family telling them of our plans to head north. It saddens me dearly to be away from my family, but I cannot return home. This time, I have pondered my choices. I feel that this decision is best for me. As for Ed, I am not with child, so that is a blessing in itself. I think that it is highly unlikely that I could ever have children since I do not have a flow. I am a broken woman, which makes me feel as if I must prove myself in other ways. However, on the other hand, it gives me a freedom of sorts to be more independent.

Bill keeps to himself. He has not asked anything of me and talks so little that I know nothing about his family. Is all I have heard him say is that he has too many brothers and sisters, and they all live in Indiana. I assume his parents are still alive by a comment I overheard. If this is the man I knew in Flagstaff, he seems different somehow.

8th March 1896

As the ship pulled out of the Los Angeles harbor, my heart raced, and I thought of Miss Weatherford and her prediction of me being a world traveler. Seattle, here we come. Look at me, daddy – I am on a real ship!

9th March 1896

The Captain and I have become close. I adore hearing his stories, and he delights in hearing mine. I have never met a man like him. He looks so distinguished in his uniform. I think he is the most good-looking man I have ever seen. He makes me feel like a lady. We sit at his table for dinner, and he often will reach over and stroke my hand under the perfectly ironed cloth. I return the affection to him.

It excites me in ways I have never felt before.

10th March 1896

Bill is oblivious, playing poker until the wee hours of the morning. This gives me the freedom to do as I wish. Since we have our separate rooms, he does not see that I have not been in my bed for two nights. The Captain says that I am a most unusual woman. Intriguing is one word he used. If only Tillie and Nellie could see me now, I should think they would be most surprised.

13th March 1896

We spent our last night together in bliss. How perfectly wonderful to be with someone you have no commitments to uphold. No future, no past. A secret tete-a-tete.

The Captain and I said our final good-byes in his private quarters. I shall say no more. If Bill caught on to our infatuation with each other, he never uttered a word to me. He is very respectful of my privacy, which; I appreciate. I am not in a place in my life that I need fathering. LJ, to be honest, I think I would resent him for it. He certainly had his full independence onboard the ship.

I shall put the memory of this in a special place.

17th March 1896

Seattle is a large city. A harbor town means that people arrive here every day from all over the world. There is a significant diversity of people; some stepping foot onto American soil for their first time. I am excited to be here but I am, also anxious to get on with our journey.

19th March 1896

I just finished the most extensive shopping spree in my life. We purchased provisions here so that we could get the best choice. Now, we have to wait for the tracks to clear of snow so that we can travel by train again. Possibly, we will buy our pack animals in Rossland. It is a town just north of the US and Canadian border above Idaho. It is a town that is similar to Flagstaff, or so says Bill. Logging and mining are the primary industries there. I cannot tell if Bill is insensitive to relaying plans to me, or if he thinks I can read his mind.

5th April 1896

We have arrived in Rossland, British Columbia, on a cold, snowy April evening. The narrow-gauge train is just pulling into the station. Our stay in Seattle lasted a few weeks longer than Bill had hoped. The winter was harsh.

Bill, having been to Rossland a few years before, was excited to return. This was another chance for him to strike gold. He thought that by bringing me here, I would grow tired of mining, grow homesick, and want to return home. It was self-sacrifice on his part. He could go to South Africa next spring.

After exiting the train in Rossland, Bill secured rooms for us at a hotel. Curiously, it is named the Hoffman House, indeed! I felt that was a good omen. It would be a temporary place to prepare for our expedition. As I looked around the town, I could feel a familiarity; it seemed so similar to Flagstaff, surrounded by mountains and trees. I feel comfortable here. Then I found out from Bill that we would not be staying in town. We were to make our way farther north along the Columbia River.

Bill awoke early this morning. He came to my room to awaken me, which is highly unlike him. Usually, he awakens and leaves without a single word to me. He felt I needed to go with him. Later, I found out that we were going to obtain our mining licenses. The Canadian government made a law that every miner must have a permit to stake a claim.

Upon arriving at the Office of Mining Licenses, we were surprised to see a slightly longer line of people than we expected, waiting to obtain licenses. When our turn came, I was standing next to Bill when the man behind the desk assumed that we were married.

"No," Bill said emphatically. "We are just mining partners."

The man looked at me, inspecting me with his eyes as if I were up for sale in an auction.

"Miss, have you ever done any mining before?" he questioned me.

"No, sir, this is my first time," I said proudly.

"Gentlemen welcome the new lady miner," he said teasingly. The room filled with laughter, and all eyes were on me. I had a choice, LJ; I could cry or laugh along with them. Therefore, I chose to laugh at myself, and I curtsied to the men.

"Pity, if you were married, it would be a different license," the man said, scratching his beard, "You could each get two stakes instead of one."

Bill grabbed my arm, and away we went without obtaining the licenses. I started to protest but soon changed my mind when I saw that a man was following us.

"Bill Shroyer," a man said, "I thought that looked like you ahead of me in line. Then when I saw the gal with you, I had second thoughts. It's been a few years."

Bill and the man stood and talked for some time. I grew bored and said that I was going back to the hotel.

When Bill returned, he excitedly told me that he had news of a stake that was for-sale northeast of here. I was interested in hearing all about the investment. It would take money and plenty of it to purchase the stake, but it could pay off double or triple for us if we were lucky.

"One stipulation, though," said Bill, not wanting to get my hopes up too high.

"Stipulation, what do you mean?" I asked impatiently.

"It's a big stake, and the Canadians are now controlling what each person can have. It seems that a couple," he began to say, almost stuttering, "Never mind…never mind…" He did not remember that I had been standing next to him in the Mining Office. I heard the man say that if a man and woman are married, you get double the stake.

"Are you suggesting that we get married?"

"No, I was just telling you the law," he said. "I never said anything about you and me getting hitched."

"Why not?" I asked. "Is there some reason why I am not good enough for you?"

"Now, I never said that. Do not go making something up. Furthermore, if we were to get married up here, it would just be for your protection. We will have an agreement. A single woman ain't safe. You saw those men eyeing you and catcalling to you in the license office. I'd marry you in an instant to keep you safe," he said, almost relieved to get that off his chest.

He then confessed to me by saying, "First, I have to tell you something, Elisabeth," he said, staring down at the floor. "I loved your mama. She was a right fine woman. I would have married her if she had had me. She was taken away before I could convince her. I stuck around to watch over you. Your family became my family. That is why I cannot let anything happen to you. You are like the daughter I never had. No one needs to know any of this except you and me."

LJ, Bill told me more than I had ever imagined he would. With that knowledge, I agreed that I would marry him, with the understanding that when I went back home, no one ever had to know. I would be free of him to marry again. No strings are attached.

7th April 1896

I am now a married woman. We found a Justice of the Peace to marry us. We had a lovely dinner together and then retired to our room that the Mrs. had made up for us. I do not seem to do anything the standard way, do I, IJ? I officially left Lizzle Hoffman behind and have now become Elisabeth Shroyer.

I was determined to respect my husband, knowing that with marriage, it was expected to share the bed to seal the union. I would wait and see what Bill wanted - for, after all, I was his wife now.

We drank the champagne Mrs. Hoffman had provided for us and toasted our new life together. For richer or poorer… we dropped the poorer and toasted to affluence! Laughing over this, he kissed me tenderly on the lips and then moved away from me. I felt a little rejected and disappointed. An agreement was an agreement, and he was upstanding enough not to betray his word, no matter what. I highly respected him for that. Our bond in trust was sealed. As my father used to say, "A man's word is really all a man owns in this life." I slipped into bed, feeling the effects of the Champagne.

Meanwhile, Bill made himself comfortable on the settee. Later, I heard him steal out of the door. I knew, at that moment, that he needed to be apart from me to keep his word. Not being able to go right back to sleep, I decided to write my thoughts down. A woman has an expectation about "that special night." Moreover, I am no different from any other woman.

8th April 1896

We went again to the Office of Mining Licenses and announced to the clerk, from yesterday, that we were married. We got our mining licenses for the same stake. Now, we just need to find gold.

Bill decided that I should tell my family. WHY? I retorted back to him that he should be doing the same thing. He muttered something that sounded like they would not be interested, and besides, it was none of their business. He would just send money home to them when we struck gold. I was curious and knew that I would bring the subject up again one day.

I gathered a pen and paper from the lobby of the hotel. I quickly composed a letter to my family. I explained our marriage arrangement and my plans to remain in Canada and become a miner. I knew that Tillie and Nellie would be shocked at the news. They knew more about mama and his relationship than me, and she would think it reprehensible of us. They would miss me dearly. We had never been apart for very long at a time. My brothers would be surprised, but none would condemn me for my decision to marry. As far as being a miner, they would be wishing it had been them in Canada staking a claim.

13ᵗʰ April 1896

I will bring you up to date since we have been so busy. After many days spent loading our supplies and obtaining pack animals, we were ready to head out on the trail.

My new home is to be a durable canvas tent, my makeshift kitchen, a window to the world. I am ready mentally and emotionally. We would place a canvas partition between us, both having privacy but not giving an indication of our separate lives to the outside world.

I learned that the men head out early in the day to mine, leaving the women to take care of the housekeeping. As I quickly realized, a woman's job was to do laundry, cook, repair clothes, and be a nurse. When I finished my chores, I could attend to what I came here to do- mine for gold.

You should have seen me, LJ; I found myself in a stream of water that was frigid from snow runoff that my toes had no feeling in them. I was subsequently so intent on finding the gold that I did not notice my feet were beginning to get frostbite. I filled my pan with rocks from the bottom of the stream. I knew that my first gold nugget was there, just being elusive. If only I could find gold. The thought took over my mind, and I could think of nothing else. Gold consumed my thinking. I was bitten by Gold Fever!

Suddenly, I spotted a shiny rock sitting in the sift pan, almost teasing me. I reached into the pan, ready to pick it up when Bill called to me. I jumped, releasing it into the air and spilling its contents into the stream. I let out a cry that sent him running to my aid.

Thinking that I was injured, he came running until he realized that I was okay. I was submerging my head into the stream to search for the piece of gold. Stubbornly, I would not surrender the nugget without a proper search.

Bill, tugging on my arm, managed to pull me from the water. I looked like a small, drowned rodent. My hair was wet and down in front of my eyes. I clenched my hand tight, causing it to turn pale white. I began to shake violently from the cold and started to feel the numbness in my feet.

He picked me up and started to carry me back to camp. As he climbed over the rocks to the bank, we both went down to the ground. I, still holding my fist tight, tried to get up, I quickly found myself sinking into the mud. Soon, both of us were covered in mud from head to toe. We looked at each other and began to laugh. I then opened my hand to show Bill the oversized gold nugget that had started the whole fiasco.

"That's my girl. You show the world that you can do a man's job. It is a beauty. It looks like it may weigh a few grams. Now, let us get you into some warm clothes," he said endearingly.

I sat by the fire that Bill had stoked, eyeing the nugget, thinking how beautiful the gold was- a bright shiny color like the warmth of the Sun. It would bring the right amount of money if one were to sell it. I have already decided to save my first piece of gold for good luck. I will sell the next one I find, but not this one. This one is my proof to family back home that I accomplished what I set out to do. I slept that night dreaming of gold and riches.

Gold is precious to man; more valuable, it seems, than man's relationship with himself.

CHAPTER TWENTY-THREE

Move North

22ⁿᵈ April 1896

LJ, I wake up early to finish my daily chores. Then I can go to the stream and pan for gold. Bill has done better than I have, although he has had more experience. He is very patient as he sifts through the sand and rocks. I observe him, trying to learn from him. He is so muscular for his age. I compared him to George, and I have to laugh. George looks like the bear in the store window, soft and cuddly. The days are growing longer, which is nice since that allows us more time to pan.

We have fellow miners camped close to us. Women are scarce in these parts. It is why Bill insists that we share the big tent. A large sheet of canvas separates my cot and belongings from him. I keep my clothes inside a trunk, and on the top is where I have placed my hairbrush and toiletries. I think I shall purchase a doily in town next time we go. You would be impressed at how few clothes I have now. This means that mending is most important. I thank my mama, with every stitch I take, that she had the forethought to be persistent with me and force me to learn such a mundane task.

To our neighbors, we appear to be loving newlyweds. His morning kiss on my lips has become a ritual that I return with a kiss back to him. He is forever telling me to be careful.

"Don't be overly friendly with any man. Married or not, a man may take your actions as flirtatious."

I keep my distance and only speak to them when Bill is next to me. We sleep with pistols beside us to protect us from man and beast. We have more than enough food supplies to last us several months, as we live on fresh fish and game. I cannot wait for the berries to come on, as Bill makes me eat the watercress for nutrients.

10th May 1896

We have had some problems with the men next to us. We have moved our camp farther away up on a hill. We can see them better than they can see us, from where we are now. There are tall thickets all around, and it stays light all but a few hours. We are fearful of leaving our camp to go to town to the Assay Office. We have to hide our finds carefully.

One day, Bill was hunting, and I was down at the stream panning; however, I always carry a basket of clothes with me so that I appear to be washing instead of panning. I heard the sound of rustling in the grasses. I hid my pan inside the laundry and placed my hand inside my pocket on the pistol. I headed back to camp. Hindsight tells me now that I should have stayed by the stream and not gone to the tent.

As I opened the flap of the tent to enter, I felt a blow to my head. I was out cold. The next thing I remember was Bill holding me and praying. Were we dead, because before now I had never heard him pray? Admittedly, a man like him only prays when the Lord is standing in front of him, deciding if he should go to heaven or hell.

The way my head throbbed, I was sure I was in hell. I had a strange sensation between my legs, and I felt sticky. A sudden realization came to me that my body had been violated. I seized with pain in what seemed like every inch of my body when I tried to move. Not only was I in pain, but I was humiliated. How could this happen to me? I am so careful and aware of my surroundings. I feel anger and rage. I have never seen Bill so distraught. He left me with another pistol. I can only imagine what his intentions are now.

Bill informed me that he would pack up tonight, and we will move at first light. I inquired if we should notify the authorities back in town, and he told me that would not be necessary.

15th May 1896

My arm is strained, I will not write much today. I have bruises on my face and body. I am alive. My rapist did not kill me. That night, I dreamed I heard wolves howling off in the distance. I asked Bill if they were coming for me, and he said for me not to worry about that. He also said that I did not need to worry about the men. He took care of them. I said a prayer thanking God for Bill and asking to keep him safe.

We made our move quickly and quietly, not wanting to bring attention to ourselves, or the other miners. We are in search of a new area to stake a claim.

23rd June 1896

We are in a mining camp in Salmo, British Columbia. I know that it is summer, but the temperatures are cold. We had a few snowflakes during the night. It is nothing that I cannot handle. I have a nagging desire to get a gold pan and sit by the river. I now understand the term "gold fever." I liken it to the devil holding out a piece of candy to a child who cannot tell him no. It is there in the water calling your name and teasing you to come to find it.

We have not had a claim since early May. We have been traveling east. I have overheard him mumble to himself about the Columbia River. He watches his back closely and is cautious of making eye contact with the Canadian Mounted Police. I have a new respect for how vulnerable a woman is when men in a wilderness surround her. I have vowed to myself that I shall always be on guard and take measures to protect myself, anyway that I must. My pistol is my protector, and I will not hesitate to use it.

4th July 1896

I had a bit of homesickness today when I thought of Flagstaff and the delightful, fantastic celebrations we would have on this day. I wondered to myself if my brothers competed in any of the rodeo events, and then I caught myself thinking of Ed. I was careful not to mention my thoughts to Bill, as he would immediately take it as an opportunity to try to convince me to return home. Especially now, he is on edge constantly. He trusts no one.

I remembered my father mentioning his homesickness during the Great War. He said that he could not dwell on it for too long. A short snippet of time was all one could allow yourself; otherwise, you would be sucked in like a whirlpool in a river, never to return. Many men suffered worse from homesickness than most diseases.

18th July 1896

I make every effort to impress Bill with my tenacity and strength. I do not complain or rebel when there is work to be done. I feel that he is preparing to move farther north. I have no friends since the majority of women are harlots, so I do not have anyone to hear gossip. It is lonely out here, but I am a survivalist. Money is always a concern, for you carry it all with you, and if you are robbed, you can lose everything in an instant. One constantly puts on a charade that you are penniless.

23rd July 1896

I felt brave today and asked Bill about our plans. He told me very quietly, and with the utmost confidence that we would be leaving shortly. He has arranged a passage on a boat to take us to Dawson City. He feels confident in my ability to travel further up into the Yukon Territory.

We will pack up and head Northwest, taking the All Canada Route, traveling north up to the Columbia River. Dawson City is some eight hundred miles away with winter looming. If we left now, we would be there in a few weeks.

2nd August 1896

We are not the only ones moving north. Upon boarding the boat, we found it was full. We noticed that people arriving late were turned away. It could be weeks or months, depending on the weather, before another boat set sail. Lucky for me, Bill had a reputation for arriving early. It was an adjustment for me to be punctual.

3rd August 1896

The trip was not easy, especially for a woman. I watched women with infants and small children who were ill themselves but had to care for others. I discovered that I also suffered from motion sickness. Bill, playing nurse, did not leave my side. He was not like the other men who ignored their womenfolk. I am sorry LJ, but the waves are too strong for me to continue writing.

Late August 1896

Stepping foot onto the solid ground was cause for celebration. We made our way up to the Columbia River to the town of Prince George. I learned that it was an old town that had been established before 1800. We were still 250 miles away from Dawson City, and it was already late August. We would continue by water when we could, but as we get closer, we will have to trek over the mountain ranges.

September 1896

I missed my birthday somewhere along the endless trail. I turned twenty in the middle of the Yukon. I had plenty of time to reflect on the past. My mind would wander back to my childhood in Flagstaff. Without even realizing it, my mind took me back to my mother's death. I felt the wet tears streaming down my face. The cool breeze got my attention and brought me back to reality.

Going was slow, even though we were healthy adults. We had empathy for those traveling with young children or those who did not have the stamina. Bill said that we were at an advantage since we were from a higher elevation; our bodies were accustomed to less air.

The trek was tedious.

The darkness seemed to be all around us with less daylight.

New life, new world, new experiences that all help to shape me.

CHAPTER TWENTY-FOUR

Roadhouse

6ᵗʰ October 1896

After arriving at Dawson City in early October, the days had even less sunshine. Blackness consumed us. I found that the obscurity bothered me the most; I realized I was a woman who liked the feel of the sun on my face. I was surprised to find that the area had more women like me than I would have ever imagined. Strong women: to which I could relate. I immediately felt powerful and eager to settle down here in Dawson.

10ᵗʰ October 1896

Bill is preoccupied with securing a stake. I have learned, through women's gossip, of a bountiful claim recently struck. People are arriving who are already near, but there is a fear that people will descend on the area from all over, to strike it rich. It is to our advantage that we are already here.

11ᵗʰ October 1896

The beauty of the area mesmerizes me. I wanted to explore and found a large group of people had gathered at a sleigh. Curious, I asked them where they were going. A young woman in the party enlightened me that they were going above town to watch the Northern Lights and asked me if I wanted to join them. I readily agreed and set out in the sleigh to the top of the mountain. I felt as if I were undoubtedly at the top of the world now.

The night sky came to life. Green and purple colors danced in the skies overhead. It was like nothing I had ever seen before. It seemed almost magical. I was transfixed by them when I suddenly found my mind wandering to memories of Ed, wishing he were here beside me to witness this beautiful show of nature. Guiltily, my mind changed to thoughts of Bill. I realized that in my excitement, I had forgotten to tell him where I was going. He would be busy trying to secure a stake from the locals inside the saloon. The saloons in town, it seems, is where all business transactions occur. With any luck, Bill would not even realize that I had been gone.

I am feeling somewhat giddy at the fact that I was not scared or apprehensive once on my escapade. I am not afraid because of my earlier incident. I have survived!

15th October 1896

I told Bill about my adventure to see the Northern Lights. After a short lecture about the importance of me not wandering off, he started telling me the story of the lights.

"Those lights are the hearts and souls of the animals we kill."

"Or, maybe, they are the hearts and souls of people who have died," I added. "Yes, I like that very much." Bill laughed at me. He said he loved my outlook on life. He had grown very fond of me over the last several months.

I felt brave enough to question him about his luck in securing a stake. He answered quickly, "Yes, and it includes a roadhouse."

I surprised him when I said, "I can run the roadhouse when I am not helping you at the mine. What kind of mine is it?"

"Gold, of course," he teased, knowing my real question. "It's a placer mine."

"When can we get started?" I asked excitedly.

"Right now, we can start getting supplies ready." He was also excited. "Let's get busy."

"I don't know what we need for the roadhouse until we get there," I said, thinking aloud. LJ, the thought of running a roadhouse makes me feel alive. I will have a purpose and something to do to keep me busy. A roadhouse would be mine. I should explain to you, LJ, that it is a lodge type structure where people stop to eat and warm themselves as they travel. I would have new people to meet and have conversations with and take care of. It is perfect timing since news of gold strikes would soon travel all over the world.

19th October 1896

I was lucky to have Bill. Whatever I needed; he bought it for me. It was his responsibility, and he was going to keep me safe and happy no matter what.

I wrote letters home to tell them I was okay and staying in this area for a time. Bill took the time to say to me that he wrote letters back to his mother in Indiana. He could not bring himself to tell her that he had married a woman so much younger than himself and try to explain to her that it was to keep me safe. He had been a bachelor all of his life, and it suited him. He never answered to anyone after he left home at age twenty-three. He led his mother to believe that he was in the Yukon alone. She would never find out. He could not picture taking me to Indiana to introduce me to her. She would never understand why he married me. I told him I knew and was appreciative that he told me. You know LJ, he did not have to say anything to me, and it was something he felt he needed to do for me. Now, I can try to understand him.

22nd October 1896

We took a trip down to Bonanza Cree, where the roadhouse was located to assess what we may need. As we topped the hill in the sleigh, my heart wrenched as I spotted the roadhouse for the first time. There, before me stood the two-story wooden edifice with a gaping hole in the roof. I panicked when I gazed up at the ominous heavy clouds coming in from the northwest. If Bill knew of the repairs it needed, he did not tell me. I searched his face for a look of surprise and saw none. I asked myself why he would not say anything to me. He was one of those men who thought it best not to disclose all the details. I do not like surprises, especially when it involves my home. We will need to address those repairs immediately.

Upon entering, I was relieved to see that the inside had possibilities with some work and female touches. Outside, there was a corral for the horses. There was a fenced area for the sled dogs with a large lean-to for them to escape into from the cold night air. There was a shabby building to the right of the house where hay and other supplies are stored and a chicken coop. I thought that we would get chickens right away. I excitedly said to Bill that we would offer fresh eggs for the guests. He told me that an egg sold for one dollar each, but even those were rare. In winter, it is impossible to keep the eggs from freezing, much less the chickens.

There was an ample-looking woodpile for winter. I remarked on it, and Bill quickly informed me that it was a good start, but we would need much more than that to make it through the winter. LJ, we have much work to do in a short amount of time.

24th October 1896

A wagon load of supplies arrived from Dawson City today. The work has begun. Men came from the town to repair the roof. It was finished just in time, for we have already had our first guest. I am so excited.

4th November 1896

The snow has started to fall. I am amazed at how quickly it accumulates. In Flagstaff, we would get snow, and then the sun comes out and melts it rapidly this time of the year. Here, they say, it does not melt until late spring.

Guests, all men, have started to arrive every day. Most of the people so far are from Canada or miners from Alaska. They only stay long enough for a hot meal and then start on their way again. I seem to surprise them, being a woman and all. They ask me more questions than I can ask them.

I have had to learn how to cut the ice and thaw it for water. I also have had to learn how to pack food down in the frozen turf for safekeeping. Snow, ice, and cold are a daily reality. If only my mama and daddy, and family could see me now.

20th November 1896

Bill killed a moose, and I watched as he skinned the hide and cut the meat for storing. He told me to observe, as the next moose we got will be all on me, including hunting it down. We will consume every piece of the carcass; hunters do not discard any part of the animal.

Thanksgiving, 1896

It was a sad day for me. Again, I miss my family. I pray, I get a letter from them soon. I work hard from morning until night. Sleep is a luxury in the cold northwest. I can escape by dreaming of home.

Give thanks for the many blessings you are given and forgive those who have wronged you.

CHAPTER TWENTY-FIVE

Good People Bad People

Winter of 1896-97

The long, dark, and cold winter makes one day blend into the next. For me to survive, without going completely insane, I do not allow myself to think about what day it might be. The blackness is so depressing, and the work is hard. There is no escape. The darkness seems to make the cold feel even colder.

Oh, LJ, right now, I would give anything to feel the sun on my face. I feel like I am a prisoner in a world of gloom and men with no escape. I am alone, a feeling that is unfamiliar to me.

I have to have the roadhouse ready at all times for whoever happens by. Sometimes, it is a fellow miner passing by on his lonely dogsled, tired and cold; they come in just to warm their bodies and give the dogs a resting place. Other times, it may be large groups of people needing a place to sleep out of the cold. I always have a pot of beans with biscuits and coffee ready for whoever arrives.

Homesickness becomes exacerbated. My mind fills with memories of my sisters and brothers, and that leads me to think of Ed. I cannot get the thought of him out of my head and often wonder what his life is like now. Does he ever think of me and wonder if I am alive or dead?

The big fireplace gives warmth and light to the otherwise dark open room. There is a large table with several chairs around. On the wall hangs the heads of the massive animals killed in the past.

We often have guests who stay overnight, and it breaks up the monotony. Games, like poker and dice, are favorite gambling games with the miners. They usually obtain more gold by winning at card games, or vice versa, without going into the fields. The miners have developed a game called panguingue or pan. Pan is a variation of rummy that the men place bets on to win. Often, using up to eight decks of cards, removing the Jokers, along with the eights, nines, and tens. Several words originated around the games, such as comoque, muck, and mucker (meaning the dealer), bong, and so on. I like to play just to use some of the verbiages. We sometimes have so much fun that our laughs are heard until the late hours of the night. I especially enjoy it when many people are here since up to at least fourteen or fifteen people can play at once. Bill loves to tease me that I make up the rules of the game to use to my advantage.

There are times that Bill will stay out at the mine. He wants to hire men to help him. I will never let on to him that I get nervous and lie awake with my pistol beside me. It is our secret, LJ, since I would be weak, and I do not want that to happen.

Bill and I pretend to be a happy couple when others are around. When we are alone, it seems all we can do is argue with one another. I cannot blame him, for he tried to talk me out of coming with him. Why am I so bull-headed?

I resent that I am always the one left with the roadhouse. I paid for half of this and the mine. Could Bill be deceitful? How can I trust him? I barely know him? My mind is going crazy. He says it is a condition of the darkness. He tells me that once it stays light, my mood shall improve. I pray for sunlight, dear Lord, before I lose me in the obscurity of myself. I cannot write in you anymore, for even you, LJ, are not a comfort to me, as I cannot have a conversation with you.

If someone reads this journal, know that I was once a strong and confident woman. There are places on this earth that are not meant for humans, and if I should survive, I shall be more resilient than I have ever been.

We grow stronger with every obstacle we encounter, gaining our strength through hardships we experience.

Spring, 1897

I am noticing that the daylight lasts longer, and newcomers are arriving almost daily. Am I now considered an old-timer since I survived my first winter? I feel that I am returning to my old self.

I reread you, LJ, from beginning to end. I can see who I am through you. Funny, since you are no more than a book with pages bound together by glue, and ink scribbled on a page. I have been like the butterfly, wrapped in a cocoon, awaiting the sun's warmth upon me to metamorphose into being.

Bill returned to the roadhouse after many days away. I realized that it was I, causing his absence. I shall make it up to him by improving my disposition, for even I did not want to be around me, why should he?

At Bill's suggestion, we went to Dawson City today. We were astonished to find it filled with what they are calling the first flood of tenderfoots to the gold rush. They are people who were lucky enough to have survived traveling in the winter.

The barrage of travelers has brought with it litter and filth. I heard a story that the Canadian government required travelers to have a minimum of one ton of supplies on them to travel across the Chilkoot Trail. LJ, can you just imagine that? Yes, they do give you a list of items to take with you. Supplies left strewn haphazardly in the streets. Human feces have begun to permeate the pristine air. Running wild in the streets are the horses and mules, forsaken by their previous owners. It is pure chaos in the mining town of Dawson City.

Some women have come to the area. However, most are dance hall girls, actresses, or prostitutes, all welcomed with open arms. Thanking the Lord, Bill and I had arrived before the stampede. Greed is setting in, which brings violence and looting. Bill gave the men strict instructions not to share information with others in Dawson at the assay office. Robberies are occurring out of sheer desperation to strike it rich. Thieves are becoming commonplace. There are many more Royal Canadian Mounted Police to help curb pilfering and violence.

I sent a letter home today, reassuring them that I was alive and well. Articles in newspapers around the world, I am told, talk of the gold rush. I am sure that Tillie and Nellie are beside themselves. The postmaster said to me that mail would be arriving after the ice on the waterways thawed. The government was not prepared for an onslaught of this magnitude.

Bill and I bought extra supplies to stockpile if deliveries ran short. I walked down the street, gazing into the storefront windows. I took particular notice of a hat brought all the way from Paris, France. Can you just imagine it, LJ? The bonnet was shipped all that way? I did not purchase it, for I have no use for it here. There are too many things we need for the roadhouse to be wasting money on frivolous things.

2nd June 1897

The usual flow of people into the roadhouse was interrupted when a young man appeared. My head was down when he approached the kitchen, and I looked up. I must have gasped, thinking it was Johnny. I startled him, also. He was tall and lanky, just like my brother. I immediately struck up a conversation with him. He told me that he was a farm boy from Iowa. His name was Frank, and he left behind thirteen brothers and sisters. He was instructed by his father - who had a dream from God himself - to send his firstborn son north in search of gold. The family would be rewarded with wealth upon his return home.

I directly took a liking to him. He and I talked for hours. He appeared to be enjoying the conversation, as well as I, for he did not attempt to leave. I had not even put Bill's supper on when he appeared in the kitchen. My reaction to Bill surprised Frank, and he left immediately. I do not understand how it is that a woman cannot sit and talk to a total stranger without infatuation being mentioned by her husband. Talk is talk. With that, Frank left without as much as a good-bye. I felt as though we had known each other before. I hope to see him again. I get frustrated with the absence of longevity of relationships in a roadhouse. I must admit that it has made me homesick.

Perhaps that was why Bill was unhappy with me for the rest of the night. Was he jealous or protective? I stayed up late having to finish my chores. He made no offer to assist me with any of them.

When I finally had time to write in you, he mumbled something about me taking more of an interest in that journal than in him. If he had asked me nicely, I would have put you down and talked to him.

Does he even know what I write in you?

15th June 1897

I hurried to finish my chores today and hung a sign that said, "Closed for the day." I knew that I was somewhat audacious in doing so and that I might get a lecture from Bill. I instead do not care. I want to go sit by the stream and pan for gold on this glorious day. I do not wish to be tied by my apron strings to a stove.

20th June 1897

I have been panning every chance I get. It is rather addictive. The adrenaline rushes through my body with every new pan. Yes, I have found some gold, and I divide it equally between the two of us. It is a concept that I have taught Bill to begin. It is easier to split it now than at the assay office. He had a habit of forgetting my share.

Even with a husband, a gal has to look out for herself.

24th June 1897

I broke my own rule at the roadhouse today. I have taught myself never to turn my back on anyone who enters. Well, today I did. I got caught up in hurrying to clean up, had my back turned when a man came. He was dressed like a trapper and spoke French, which is not uncommon here, and I can talk enough to get by. He was tall and appeared more substantial in his beaver coat. He had an extensive beard and an abundant amount of dark curly hair that had leaves and twigs woven into it. He was disheveled looking.

I informed the man that I was closed for the day. I had no food or drink available. I told him that he could obtain anything he wanted in Dawson City. As I turned around to walk off, I heard a loud bang of his fist on the table. He pointed down to the table, motioning for me to put something there for him. LJ, I am so naive. He did not come for food or drink, but rather me! I began to hurry off, but with his long arms, he could reach me and pull me in towards him. He started by kissing me in a way that nauseated me. My right hand had been inside my pocket all along, holding onto the pistol that I always carried on myself. I could feel my finger on the trigger. I had not ever shot a human being before today, but I had no choice in the matter. It was either my well-being or fulfill his sick satisfaction from me. I knew I had no choice. My finger pulled back the trigger...... releasing the bullet into his matted beaver coat. My mind screamed as he jolted backward onto the floor. He hit the floor hard, knocking off the tin cups that I arranged in perfect order. It all made quite a loud sound. I took my opportunity and did not look back but ran as fast as I could out of the door and down the dirt road to the mine.

Bill heard me shouting for help as I ran down the hill. Hurriedly, he grabbed his gun and made his way past me towards the house. Is all he said to me, was "Hide, and I will be back for you." I, for once in my life, did as he instructed me to do with no question.

Bill returned to find me, still hiding behind the remains of an abandoned placer mine. This time I held a shotgun in my hand. I have never been as happy to see him as I was now. I hugged him hard as he questioned me as to what happened. He informed me that I just knocked the man out cold and grazed his side with the bullet. Bill convinced the man to leave the area and not return by the threat of the Royal Canadian Mounties.

Bill says now that we must find someone to operate the roadhouse along with me. It is no longer safe in this area. My vulnerability comes from the fact that I am a young, good-looking female alone in the Yukon.

He now knows that I can do what I need to do without hesitation.

We grow in strength with every obstacle we encounter.

CHAPTER TWENTY-SIX

A Friend Comes to Stay

The photo belongs to Garry &
Judy Hoffman Collection.

17th August 1897

To my surprise today, Frank, who I told you about this spring,
LJ, returned for a hot meal and a friendly face. My wish to see him
again came true. He was a healthy, determined young man when I
first met him, eager to begin his quest for gold. However, when he

returned today. He was a mere resemblance to himself. He walked into the roadhouse, defeated, hungry and tired. I hardly recognized him. I went to him, hugged him, and sat him down near me.

"I don't have money to stay, ma'am, indoors," he said rather ashamed. "But, if I can sleep on the floor of your barn, I'd be very grateful. I would clean the barn and chop wood or do whatever I can do to help. I'd only stay a few nights and then be on my way."

"Where will you go?" I inquired with empathy.

"Make my way back home, I'm guessing," he said somewhat unsure about his future.

I looked at Bill in my pitiful way and asked him if we could make room for Frank. It still works because I got my way.

Bill took him out to the barn and showed him where he could stash his gear. He told me that he noticed how Frank scarcely had any mining gear, compared to what he had when we first met in the late spring.

"Is that all you got left, boy?" Bill asked.

"Yep, sold some of it, and some got stolen, and some got lost. Lucky to be alive after that avalanche took me down the side of a mountain. That was when I decided to head back to civilization. I didn't want to end up alone out there and die without my mama knowing what happened to me," Frank said in a forlorn voice.

"Get some rest, and Elisabeth will have some supper ready for you soon."

"Thank you, sir," Frank said gratefully.

"I would just want someone to do the same for me," Bill said while closing the door to the barn.

As Bill was telling me about Frank, I saw compassion in him that I had never seen before. I rather like that side of him. Could that be how he was with my mother?

1st September 1897

A few days have turned into several days. I am growing accustomed to Frank being here with us. Bill seems to accept him, which makes me happy. Although he is not of sizeable stature and intimidating, I feel safer with him here. He is the right company for me.

5th September 1897

Today is my twenty-first birthday. I am happy with my life at present. I have decided to go to mine. Maybe, my birthday will make my luck prosperous today, and I will find a big nugget. The miners down from us brag that they have a suitable vein, but don't we all? I would never admit to not finding anything. Frank feels comfortable and well enough to run the Roadhouse. So, happy birthday to me.

Guess what, LJ? Frank made me a cake. Nothing fancy, but the gesture was nice. Bill forgot my birthday and said sorry, kissed me on the cheek, and then pulled a fair-sized nugget out of his pocket for me. I wonder if he was going to keep it for himself and then got to feeling guilty for forgetting what day it was. Hmm… I will not think about it again today. I wonder why I find fault with Bill and not with Frank.

20th September 1897

Bill came down sick with what the Doc said was dysentery. I have become a nurse to him, taking up most of my time. He cannot keep anything down on his stomach, and he has diarrhea. I have never seen anyone as sick as he is today. The Doc says he should recover if not given harmful food or water.

Frank has proven to be just what we needed for help. He is a trustworthy, hardworking young man and is building an addition to the barn. He is very clever.

24th September 1897

I laughed today as Frank was building his lean-to.

"What's so funny, Elisabeth?" Frank wondered.

"I have begun calling this place "on to," I said.

"On to what?" he asked curiously.

"Well, everybody who stops here is "on to" someplace else. Therefore, I nicknamed the place "On To." I think it is rather clever.

We laughed together. It feels good to have a friend with whom to share a chuckle with daily.

25th September 1897

Bill is feeling better now that we have found cleaner water for him to drink. It is a lesson for us all on freshwater. He filled his canteen with contaminated water. I put the container into boiling water for a while. I sure do not want to get sick like that.

He felt better tonight. He hugged me and told me, thank you. Frank goes down to the mine to keep an eye on things for him. I think he is going to stay with us for a time. He makes us better people.

30th September 1897

Frank appeared with a sign he had made for the doorway that said, 'Welcome to On To.' He placed it just under the sign that said Shroyer's Roadhouse. I was thrilled with the gift. Bill just shook his head. He says he was amazed at the crazy things that a girl can get people to do for her. I am proud of the sign hanging above my doorway; 'ON TO.' When I kissed Frank on the cheek, he blushed.

2nd October 1897

Patrons of the roadhouse asked me about the sign, and if that was a local Indian word and if so, what it meant. I laugh and tell them the story of everyone being on to someplace else. How funny is that? When I told the men, they laughed. Having laughter in our home is good. We are our own family.

8th October 1897

Frank has taken on many of the outside chores for me. He has made my life happier and more manageable. I prepare the food for the guests. Men want a home-cooked meal from a woman. I get time now to go down to the mine.

The days are considerably shorter now, and I am dreading the long dark winter. If Frank stays on, I will at least have someone to visit with.

Tonight, I overheard a guest speaking German to Bill. He was getting frustrated not being able to communicate with the man and his family. I came out and could understand the man and manage to converse with him. Bill did not know of my ability to understand the language. Both Bill and the man were pleased to have an interpreter. The man brought his entire family with him in hopes of striking it rich.

Even the mayor of Seattle walked away from his job and traveled north, looking for gold. The author, Jack London, stopped by one day while traveling in the Yukon.

I like to listen to people tell me their stories. I feel like they have kept them so hidden away, when they see me, they let down their guard and just start talking. I have a good way of listening. People trust me. Often, the conversation is about home and loneliness.

30th October 1897

I got a letter from home today. I could smell Tillie; I swear. I have a new nephew. The Gregg family is growing in size. He was born last December. He is a very energetic little boy. She stays busy on the farm.

Tillie told me there are a few streetlamps in town, and businesses have telephones. A few of the more affluent people have them in their homes. She says that when I come home, I will see many changes.

There is a teacher's college being built. Can you imagine? That will bring many people to town. It is right next to our school. I miss home.

Someday, I will return.

Christmas, 1897

My second Christmas was spent in the Yukon. Last year, I was so miserable that I did not care about what day it was. At least, I am accustomed to it being black all day. Frank is excited to have someone to share the day with also. He is as homesick as I am. We cry on each other's shoulder. I love that man. You know, like a brother. I do not feel attracted to him like I did the Captain. He (The Captain) aroused feelings in me that I did not think I was capable of having. Do not get me wrong; I love Bill, too. It is just that Frank and I have more in common with each other. He is my best friend. We laugh at the silliest things. I will confess to you without him, I would not still be here. Bill enjoys his company more than he will let on. I think he is jealous of our friendship.

Merry Christmas, my dear LJ. What would I do if I did not have you?

Dear Traveler, may you find happiness as you travel to your "on to" place.

CHAPTER TWENTY-SEVEN

Jealousy and Robbery

Spring, 1898

LJ, I miss my sisters. I need a woman who knows me to talk to about men. I declare they are demanding. I could write to them; however, the mail is so slow that by the time I received a reply, one or all of us might be deceased. You know what I mean, not really dead. I would hope an argument would not be a cause for that drastic a measure.

Frank always takes my side during an argument or so claims Bill. He is grumpier than usual. He never discusses his feelings with me, where Frank is always open with his. I am caught in the middle, trying to please both men.

After spending the winter with Bill and me, Frank asked me to explain to him the relationship between us. He scratched his head and said that it was like no marriage he had ever seen before.

I explained to him the best I could. If I had a normal relationship with Bill, things would be more comfortable, or so I think. Bill vowed to take care of me and keep me safe. He has definitely held up his end of our agreement. I am content most of the time, convincing myself that if I could not be with Ed, I would survive by not getting romantically involved with anyone. I will stay with Bill and care for him, richer or poorer or sickness and in health. I made a vow.

He seemed content with my explanation.

Today, I just blurt out in frustration, "I wish you two would settle your differences. You act like two jealous boys." You should have seen Bill give me a face and said: "You treat him better than me, seems I can't do anything right, and everything he does is all right by you." Bill seemed more tired and cranky than usual.

"Now Bill, you know that isn't true," I said, defending myself. "Frank works hard around here helping me; maybe it would be better if you two went down to the mine and worked together. Frank probably gets a little bored here, only helping a woman all the time. You know he's an able-bodied worker, and two extra hands and eyes might be precisely what you need."

"All right, then tomorrow Frank, you get up and go down to the mine with me," Bill said curtly.

"Mr. Shroyer, I will show you that I am a good worker," Frank said.

I told them that I was proud of both of them. The things I have to do around here for some civility. I am again thankful to have made it through another winter.

I have been gone for two years now. Oh, my.

15th July 1898

Frank was up early getting chores done around the roadhouse and preparing for the day at the mine. When Bill got up, Frank already had the dog sled loaded.

"I think we've got everything, Mr. Shroyer," said Frank proudly.

"What about grub?" Bill asked Frank.

"Mrs. Shroyer said she'd bring us down lunch."

"Elisabeth, you don't need to be catering to us. You have your work to do," Bill said gruffly, placing his tools inside the dogsled. You should have seen me, LJ; I gave Bill a look that made him change his tune.

He then told, Frank "If she can't pan for gold today, we will have one madwoman on our hands. Let me tell you, Sonny boy, you've got to keep them happy."

"Yes sir, Mr. Shroyer."

Maybe Bill is jealous because Frank and I are both young and energetic. He confessed to me that he even liked Frank better than he liked the arrogant Ed Geddes. Bill said he could never put his finger on it, but something about that man was unsettling to him. He was glad I had him out of my system for the last time. If he only knew how often, I still think of him.

The day was quiet, and I was alone when the mail carrier came upon his dogsled. He surprised me with a letter from home. It was from Tillie and quite lengthy too. I was excited to read the letter.

Dearest Sis,

> *Letters are few and far apart these days. It is with a heavy heart that I tell you the sad news of baby Emmett. Emmett died from complications of his Spinal Bifida. Poor Nellie is simply beside herself. We laid Emmett to rest in Calvary Cemetery just below Mama's grave. It was a beautiful service. Young Nell took the loss of her brother very hard. She is such a sensitive little thing.*
>
> *Bert found himself a sweet young woman named Nora Fredrick. Her daddy had land in Pomona, California, before settling here. He had a large orchard over there in California. Her Mama's family is from the Tonto Basin, cattle ranchers. Their last name is Cline. Jesse has gotten to know them from dealings in town. She seems like a charming girl. Maybe now, Bert can grow up, stop all that fist fighting. He and George traveled down south to Rimrock in the Verde Valley to visit her family for a week. I imagine there will be a wedding soon.*
>
> *George says the Indians still fight with the settlers in the Verde. I would not be at all surprised if Bert did not move down south.*
>
> *Johnny is ornery as ever. He did manage to win himself twenty-five dollars on the Fourth of July bull-riding contest. He is still ranching for the Hashknife out in Winslow.*
>
> *You asked me for my recipe for Mama's potato soup with rubbins. It is so easy and tasty on a cold day.*
> *2 to 3 stalks of celery, diced.*
> *1 onion peeled and chopped.*

Now put that in your pot with a big cube of butter to soften the celery and onion.

Peel and wash two or three good-sized potatoes. Cube them into bite-sized pieces. Place them in the pot with the onions and celery. Cover it all very well with water, salt, and pepper. Boil the potatoes until they are just starting to get soft. About ten minutes or so from being done.

In a bowl, put one-cup flour, salt, and pepper and crack an egg into the mix. With your hands, "rub in" the mixture to blend. Hold your hand over the pot and rub the dough into little dumplings. Now, be sure to put whatever flour is leftover into the pot at the end to thicken the soup. Cover and boil hard for about ten minutes. Do not forget to stir the pot because it can stick. Check your potatoes and rubbins to make sure they are done. Add a couple of good splashes of cream at the end and another pat of butter on top. Remember, it is always better the next day after it has sat. Mine never seemed as good as mama's, and I always teased her that it was the taste of her hands and the love in her heart that made it good.

Oh Lizzie, it just is not the same without you here with us. I miss you, dearly. Do you think that you will ever come home to us?

Your cherished sister, Tillie

Tears ran down my cheek as I put the letter aside and said a prayer for baby Emmett. My dear Nellie, her loss must be significant. We all knew the poor thing did not have long on this earth.

Then I tried imagining Bert with a woman. Bert has always been a loner; this girl must be unique to get his attention. I am happy for him. I cannot let myself dwell on how homesick I am. Letters from home are nice to receive, but afterward, they always make me feel sad.

I almost forgot their lunch! Tomorrow I will make potato soup for them.

20th July 1898

LJ, things have been hectic these last few days. Therefore, I shall start where I left off. I, not wanting to be alone anymore, because of the sad news about Emmett, gathered the dogs together and drove them down to the mine. When I arrived, I looked for Bill. Frank told me that Bill was not feeling well and had gone to the tent to rest.

"Bill, are you alright?" I inquired outside the tent. "I brought you lunch down. Are you hungry?"

I waited for a few moments before entering the tent, only to find Bill on the cot; he was profusely sweating and had the chills. Quickly, I called Frank for help. I had to get him into Dawson City to see the doctor. I asked him if he thought it was dysentery again, and he said no, he had terrible pain in his back.

Frank and I, having secured Bill into the sled, drove the dogs at top speed to town.

We pushed our way in, insisting that the doctor saw him immediately. The doctor stipulated that we leave him overnight for treatment. As I protested, Frank took charge. He knew that Bill did not trust some of the new miners. With him out of commission, Frank had to take charge. He left me to stay with Bill while he went back to the mine. Little did I know what Frank was going through at the mine.

The men at the dig were surprised to see Frank appear so close to darkness. They were preparing to leave with our mining equipment and Bill's gold. Thieves! He suspected them all along, nothing specific, just a gut instinct he had about those three.

"You gonna take us down? It is one against three. You are outnumbered. Come get us," goaded the men.

"Leave the gold and equipment, and I will let you go," Frank bargained, holding the shotgun pointed right at one of the men.

With that demand, the men, having indulged in Bill's supply of whiskey, started to laugh at Frank's foolish claims. "Take your pick, son."

Frank assessed the situation, agreed, shaking his head. He would defend the property with his life. He reached down, slowly feeling the rifle by his side. He had never shot a man. Nevertheless, he was now willing to do so. He pointed the gun up, his hand shaking. He knew he had to be fast to surprise them. Time seemed to stand still.

The gun fired off onto the ground, scaring the horses that lead the wagon. The horses flung back on their hind hooves and overturned the wagon, throwing one of the men to the ground. His legs, trapped under the wheel, left the other two men trying to secure the horses when Frank began shooting at them. He took several shots in the darkness, the men returning shots at Frank. Suddenly, it grew quiet; only the sound of men running away. He was dismounting the horse when a bullet struck him in the back. Frank fell to the ground, injured but alive. He would lie still until the men had run off. He saved the equipment, but probably not the gold.

As daylight exposed the mayhem, the placer mine was in ruins. Frank lay upon the ground surrounded by pickaxes, shovels and gold pans strew about. The tent, although in disarray and ripped apart, could be repaired.

The appearance of other miners from the area surprised Frank. They had heard the commotion in the night but had waited until light to offer their assistance. Frank told them the story, and the men vowed to capture the other two thieves. The other man, trapped by the wagon, would not be going anywhere until the Royal Canadian Police arrived.

Frank was brought into the Dawson hospital. Hearing the commotion, I came out to investigate. I was surprised and grateful to Frank for his bravery.

Bill was still in pain due to kidney stones. He would recover after he passed the stones. Although grateful to Frank for defending the mine, Bill questioned Frank as to why he did not shoot the bastards. He also asked who was at the mine now. Bill, all the while, was preparing to leave the hospital. He was complaining that there was work to do. "No time to dilly-dally around this place."

I tried to convince the man to go back to bed. Stubborn as he was, he collapsed to the floor.

Profanity-filled the hospital room as Bill rubbed his bloodied head. "I guess you get your way this time, honey. I will do what the doc says. You just get out there to the mine as quick as you can. Save the gold that is in my tobacco tin under the bed."

"Not until I find out how Frank is doing." I was not leaving until I knew Frank's condition. After examining his wound, the Doc said that the bullet wound was superficial. Frank was cleaned up, and he insisted on going with me out to the mine. Therefore, away we went back to the camp. I have not had this much excitement in a long while.

Yes, Bill recovered from his kidney stones after about a week of pain and sickness. The placer mine was in pieces. Bill was distraught by his missing tobacco can. I could not believe it when he told me that he thought it would be easy for Frank to find it and just happen to put it with his things.

Luckily, his inner voice convinced himself not to accuse Frank without proof. However, he said to me, 'If I ever found out that Frank had taken it, why... I'd have no choice but to kill him; same if he touched you, Elisabeth.'

Bill said he was ready for a move from this place. "Time to move on." He started tearing down the water shaft. A shiny piece of rock fell out of the hillside as Bill pulled out a timber.

"What in God's name is that?" he said, reaching into the mud. Pulling the muddy piece out and washing it off, he mumbled, "By gosh, looks like gold to me," as he squinted his eyes to inspect it. "Gold! Damn it to hell! Now, I cannot be too mad at those men; it was there all along. They just helped me find it."

Bill was still laughing when I arrived back from tracing the men's steps from the previous week's attack.

"What on earth are you laughing at?" I asked, rather perplexed. "I have a surprise for you."

"I have one for you, too," he laughed, holding the nugget in his hand.

"I found the tobacco tin, full of gold," I boasted.

"I found a big nugget in a vein," he boasted back. Running towards each other, we flung ourselves into each other's arms. We stood, hugging each other for an extended period. I thought to myself that it felt good to be in Bill's arms. Hugs were what I had missed most in our relationship. When I thanked Bill for hugging me, he agreed that he also enjoyed it. Then he proceeded to blame me for never wanting his attention. He mumbled something to the effect of never being able to figure me out.

The find proved to be prosperous, and Bill made Frank a partner in the mine. I could not be happier. The three of us could send money home for the first time since our arrival. For those that were left at home, the payment was much accepted. For us, it seemed to lighten the guilt of being away from them.

We decided to invest a little of the money into the roadhouse that required repair. We discussed selling the roadhouse or closing it up completely. We decided that we would do it for one more year and then maybe move on. Bill cannot stay put. He is always on the lookout for a more significant strike. Knowing that we would not be doing this for the rest of our lives eased some of the stress. We could take each day as it came. As for me, I still have not decided if I want to stay or go home. This has been a real adventure, LJ.

Jealously is a deadly sin and turns right into evil.

CHAPTER TWENTY-EIGHT

5th May 1900

Four years have passed since Bill and I settled down around Dawson City. We have seen many changes while chasing the elusive dream of striking it rich and suffered many hardships. Word had gotten out that there had been a strike southwest of the Bonanza goldfield in Quartz Creek. This would mean relocating forty-five miles away.

I thought that maybe a change would do Bill well. The boom days of a roadhouse were ending. The people who stayed have built homes for themselves while others have gone back home. The gold rush was winding down.

I have grown accustomed to my life. It sounds rather odd to say, thinking back to my past. Without you, LJ, I would have forgotten much of it. I can go back and read my journal about me.

I remember the day I got you. I was so excited. Birthdays were happy times. We were a large family, so most days mingled into one another, but a birthday was a day for me. I always felt special then.

1st December 1900

We have spent the winter in Dawson City. I was ready for a change. To come home to a real home and take care of just my husband would be an adjustment. However, I would not miss my days of cooking for others.

Frank has decided to return to his family in the summer. He has stayed four years. His mother is ill, and he needs to see her again. There is so much to do for entertainment in Dawson. We have every form of fun available. We have a bowling alley and an arcade.

They even let us, women, into play. The time passes quickly.

I have made women friends again, and we like to go to the opera house. Sometimes, we can watch a picture show about us miners here in Dawson. They call us 'hardy people of the north.' It makes the time pass quickly. Tillie and Nellie watched one of the Yukon, and Nellie wrote me a letter afterward. She told me about how proud she felt having her baby sister be so strong and brave. I guess I never thought of it that way before. I just get up every morning and do what I have to do.

We also have a telephone line now. We all gathered out in front of the telephone building while the first call was made from it. It is incredible to think that we can visit with family in Flagstaff and hear their voice on the other end.

LJ, it is because of the telephone that men like Frank have decided to stay on a little longer. He now says he will go home next summer. I am glad he is still here with me. He is my best friend.

12th December 1900

Today, Bill came running into the house. He was downtown when the telephone operator saw him. She seemed distraught with some news for me.

"Just tell her to get down here right away so we can make that call back to her family. Something bad has happened," as she pleaded for Bill to hurry.

I ran down the hill, practically sliding on ice on my rear end most of the way. I could not fathom what could be wrong in Flagstaff.

Nervously, I took the receiver from the operator and held it in my hand, trembling all the while. A familiar voice on the other end reassured me that she would connect me immediately with my family. "Hello," said Jesse, as nervous as I, on the other end. "Real bad news, Lizzie, Little Nell is dead. She got sick with tonsillitis at school, and before Nellie could make it to Albuquerque to be with her, she died."

I had sunk to the floor of the telephone office. Bill was there to pick me up, as my grief was overwhelming. I was in shock. My poor little Nell, dead. First Emmett and now Nell. I may as well have been on the moon; I felt so far away.

Spring 1901

These last few months have been hard on me. I spent most of the winter in bed, not wanting to have any visitors. I am thin, and I can feel bones that I did not know I had. I cannot eat or drink. It is cold outside, but the sun draws me toward it. I long for Flagstaff, where even on a cold day, the sun warms your face.

Today is the first day that I have felt like writing.

Bill is beside himself, offering to take me back to Flagstaff immediately. I argued that such a trip in winter would be too hard for me. I agreed to leave after the spring thaw. Frank was worried about me, also. Neither man can cheer me up.

Spring came and with it was time for Frank to leave. He made his travel plans. He has convinced me to go with him up to the mountain to watch the Northern Lights one last time with him. He knows I loved watching it, and I could ask the spirits to take little Nell and Emmett up to the higher spirits.

10th May 1901

I am accompanying Frank up to the top of the mountain. I am weak and know that the trip will be difficult, but worthwhile. I am longing to watch the Northern Lights one last time, so we have picked a day for our hike. We agreed to take our time going up the mountain with a pack mule and stay overnight for the show. Bill is not interested in going with us, as he has business to finish in Dawson.

12ᵗʰ May 1901

How do I begin to put my final days in the Yukon on paper? Frank and I started our journey on a beautiful spring day. The hike led us around many streams and over snow-packed mounds. However, flowers and green grass were popping through the earth with a promise of better days ahead.

The view and light shows were glorious. My spirit felt enlightened. I thought to myself that this was what I needed. We made our camp and snuggled down for the night. We laid staring up at the night sky until sleep overtook us.

Just as the sun appeared in the eastern sky, we could hear a baby moose bellowing for its mother. Everyone knew to stay away from the moose, especially in the early spring, when the calves were born. The moose, known for their protectiveness of the young, would defend the babies with their own lives.

As we made our way down the mountain, Frank, being curious and just wanted to observe the young calf, ventured closer. Afraid that we would be seen by its mother, I was warning him to hunker down behind a tree as I hid behind a large blue spruce tree.

After a while, Frank observed that the calf was mired down in the muddy ground. He made his way down to it. I was protesting at every step.

Suddenly and without warning, the adult moose appeared with its ears pinned back and head flailing back and forth. It began stomping its feet and grunting horrifically. Frank froze in place in the open field. He had nowhere to go.

The baby calf grunted back at its mother. Frank lied down on the frozen earth covering his head with his arms. Hearing the sound of a pistol firing off in the distance spooked the adult moose. Frank, also startled, stood to see if help was arriving. The moose, only viewing Frank, charged toward him. He instinctively began to run away from the area. The great moose struck him as if he were nothing. Frank's lifeless body went flying through the air and landed brutally hard a distance away from me. Helpless, I lay quiet in the thicket of the trees. I could not leave the safety of the trees, or I would be next, I had no choice but to stay quiet. I knew that if Frank were not already dead, at the least, he was gravely injured.

The forest was quiet. There was nothing to do but wait it out until it was safe enough to make my way down toward town or help arrived.

It seemed like hours that I lay beneath the spruce tree. Suddenly, the moose was on the move. Someone was coming, I thought. I should warn them, do something. I recognized Bill in a search party for me.

"Lord, do not take Bill," I prayed aloud.

Humans outnumbered the giant moose. The animal did not have a chance against a dozen or more rifles. The moose fell to the earth like the sound of a large tree toppling down. Then silence. I let out a sigh of relief and called Bill.

He ran to my side. I had lost weight during the past few months and felt like a small child in his arms. I wrapped my arms around his neck and began sobbing that Frank was gone. In the blink of an eye, he was taken away from me. My grief was overwhelming.

"Take me home, Bill," I pleaded.

"Yes, Elisabeth, we are going back to civilization," he said as he carried me down the mountain.

"No, Bill, I mean to take me home now, back to Flagstaff," I said in a frail voice.

Why do we humans think that we can win over Mother Nature's power?

CHAPTER TWENTY-NINE

Returning to Civilization

20th June 1901

The train, arriving from the east, pulled into the station in Flagstaff on a crisp June morning. No one knew that we were coming home. We had taken a side trip to Iowa, delivering Frank's body to his mother, and then attended his burial. Frank became a part of our family. Both of us felt Frank's death. Bill took his death harder than anything I had witnessed of him.

Bill gave his mother his share of the strike. He explained to her that Frank was like a son to him. His mother was grateful for the financial help.

His family buried him in the family plot. It surprised Bill and me to be welcomed so warmly by members of the community. Frank had been a good son and had often written to his mother. She, in turn, would read his letters aloud to the community. Everyone was interested in following his stories of the Yukon and his life with Bill and me. Bill was surprised to learn that Frank held him in high regard. Wherever we went into town, people treated us as if we were notoriety.

I was beginning to feel more like my old self again. The women of the community all saw to it that I was fed well while I was there. I arrived undernourished and looked like a skeleton of my former self. All were concerned about my health.

Bill spent much of his time talking to the men; they had many questions for him regarding daily life in the Yukon. Of course, when he bought rounds of drinks for the men, he became very popular. Bill had never been one to over-indulge in alcohol, as some men did. This was a rare occasion for him, and I was not caring. It was all I could do to keep my composure.

A large group of people turned out to wish us farewell. I had a deep sadness in my heart as the train pulled away from the station. Now, it was my turn. I was headed home.

Back in Flagstaff, Bill and I checked into the Weatherford Hotel on Leroux Street and Aspen. I wanted to look my best when I saw my family for the first time in over five years. I was busy eating everything in sight to plump up for our meeting. I soon discovered it was impossible to hide in this town from people who knew us.

George, being the family patriarch, came to visit us first. He understood the importance of being alone and appearing when one is ready. He took the news back to the family, who was waiting anxiously for his return. I do not know who was more excited, my sister or me.

Tillie sent a telegraph to Nellie with the news, and it seemed that she must have taken the very next train out of Yucca headed east. She was in town by the time I was ready to make my appearance.

Johnny was notified. He had been out on the range and came into town to greet me.

We were asked to have dinner at Tillie's house on Sunday. Bill and I agreed. Bert had wanted the meal at his home on Dale Street since the house was large. I was the one who said I did not want to meet my new sister-in-law with an apron on. We decided on Tillie's for dinner, even if it was about three miles north of town.

I had not seen their cabin for many years, and there were many changes made to the property. I was shocked to see so many children playing outside.

"Who are all of these children," I asked George. "Do we have other folks visiting today?"

"No, Lizzie," George laughed. "These kids are all family. Wouldn't mama be happy today?"

Goose pimples appeared on my arm as I thought of mama. "I think that she can see us and is very happy."

The family greeted us with many hugs and kisses. Just as I predicted, Nellie and Tillie were in a dither about my gauntness. George made them promise not to preach to me about it.

"You know how Lizzie gets," he pleaded with his sisters. They promised him they would handle me with kid gloves.

It did not happen, but I could not blame them when I saw myself in Tillie's big mirror. The two of them had a little more weight on them than they needed. It was common after giving birth to several children. Tillie had three children; Nellie had Georgie and baby Marguerite, and Nora, the new sister-in-law, had given birth to two babies; the boy died as an infant, and Ella was a rambunctious little girl. Nora was pregnant again. The Hoffman family was growing in size.

We visited all day and into the night. I was happier than I had been in months. My sisters did not want to leave my side for fear that I would suddenly be gone. I was content to sit at the kitchen table and visit.

30ᵗʰ June 1901

The headstone had arrived for little Nell, who had died six months prior. The family decided that they would have a small service for her after I returned home. The burial for Nell was in Calvary Cemetery next to her baby brother Emmett and at the foot of her grandmother Mary Josephine. I continued to grieve for all the lives lost. All died too early in life.

14ᵗʰ August 1901

Bill and I continued staying at the Weatherford Hotel. I had not asked my family if they had seen Ed recently. I did not want to know if he was still married or not. Besides, a married woman asking about a man was inappropriate. Bill had been good to me, and I owed him that much for bringing me home.

I knew that Bill had left the Yukon, just as news of more gold strikes was being found near Juneau. He reads the newspaper's front to back, not missing any story on the North. I knew that he was anxious to return. I would find Bill sitting quietly in the corner of the hotel, reading the newspaper. It was his way of staying in touch. He did not wish to cause an annoyance with my family and me by demanding a specific departure day.

However, he was getting anxious to leave.

19ᵗʰ August 1901

George had noticed that Bill was becoming irritable staying in town. He asked his brother-in-law to go with him to look at some property that he had wanted to buy. Mr. Schultz had a property northeast of Jesse Gregg. All the men know each other, and maybe in passing, he could obtain information on the length of our stay. After hearing nothing, George came out and asked him directly.

"George, I wish I knew," said Bill rather forlornly.

"Lizzie said it was up to you. She said that she would know when you were ready."

"I would like to get settled before winter sets back in. I worry about taking her too far away from civilization," Bill explained. "Something inside her changed after Frank died. She has lost her spirit for adventure. I sometimes think it would be best if I left her here for a while to recuperate."

"You know you can leave her here with us," said George, thinking that his youngest sister would be madder than a horny toad.

"She will be in good hands, but I would let her make that decision. You won't go running out on her without her approval?"

"No, I won't leave her behind if she wants to go. That is good advice from a man who has never been married. You are wasting your skills. Are you ever going to get hitched?"

"Not this late in life, my friend. I've raised this family and am quite happy on my own."

Bill returned to the hotel with his mind made up. Tonight, he would take me out for a nice dinner and talk it over.

"Get yourself up and dressed really pretty. I want to take you out on the town tonight."

"I don't feel like it tonight, honey," I retorted.

"Plans have already been made. Come on now," trying hard to convince me.

My thoughts began to turn into panic. What would I do if I saw Ed at the restaurant? It was night, and that is when he would come into town. My heart was pounding as I dressed.

Bill took me to my favorite restaurant, The Coconino, which was on Railroad Avenue, just down the street and around the corner. Woo-Yen, the proprietor, had been in town for years and was happy to see me.

As we entered, I was relieved to see no one I knew in the restaurant. I could relax and enjoy myself.

"You been sick, Miss Lizzie?" Woo-Yen questioned me and then went on to say how beautiful I looked.

"Yes, but getting better now," my voice stopped… Was it him? No. Then I heard his voice. I immediately wanted to take flight. Bill laid his hand on my arm, silently signaling to me that it was all right, do not panic; he was trying to calm me down without uttering a word.

Ed was drunk, as usual, with several women on his arms.

I felt nauseous, light-headed, and suddenly afraid. Was it Bill I was fearful of or Ed? I wondered to myself.

Ed had grown older, but he was still the best-looking man in town. Should I speak to him or ignore him completely, hoping he does not see me?

Ed saw Bill first. Approaching the table, Ed stumbled and fell into the chair next to our table. He laughed at himself and managed a hello. Then slurred rudely, "Hasn't this man been feeding you, Mrs. Shroyer?"

"Ed, do not speak to my wife like that again, sir," requested Bill politely. He never wanted to provoke Ed but wanted to calm things down before things got out of hand.

Ed, who never missed an opportunity to be provoked, stood up and laughed at Bill, then turned to me.

"Liz, you look like the other side of death. Is all the food there frozen?"

The women let out a cackle.

With that being said, Bill stood up and asked me if I was ready to leave. I nodded my head, yes, afraid to speak.

"Did I say you could leave?" Ed was bullying Bill. It was obvious that Ed was trying to provoke Bill into a fight.

"Let's go, Elisabeth, before I decide to teach this man a lesson in manners," Bill said, growing angrier at each passing minute. Woo-Yen was watching from the kitchen, hoping that there would not be a fight in his restaurant.

"So, your name is Elisabeth now, Cyclone?"

I, speaking in a diminutive voice, asked Ed to let me pass. "Leave us alone, Ed. We have no fight with you. Leave the past behind and let us leave. I have no desire, and neither does Bill to fight with you. I have been ill, but I am now well enough to return to the North. In fact, we shall be departing soon."

Bill got his answer without even bringing up the subject.

Deputy Sheriff Pullium had just happened to be doing his rounds in the area of the restaurant when he suspected possible trouble. He said hello to everyone, including Ed, who had his fist up, as if to fight.

"We were just leaving, deputy," informed Bill.

The next day, Bill went to the train station to purchase tickets. The family was shocked at the news but understood that we needed to return north before winter.

I reluctantly gathered my things and said a heartfelt good-bye to everyone.

The train once again pulled away from the Flagstaff station with me saying my traditional farewell to my majestic mountains.

Know from experience when it is time to leave; let nothing hold you down.

CHAPTER THIRTY

10th August 1901

The return journey was harder on me than any other trip. My mind kept going back to Ed. I was concerned that he was consuming too much alcohol. I wondered if he was happy with his life. Had he succeeded in becoming a ranch owner? I never got the chance to find out. I wished him the best and hoped he was happy.

Life in Quartz Creek was mundane to me. I lost my drive for mining.

"Shouldn't Elisabeth be getting better by now?" Bill asked the town doctor who administered laudanum for my depression.

Then I heard the doctor whisper to Bill, "It could take years. Why I have seen some women get so bad that the husband has to put them away in an asylum. I am just saying, Bill, do not rule that out. If she gets worse, you may not have a choice," the doctor explained.

Not me, I thought to myself.

Thanksgiving, 1901

Bill was growing tired and discouraged. He retreated to his stake for weeks at a time because he was hurting. Frank was like a son to him; he mourned the loss. We were of no use to each other.

Why haven't we seen it before, LJ? Without Frank, we may have gone our separate ways long ago. He kept us together. He was the glue in our relationship, just as he had been with his parents. Frank's father left his mother soon after Frank left home. That was it, I had no one to care for now. I lost my purpose in life.

Bill recognized this and asked me if I would like to have children. When he brought up the subject, I laughed at him and told him no. "This is no place to bring a baby into the world," I answered, pointing out that the rest of my family had done well with producing heirs. My parents, by now, would have nine grandchildren, with Nora, expecting baby number ten in February. I never told him that I could not have children. Since we had never been together sexually, I did not feel the need.

Luckily, for me, Bill heard of a strike in Alaska. He wanted to go into that area. I agreed to go if I could live in Valdez. It is a booming town. I would be closer to civilization, and there would be more I could do. Bill can come and go as he pleases, while I stay in one place. I will make friends and be social again. Life is coming back to my empty soul.

Spring, 1902

We settled into Valdez before winter came. Like every mining town, alcohol was a problem with the men. I joined the Temperance Movement. Bill knew that in the back of my head, I was helping Ed. He cannot fight my feelings.

He is away more and more. Bill was entertaining the idea of going to Juneau while I have my own life. He will come and go as he pleases, as so many men do in this area of the world. We will live estranged from each other.

Therefore, I will live in Valdez with Bill returning to check in on me and give me money to live on. I furnished my new house with pretty things. Living in the Port of Valdez puts shopping at my fingertips. There are new arrivals weekly of clothes and furniture. People living away from civilization, but they no longer have to do without the more elegant things in life.

New Year's Day, 1903

Christmas came and went without a word from Bill. I worried about him being alone, hoping that he was not injured or worse yet, dead.

I spent my time at supper clubs where they were singing and dancing. Then sleeping until noon and going to bed in the early-morning hours. Attending one social affair after another. It was a significantly different lifestyle than the one I had in Dawson City.

I finally received word from a shipmate who had sailed from Juneau. Bill was there and healthy. He sent a message that he would come to see me after the spring thaw. He sent a present to me by way of the shipmate.

"Mrs. Shroyer, your husband, asked me to give this to you," the young man said, in a very official voice.

I thanked the young man for doing the favor for Bill.

"Oh no, ma'am, it was no favor. Your husband paid me well and told me how important it was to him for you to get this," handing me the gift. I thanked him again.

I was surprised by its weight. What could it be, a big chunk of gold? Carefully, I unwrapped the gift. I was delighted to find a beautiful Russian gilded egg. He remembered that I had seen one in a store in Dawson City a few years ago. My life then had no place for such delicate beauty. Now, I could place it on my mantle and enjoy it.

Bill has not forgotten about me, I thought. Christmas had come after all.

13th May 1903

Bill did just as he had promised and returned to Valdez from Juneau by way of a ship after the spring thaw. He had taken on a partner, a young man he had met in a saloon in Anchorage. The man's story was much like that of Frank's. He also left home in search of gold, leaving his family behind. Alone and homesick, Bill recognized the man's distress.

"I can always use an able-bodied hand to help out," he told me.

"I have not forgotten how difficult it is to work a strike. I am relieved that you are not alone and have someone to help you should you need it," I said understandingly.

"You are looking well, my dear," he observed, looking me over from head to foot. "The doc thought I could put you in an asylum."

"What on earth for? Did you think I had gone daft?" I said, my voice quivering at the thought of an asylum. Can you just imagine, me in an asylum, LJ?

"We thought that you had lost your mind, and I wouldn't be able to care for you," he explained.

"So, you leave me alone? Being by myself here for too long would have surely made me go crazy," I said.

"Elisabeth, I am not staying in Valdez," he told me.

"I am not going to Juneau," I returned. "Nor will I stay here, alone."

"You will return to Flagstaff? Stay as long as it takes you to decide what it is you want out of life. We have had our time together, and it was wonderful. We can always get an annulment if you should find yourself wanting to remarry. You will never be happy until you are with your cowboy," he said, surprising me with his keen observation.

"How did you know that I still have feelings for him?"

"I know you better than you know yourself, my dear wife," he said. "Now, kiss me good-bye and go make your plans to return home."

I have booked passage on a ship going to Seattle. From there I will travel to Los Angeles and home.

I had seen as much of the world as I wanted to right now. Maybe later in my life, I will travel again, but for now, is all I want to do was be back with my family.

I was going home… my majestic mountains would be awaiting my arrival.

When the heart is sad, love and friendship are the only medicine it needs.

PART III

SPRING VALLEY

Jesse Gregg, Tillie Gregg Lizzie, and unidentified man

The photo belongs to Garry & Judy Hoffman Collection.

CHAPTER THIRTY-ONE

Home Again

1ˢᵗ July 1903

Let me begin by saying to you, LJ, that we have had quite the life, you and me. We have traveled to the top of the world and back. We are survivors. I am proud of my life. I did not become the person, i.e., ordinary homemaker, that I was terrified of turning into. I feel reflective today as I sit on Tillie's porch in this beautiful valley with a most spectacular view of my mountain.

The summer rains are here, which, at times, will hide the mountain from sight. Then, you look up at her, and the sun is out, shining on her majestic peaks. Beautiful, San Francisco Peaks! I shall never tire of looking at her. Only when you leave and return, do you realize what you missed the most. I love Flagstaff and the surrounding area. It is God's country.

Today, I think I will borrow a horse from Jesse and ride to my heart's content. I feel the urge to ride fast and hard, pushing the steed and myself to race with the wind. I will not be afraid to let my hair down and tempt fate with our speed. For I, Lizzie Hoffman, am a woman of immense strength and beauty, and I shall let no man rule over me. I am independent and courageous and had my past documented with you, my dearest, LJ. As I read back on my life, I have to say, I have been blessed with family and dear friends. I could not ask for more than that. Amen.

2nd July 1903

My ride was as fantastic as I had hoped. I followed the Beale Wagon Road west, stopping only to let the horse drink from the nearby water tanks. My only wish was that it would stay light like in the North. I could have ridden all night. I saw no human on my outing, so I removed my blouse and camisole and galloped with my breasts free. Invigorating and unrestricted. I rather felt like Lady Godiva. Tillie and Nellie would surely lecture me on being a lady and following proper etiquette, even when one is alone. Absurd notion. Not that I should do such a thing in public, mind you. In this situation, I am at liberty to do as I choose.

I know that if I had a daughter, I would teach her to be curious and independent. A son, I would teach him about women and be mindful of her feelings and much-deserved freedom like a man. I have witnessed too many women enslaved by their own husbands as if they were property. My poor sisters pretend to be happy enough, but are they? What if they were given the same freedoms as I have had? Would they want more out of their lives? I think so. They question me on what my life was really like. I begin to tell them, and they balk at me. I believe that women are easily persuaded by men not to accept new ideas. I tell them that Eve was freethinking, and they lecture me on sin. Enough of my rambling. Wars would not come about as quickly as they do now. We shall have peace.

5th July 1903

The celebrations of the Fourth of July were, just as I remembered them; Only bigger and better. It is nice to see Indians like the Navajo and Hopi get involved. I could watch them dance around campfires all night. In fact, I did stay until it was over. I was unescorted. Well, not at first, but Tillie had to take the children home. I did not wish to go with her to wash faces and hands and change diapers. I should instead prefer to plow a field and plant potatoes, herd and milk the cows than stay indoors to cook and tend the house.

I shall have to begin looking for my own place. Too bad George had to sell Mama's houses; I should have liked to live in one of them. Oh well, the family needed the money he made from them. I shall put home searching on my priority list. I desire more independence.

8th July 1903

I escaped with my brother Bert to help him drive his wagon. He is a drayman, which means he carries goods for people wherever they need them taken. I asked him if he would take me along to the Canyon next time he goes.

My only wish was that my brother Johnny was here. He has gone south down to the Clifton-Morenci area. He left before I came home. Tillie says that since the Hashknife let go of all those cowboys, the men have to go off the mountain to look for work. He might get on with the mines or ranches. We did receive a picture of him. He thinks that he looked debonair, but I cannot help but laugh when I gaze at it. He must have a girl he is crazy about down there.

4th August 1903

I decided to rent a room in the boarding house. I have lived there on two other occasions, so it feels like home. I do not require much to make me happy. I come and go as I please, and the Mrs. cooks a good meal. For the time being, this is home.

LJ, you should see all the rain we are getting. At times, it turns to hail, and then everything is white like snow. I just looked out my window, and I see the street's flooding. It looks like it has taken up the wooden sidewalks. What an awful mess. It must be coming from the Rio de Flag.

I talked to Tillie on the phone, and she said the storm came in above them. She said for a few moments it reminded her of Kansas. It was as if a cyclone hit with the devastating wind blowing trees down. Then the rain came in a deluge. The garden was just getting ready to pick, and she thinks all is ruined. It is too late to start over.

1ˢᵗ September 1903

Johnny surprised everyone last night when he arrived by train. He was in between jobs and wanted to come to see me. He was surprised that I was not living with Tillie and asked me why I was not there with her. I explained my reason to him, and he said he understood. I told him that if he did not understand, then no man would. He and I are too much alike. He told me that he had an offer with the copper mine. He would rather it was gold, he said. I showed him the first gold nugget I ever found. I could see that it would not take much for him to get the fever.

We went out to Tillie's, where she had cooked us a meal. She told Johnny that food was the only thing that brings me out her way.

The first thing she said to him was to "Take those boots off in my house." You know Tillie and her neat as a pin house.

Johnny began removing his boots when he noticed our nephew, Jimmy, sitting on the floor in a corner, building a log house. Johnny aimed his kick precisely at the log house. The boot, flying through the air, landed exactly in the middle of the log cabin.

LJ, Jimmy was so angry with Johnny that he yelled at him, "Uncle Johnny, you are mean! Why did you come here, anyway?" His laughter filled the room. I was so angry at my brother.

Tillie lit into him too and said, "Johnny, you ought not to act that way in my house."

"You are my sister, not my mother, woman!" he said rudely. Turning his head toward me, he saw I was unhappy with him. However, I understood him completely. If I had been a boy, I would have been just like him. I did feel sorry for little Jimmy, though.

Johnny then asked me if I was going to the dance tonight at Babbitt Hall. Before I could answer, he blurts, out "I'm going- he spoke up and said, "I have not been to dance here in Flagstaff for years. If all those women I used to know are not married yet. Come with me, sis?"

Then Jesse piped in with the standard question that sent Johnny into another world, "When you going to settle down with a good woman, Johnny?"

Johnny laughed and told him that no-good woman would have him. He was single, and it would stay that way.

"Just leave him alone about it, Jesse," Tillie said, defending her brother. "What will be, will be. If the Lord wants him to marry, he will marry."

Again, Johnny retorted and said, "The Lord, he ain't got nothin' to do with it, Tillie. Besides, it is more like between the devil and me. I've killed so many men; the devil is just waiting for me to get there."

"Johnny!" again protested Tillie, "Not in front of the children."

Ah, family, some things never change. I love them both. We then changed the subject back to the rainstorm. Jesse said that he watched an eight-foot wall of water come down the Rio headed right into town. He called the sheriff to warn him, but it was too late to save anything. The town was a mess.

We left together, saying our goodnights. Tillie cornered me to ask if I was planning on going to the dance. I said yes, not wanting to lie to her, and she just asked that I called her tomorrow. I saw a bit of regret in her that she was not free to get up and go when the mood suited her. I missed the good old days when she and I would go together.

As Johnny and I rode into town, we made our way past Bert's house. The children yelled at us as we went past. They were out playing in the mud and water in the Rio behind their house.

I had to make Johnny stop and say hi to our nieces and nephews. I asked him if he had seen Ella since she was burned a couple of months ago.

"I saw her right after she was burned," said Johnny. "Teach that little girl a lesson not to be lighting a stove with a piece of the pitch." I was put out at him and his lack of caring. Ella's face was severely scarred on her left side. I could not help but think of how tragic it could have been. It brought back that horrific night with mama and seeing her burned.

"You weren't there the night that mama died," I sobbed.

"You are going to always try to make me feel guilty about that night, Lizzie," Johnny said as he galloped away from Bert's house in a mad dash, leaving me there. I was furious at him. How dare he treats my nieces and nephews that way? I may not want children myself, but I refuse to have him be rude. I am still feeling the loss of little Nell and Emmett.

It was still early in the day. The dance would not start until nine, so I went in to visit with my sister-in-law Nora. No use to hurry when it would last until dawn, anyway.

Be confident in yourself to bare it all when the time is right.

CHAPTER THIRTY-TWO

The First Encounter

Night, 1st September 1903

Remind me again, LJ, as to why I would ever trust Johnny to escort me to a dance? I am already late, and I know that he is sitting upon a bar stool downtown, not even thinking of me. My face powder will be old by the time he remembers me. A girl dresses up and gets beautiful for what? Men!

2nd September 1903

I took myself to the dance. I hate being late for social events. It is a pet peeve of mine. My brothers and sisters must relish the idea because they are always late. The family code is, never to hurry. They will all be late to their own funerals; I swear. Walking to the hall, I saw several people that I knew, many of whom I had not seen for years. I made my way around, as I usually did at dances, feeling very comfortable in my surroundings. Being back in a friendly place was good. As I glanced around the room, I searched for a familiar face. If Ed was there, I wanted the first glimpse of him before he saw me. He was nowhere to be found. I found myself feeling disappointed.

As I walked over to the refreshment table, a group of women were talking and noticed me standing there, when one woman quickly said, "Oh, I know who you are here to see."

"Who might that be?" I said in a curt voice.

"Why, it is the man I am looking for, too? Aren't all the women waiting for that scoundrel?"

I responded with, "Aren't all men scoundrels?"

"There is the man of the night, and he just walked in with Clara Fine hooked to his arm," said Helen Turner, looking right at Ed. My face turned bright red.

"Yes, he is a popular one," I said, turning away from him. Clara and I had been friends in our youth. I turned around very quickly and saw the couple walking into the hall. Not wanting Helen to get any ideas, I promptly informed her that I was a married woman and not looking for any man. My husband was in Alaska.

"Why did you come?" asked Helen, being very nosy.

"Well, I came to see you." I snapped back, grabbing a glass of punch. As I walked away, I could hear the two women giggling, but things like that did not faze me; it just gave me more strength. You would have been proud of me, LJ.

Ed had not noticed me, as his eyes were on Clara; or should we say on Clara's bosom, which left nothing to the imagination. I walked right over to Ed and Clara and gave them a very warm hello. I was enjoying the look on Ed's face when he saw me standing there.

"Liz! I did not think you would make it tonight. I saw Johnny downtown, and he had not even seen you. Johnny didn't even know where you're staying," Ed said in defense of himself. "Where is Bill? Is he here with you?"

Clara butted in with a "Why, Mrs. Shroyer, how good it is to see you. I heard you were a miner in Canada or somewhere on earth that no respectable woman would go."

"You mean, Clara? You will take all the gold in the world, but you will not go dig it up for yourself? I am a woman who likes to take care of myself. You would not know the feeling of finding a piece of gold out in the middle of nowhere while standing in an ice-cold stream. You should try to care for yourself once in awhile Clara, instead of having a man to do it for you," I said, as I walked away to talk to someone else. My blood was boiling. For one, Johnny never told me he saw Ed in town, and then that bitch calling me unrespectable. If I were not a lady, I would have hit her between the eyes. Men do it all the time, and I saw it often enough with women in Dawson City. I should have told her I shot a man.

Ed was speechless. Our first encounter with me being back from the Yukon went as well as our last visit almost two years ago. I danced with several of the men, all of whom seemed very anxious to see me and glad I returned home. After all, I had been a good catch, before I went to the Yukon. I still am.

All the while, I was dancing; I kept Ed within sight. He had not asked Clara to dance once, and you could tell that she was getting very frustrated. I was about to go home when suddenly I noticed the two of them seemed to be having words. I laughed to myself wondering if it was about me. Almost everyone knew that Ed, and I were once a couple. Apparently, my leaving town caused quite a ruckus for the gossipmongers. No one expected me to give Ed up just like that. Much less, that I would go with Bill Shroyer to the Yukon.

I slipped out into the fresh night air and stopped to visit with some of the people outside. Johnny happened to be one of those people, and he asked me why I was leaving. He had a few too many drinks and reeked of whiskey. He knew immediately that it was Ed.

"What's he done to you this time?" Johnny said slurring his words.

"Ed hasn't done anything to me, Johnny," I said trying to discourage him from getting mad. Is all I needed was for Ed and Johnny to get into a fistfight over me. However, before I could stop him, he went into the hall and punched Ed right in the nose.

Onlookers were flabbergasted when they realized it was Johnny Hoffman causing problems again. I was so embarrassed.

"Johnny, leave him alone. He has not done anything to harm me. I came by myself, I didn't come with Ed," I said trying to coax Johnny out of the hall.

"He and I never squared things up about you, Lizzie," slurred Johnny. I have never forgiven him for causing you to leave us for all those years."

"Gentlemen," said Mr. Hawk, "you will have to take your difficulties outside. We will have none of that roughhousing in this hall tonight. Now, take your fight elsewhere."

Ed immediately apologized to Mr. Hawk for the altercation. Furthermore, he quickly removed himself from the building. Johnny stayed and wanted to pick a fight with Mr. Hawk. I left the building again, and this time had made up my mind just to go straight home. I could see Ed was walking downtown towards the saloons. I had an urge to go running after him, and then quickly changed my mind. I would not run after any man again, especially Ed Geddes. Nor would I ever leave town once again because of him. This was my town, and I was here to stay.

The muddy street was hard to walk on. My boots kept sinking in the sludge. It was dark, and I could not see where I was going. I made my way up the street by instinct.

"Liz wait, I'll give you a lift the rest of the way to your brothers'," a familiar voice said. Then his horse whinnied, so I began focusing my attention on the animal.

As I was stroking the mane and talking sweetly to the horse, I uttered, "Too late now, Ed; we cause each other enough problems. Besides, I am sure Clara is waiting for you to take her home. I can take care of myself and find my way home without your escort." You would have been proud, LJ, the way I ignored him. You could feel his jealousy of the attention. I was paying his mount and not him.

"Come on, Liz, give me a chance. I went to that dance alone, and Clara hooked on to me like glue," Ed said, trying to convince me to stop. "I can't stand it when you treat me that way. However, if that is what you want, I'll just turn around and go back to the dance with Clara."

"How would it look for a married woman to be seen with another man? I have my reputation for being concerned about." I really acted the part.

"Then why is your husband out running around with all those Eskimos?" Ed asked curiously.

"I don't believe that's any of your business, Mr. Geddes. Bill and I have decided to take a much-needed break from each other. Living in close quarters for all those years, makes a couple need some time apart. Besides, I wanted to be home with my family through the winter. I have plans to travel to Valdez in the Spring," I said, turning for the door handle.

"Liz, please, I'm not a man to beg, and you know that. I just want to know if I have a chance to ever be with you again."

LJ, I never expected, nor was I prepared for him to say that to me, not tonight.

"Wait. I just cannot endure seeing you with another woman on your arm. I left you because of what happened all those years ago, and to see you tonight brought it all back," I said, trying to hold back real tears. "I cannot do this anymore. Now, excuse me, I am going home."

"I'm so sorry, Liz, you know how much you mean to me. I cannot just forget all about you. I have tried for seven years to forget you. Hell, I have loved only you and nobody else. I got married, but not as you think. Not because of love, no ma'am. After I had sobered up, I had begun to wonder why I had gotten hitched," Ed said honestly. "Besides, it was over long ago."

I was touched. No one has called me Liz for years. I knew that I had not escaped him, even after going away to the Yukon.

"Liz, if I can get your permission to call on you one of these days, I would like that very much, even if it's just friends. I wouldn't expect anything else."

I left him with a, "We'll see."

I know now that one day I will have Ed; it is just a matter of patience. I have waited this long; I can stand by longer. No use throwing him a life preserver this early in the game. Let us see if he can swim. I will drag this out, and if he wants me, then he can earn my love.

A broken heart by the same man once is bad enough, but twice is inexcusable.

CHAPTER THIRTY-THREE

Return of the Black Onyx Horse

5ᵗʰ October 1903

Fall is my favorite season. The aspens are changing to a beautiful gold, and the oaks are a simmering red. I can remember the little girl who would tramp up Leroux Street, crunching leaves as she sauntered up the road. In so many ways, it seemed like just yesterday, but so many years have passed and so many tragedies.

I received a letter from Bill. He had gone back to Valdez to sell the house and has made up his mind to stay in Alaska. He had killed a black bear, which he turned into a warm winter coat. He asked me to consider coming back with him, but he would understand if I stayed in Arizona. His advice to me was, to follow my dreams and not his. He expressed how he appreciated me, that I had meant the world to him, but had never found the words to tell me. I have not at any time known anyone that painfully shy before in my life. I realized that all of those years, I just needed him to say, I love you, and talk to me. We would have made it work out. His letter was beautiful and from the heart. If I had known, I would have written letters to him all along. I replied to Bill and thanked him for the opportunity for me to return. I explained to him that I would need more time to decide. I would always worry about him up in the cold, Northwest where there were still dangers. I wondered if he had ever told his family about me. I never fully understood why he kept our marriage secret. I am not someone who people are ashamed to be with. I know there was a substantial age difference, eighteen years, but it is not uncommon. Perhaps he was married before. I will never understand. We did not grow wealthy, but we struck gold together. We accomplished what we set out to do. He became my father in a way.

Having the letter from him gave me more strength and determination to see Ed again. If I can forgive Bill, then I can forgive Ed. Maybe, I am the difficult one?

10th October 1903

Nellie is coming to visit. Since I have not admitted to anyone, but myself, that I am here permanently, everyone is afraid that I shall up and leave. I cannot spend another winter there. Because everyone thinks, I am fragile, my melancholy, no one harps on me as to what I am doing. I will use it to my advantage.

It will be interesting having all those babies around. We have a baseball team of our own with all those kids.

12th October 1903

Nellie and the kids arrived. We sure can talk a lot between the three of us. Tillie mentioned her last trip to the Grand Canyon, and I said how I had not been there in years. Nellie said we should go up there to visit. It just snowballed from there. Nora took on the daunting task of offering to care for three babies while we were gone. George, not wanting to be left out of an adventure, is going along. Bert said he could take us up in his new coach if we did not mind riding with a few supplies. We decided to stay one more night, while we were there. We can take the train back to Williams.

Nellie had a friend there that she wanted to see, so now we are staying at least one night in Williams before catching the train home. Wow, these ladies are planners. I wonder whether they will boss us around and order our food for us too. Ha-Ha. Of course, I thought of Ed and am hoping I run into him along the way.

I daydream about him being on a beautiful stallion riding along beside the train calling to me. I jump from the train and onto the horse, clutching onto him as tight as I can. Then we ride off into the sunset. I just wrote a moving picture show! I can dream, even if my thoughts are only an illusion.

Of course, we kiss. It is my imagination, or are you are a romanticist at heart, LJ?

14th October 1903

I went out to Tillie's house today to look through my trunks. She had them moved to her cabin when they sold my house in town. Silly Tillie, she knew I would be back for them. Anyway, I wanted to see if I could still fit into my riders. For now, I can, but if my sisters keep feeding me the way they do, I will not be able to for long.

As I was looking through my trunk, I saw a somewhat charred wooden box. It was familiar to me, so I opened it. I guess the contents surprised me because I let out a squeal. Tillie poked her head around the corner and asked me if anything was wrong, and I motioned for her to come over. I removed the lid again and showed her the contents… it was my black onyx horse packed inside gray cotton. You could smell soot on it, even to this day. It survived the house fire.

Tillie confessed that Johnny had found it one day when he was over at the property trying to clean up. He asked her for advice on what to do with it. She told me that she took it and kept it for me. She then asked me how I felt about that.

I confessed to her that even I do not have an answer to her question. Surprised, saddened, and also excited. To find something that meant so much to me at one point and then fearful of it, is confusing to me. I will not get rid of it now. It is a keepsake. For the time being, it shall sit on the little shelf in my room at the boarding house. We leave tomorrow for our grand adventure.

I think I am more anxious about the prospect of finding Ed than the grandeur of the canyon. I have butterflies in my stomach, just like when I was a little girl. She is still inside me, after all I have been through in my life. Such a relief to know she is there.

15th October 1903

We have made it to the Canyon. What an excursion. We left from Tillie's house, where Bert picked us up and carried us to the Canyon. He said a few supplies, but really, we were loaded. We had the smaller crates under our feet. Beggars cannot be choosers. He explained that he had a few stops along the way. His new Surrey was comfortable. The seats were made of white, soft, tanned leather with a matching roof decorated with fringe that hung off the side. I suddenly thought of Bill and our time in Seattle.

We rode in a coach similar to Bert's, but we sat as far apart as possible. Sadness swept over me. I had a longing to see Bill again. I miss him.

Bert stopped at Anita to unload a few supplies. I had asked Bert to make inquiries for me about Ed. His cowboy friend, Ed Howell, told him that Ed was in Williams on business. He said what he had found out about Ed. I just smiled, thanked Bert, and walked away. I was not ready to do any explaining, although Bert would never question me about it.

The Grand Canyon was beautiful in the fall. The leaves along the rim were changing with the warm days and cold nights. Tillie was friends with the Kolb brothers, and we enjoyed visiting their studio. I could spend hours there looking at their many pictures of the Grand Canyon. Those men are daredevils. They will do any stunt for publicity. They had many questions for me about the Yukon. I am always happy to tell my tale and witness the surprise on people's faces when they put a woman in the story. I guess it is my way of bragging about how determined I am.

18th October 1903

I was anxious and nervous, LJ, when we returned to Williams by way of the train. My heart was pounding as I walked from the station to the hotel. I had been here on several occasions in the past, but never really looked at it in the way I saw it today- as a possible home. Yes! That is it! I needed a place to live even if I stayed until the summer should I decide to return North.

I was not as recognized in Williams as I was in Flagstaff. It would be just the place for Ed and me to carry on a courtship. Hmm, I rather like that plan. Should I? I felt silly as I asked the clerk at the hotel if he knew Ed Geddes. As I started to explain to him who he was, the man laughed and said, "Lady, everybody knows Ed."

The clerk gave me a couple of ideas as to where to look for him in the saloons and restaurants. I did not want to embarrass Ed by finding him in a compromising position. Therefore, I asked the clerk if he could possibly get a message to him. The clerk agreed, and I wrote out a note on the hotel stationery. In my note, I suggested that he first talked to George to get his permission if he would like to take me for dinner that evening. I did not want to offend George by sneaking around. This relationship would be in the open for my family.

I paced my room, awaiting a reply from Ed. I will have no nails left or be hungry after attacking my fingers nervously. The dinner hour drew near, and there had been no communication from him regarding the note. I, trying to be patient, could not pace the floor one more time. I went downstairs to the clerk and asked him if he had gotten the note to Ed. The clerk assured me that he had personally given it to him. My heart sank as I turned around to leave.

I heard laughter coming from the bar in the hotel and was familiar with most of it. Glancing at the bar, I saw Ed and George sitting together, drinking whiskey. Now, I pondered, what should I do? I decided to go back upstairs and lingered patiently for either George or Ed. While I waited, I put on extra rouge and made my lips a little redder. I wanted to look beautiful for Ed.

Am I going insane? I will not be treated this way by any man. That is it! Done! I am through chasing him. Wait. Someone is knocking, do not hurry. He can wait.

Postscript. It was George, and he was feeling very tipsy when he told me that he had sent Ed on his way. I, knowing the Hoffman humor, passed George at the door and went downstairs to find Ed waiting. I was always the brunt of the family teasing and was not going to give George any reward for his joke.

Ed quickly grabbed my hand and headed out of the hotel, not wanting to share me with my family. Tonight, he wanted me all to himself. Ed had been waiting on the chance to get me alone. He had one chance to make right if he wanted me.

He arranged a beautiful dinner for us. He and the saloonkeeper were friends; when asked, the cook gladly prepared a meal for us. The saloon had a secluded room in the back that had been available for intimate occasions. I was so impressed that Ed would do that for me. Years ago, I was too naïve to have recognized that Ed could be a gentle man. Miners and cowboys experience rough lives; it always surprises me when they can turn warm and cuddly.

I enjoyed the laughs and tender looks. We were very much at ease with each other. It was a comfortable relationship for both of us. There was nothing to hide or explain. We had known each other so long that there was no use wasting time on reliving the past. We would start with a clean slate.

I asked many questions about his ranch. He put the paperwork in for a homestead. He explained that he was just getting started, and there was much work to be completed. He spent all of his adult life on either cattle ranches or herding sheep. He saw both sides of ranching. He explained to me that he was a member of the Arizona Rancher's Association and traveled to help oversee the grazing of the ranch land. Sheep were notorious for eating everything in sight and leaving the ground barren. He also understood that both were necessary for the state, and they had to work together.

He admitted that I was not your ordinary woman of the day. He had witnessed me obtaining anything a man could take on and maybe do a better job of it. He knew that he could teach me the ins and outs of ranching. I stipulated that if I were with him, I would expect to be treated no differently than any of the other cowboys' excluding behind closed doors. With no exception, I would be treated as a woman of honor.

19th October 1903

I am relieved to know that we both want this time to be different, something unique. We want a chance for a fresh start to show each other who we are now. There is no question in either of our minds that we love each other very genuinely.

I watched him as he paused outside the hotel, not wanting this night to end. He took me in his arms and kissed me sensually; I had not had a kiss like that before. I could not take a breath, but I knew I was still living by the beating of my heart. If I were alive or dead, it would make no difference- I was experiencing pure happiness. After some minutes and many onlookers gawking at us, Ed released his hold on me, straightened his hat, and said good night.

"I'll be around to pick you up at 11 o'clock in the morning," he said matter-of-factly. I told him I would be ready at precisely 11 A.M. I even told him that I liked a man who is on time. He is so cute when he tips his hat.

I went to sleep that night dreaming of Ed, horses, and cattle. He was my knight in shining armor. Then the nightmare, which I had not had in years, came back to me. It began with a quarrel with Bill, begging me to leave Ed over a fight about a black horse. I awoke to sweat running down my back. I had a fitful slumber after that. Why had that silly onyx horse come back into my life now?

Ed was there at precisely eleven o'clock. George gave his okay for me to spend the day with him even though George knew he had nothing to say about it. It still made him feel important.

"I thought you might like to see the town. This is where I call home in the winter. A little quieter than Flagstaff but plenty of action going on,"

I agreed with him that I liked it also. I toyed with the thought of telling him that I was thinking of moving here but decided against it. I will check it out on my own. I worry about how a bachelor rancher like him will handle marriage. I know, LJ, am I putting the cart before the horse? I will not force him into anything. If he wishes to stay a bachelor and pursue his life of freedom, I will understand.

However, I hope with all my heart that he does not want that life any longer.

The hardest part of all is telling my family that I want to live in Williams, not Flagstaff. How do I do that? Bill said to me that we could get an annulment, but how long will that take? I will write to him tomorrow with my intent to stay in Arizona and ask him for the separation.

We never consummated our marriage, of which now I am thankful because a divorce would have been harder with the Catholic Church.

Looking back on my marriage, I was young and vulnerable. Bill saw this in me and took me on as his charge since, in his mind, he was my protector. It takes a strong man to hold a promise like that in a cold environment and long, lonely nights. There were many nights that I would have enjoyed love and affection, not to mention warmth from another's body.

Did he have someone whom he left behind in Indiana with whom he still loved deeply enough not betray her for lust? I doubt I shall ever know another man who is as strong in his convictions as Bill.

26th October 1903

On Sunday, dinner with the family, I announced that I was seeking an annulment from Bill. I expressed how he was like a father to me, and I would always have a special place in my heart for him. I am ready to move and find true love. No one seemed surprised; they all assumed that I have always loved Ed. I need to find my own way without being dependent on my family.

Oh, LJ, that was the hardest sentence I have said to them. I do not wish for them to think that I am pushing them away from me. Families have such touchy feelings. To them, I have always had my independence, but to me, I always felt as if I could only go out as far as the tether. I know the dangers facing a woman firsthand and feel confident enough in myself to handle rough situations. I could kill someone if I had to.

I asked my brothers not to mention the move to Ed until I had found a place of my own. I did not know when I would see Ed again, but I wanted to be the one to tell him.

George told me later that he had been in touch with Bill over the years, and he knew him to be a real gentleman. Bill never mentioned George's letters to me. I think that it is odd, don't you?

I love my family, but sometimes they are overprotective of me. I just want to tell them that I am not a baby anymore. The world knows me as a woman, and they cannot see me in anything but diapers!

Even as deep as the Grand Canyon is, my love for you is even more profound.

Living in Williams

2nd February 1904

Waiting to hear from Bill is difficult. You know me; I am not a patient person when there is something I really want. I am driving the mail clerk batty. I rush in to check every day, and after he looks, he just shakes his head no. I think he will be relieved when it does come, and I can stop hounding him.

I found it LJ, the perfect place for me. There is a small house in Willaims, that would be just right for a single woman. It is the cutest little cottage in the woods' west of town. The proprietor is leery of having a lone woman living in his bungalow. After I told my story to him, he agreed to let me rent from him.

I am so excited to have a place of my own. Furthermore, it is not far from where Ed lives. It is only a matter of time now: waiting to see Ed and surprise him with the news.

13th February 1904

I am settling into my new life. I am purchasing furniture with my own money from my days of mining. Let us just say that I can be comfortable for the rest of my life, as long as I am careful. I carry with me my own dowry.

I have reignited old friendships with ladies I had met years ago. I was invited to attend a luncheon at the home of the mayor. The mayor's wife, Mrs. Nellis, is a kind person, and she feels it her job to introduce new arrivals to town. Therefore, I shall attend and look my best.

14th February 1904

Entering the Mayor's home, I observed how she had decorated her parlor with red roses, obviously freshly cut and shipped from Los Angeles. You remember LJ, the beautiful fields of roses grown by the Chinese. Now, just a distant memory. Few of the ladies here, I would doubt, would pay attention to such a thing. At the least, even give a thought as to where roses come from. I cannot see many men providing the care and nurturing to roses that the Chinese express. It is an art.

I took mental notes on the luncheon so that I can look sophisticated when I give one. I have not put on many parties. It consisted of tea sandwiches, scones with a dollop of clotted cream and lemon curd, and a green leafy plant called watercress. When I ate the watercress, a lady quietly told me that it was on the plate for presentation only. I informed her that many people around the world would just as soon kill you if they knew you made trash of such a beautiful and delicious plant. You would have thought that I was threatening to do just that by the squeal she let out. It was all I could do to contain my giggle.

"Ladies, I would like to introduce you to Miss Lizzie Hoffman of Flagstaff and Dawson City, British Columbia. Lizzie has decided to make our fair city her home," said Mrs. Nellis. "You will find Miss Hoffman -or Lizzie as she prefers to be called- a woman of true character. Let us give a round of applause to Lizzie and wish her success in her move to Williams."

Considerable applause went up as I stood to thank Mrs. Nellis for the kind introduction.

"I am happy to be here and plan on staying for some time."

"Do tell us what your life was like in Dawson City. Secretary make a note to schedule Miss Hoffman to speak at one of our luncheons," said one of the women in the crowd.

"I would be happy to tell you of my gold-mining adventures in the Yukon," I gladly responded.

"Excuse me, may I ask why you do not go by your married name of Shroyer?" Asked the tall blonde woman in the back. I was surprised to see a woman of ill repute attending such a formal luncheon. I recognized the woman from a dance many years prior that Ed had been with before I left town. I know that there are going to be many women with, whom Ed has had affairs with who would challenge me. I also know that there are those who would support me: Mrs. Nellis being one of them.

"We will not ask Miss Hoffman to explain her past life to us. Please direct your questions to Miss Hoffman in private in the future. It is really none of our business," said Mrs. Nellis, being quite perturbed at the woman.

"Our sincere apologies to you, Lizzie. We would also like to encourage ladies of our fair community not to lower themselves to be rumor-mongering."

I graciously accepted the apology and sat down to enjoy the rest of the luncheon. I avoided the blonde vixen with the evil eyes. I now know that I must find Ed quickly before the malevolent woman sees him first and ruins everything. My mind was racing as I went into each saloon searching for Ed. Of all days, I could not find him.

"Where is he?" I asked one of the men at the saloon.

"He went out on a deer hunt. He should be back in a couple of days," the man behind the bar, answered. "It is an annual event, and a lot of the menfolk turn out for it."

"Thanks," I told him. I would have to wait it out and get to him before the blonde-haired woman got to him. I thought back to the Thanksgiving that we saw Ed after the turkey shoot. It was a good memory.

18th February 1904

On my daily outing to locate Ed, I overheard the news I had been waiting for. The men started arriving with their deer loaded high on the back of the horses. I witnessed this same thing a few years ago with turkeys. Each man laid out his catch so that Mayor Nellis could view them. The winner would get fifty dollars in cash. I saw Ed riding into town with his deer piled high. I stood back in the crowd and watched. Eagerly, I awaited the outcome. It was quite a spectacle to see all the deer carcasses covering the street.

The Mayor took his job as a judge very seriously. He examined each deer for size, and points on the antlers, looking over Ed's catch very thoroughly. He walked past them with his hand in a pocket, and the other side cupping his chin. He was deep in thought, pondering this major decision. He walked away and turned towards the crowd; he then announced the winner of the 1904 annual deer hunt was… Ed Geddes.

He then presented Ed with the winnings. Apparently, it was not his first time to win a hunt. There were sounds of several of the men grumbling under their breath.

The Mayor would then auction off the deer. Ed's deer was the last to be sold. I waited anxiously to put in my bid for the animal.

The bid started at one dollar. I was in from the start. Women were shocked to hear a woman's voice in the bidding war. Ed was there one minute and then gone the next. Where did he go? When my bid reached ten dollars, I heard a familiar voice raise me twenty-five cents. Then again, I placed my bid, and the voice increased it to ten dollars and fifty cents.

I turned to where the voice was coming from, and it was Ed. He was bidding against me. He tipped his hat towards me and smiled.

"Eleven dollars and twenty-five," I yelled out.

"Eleven dollars and fifty cents," he said back. I was stubborn enough to keep this bid going all night. The crowd was enthralled by the caller's voice. Ed, on the other hand, was getting anxious for the bidding to be over for this time.

When we reached my bid of sixteen dollars, Ed turned to the crowd and proclaimed me the winner.

"Sold to the pretty lady for sixteen dollars." Ed then announced to the crowd to make their way to the saloons. Drinks were on the house.

I knew I had better lasso the man of the hour before he had a chance to celebrate his winning.

"Liz, can you cook?" Ed asked me. "I know your mama was a right fine cook, but I never saw you once lift a finger to do any cooking yourself."

"Come to my house on Sunday afternoon, and I will show you if I can cook or not."

"I'd love to go over to your house."

"I will need to tell you where I am living. I moved over here a few weeks ago. I live west of town."

"Come celebrate with me. We can stash the deer in the butcher's icehouse."

"Did you hear what I even said?"

"Yeah, yeah, you live here. Therefore, you can come to celebrate with me. I need a drink and smoke." MEN! I was somewhat disappointed that I did not rate higher than the drink that day. I told myself that this was his life that I wanted to join.

He owed me nothing. It would take time on his part to get used to the idea of having a woman around him full-time. I had experience with bachelors.

"Let's go celebrate," I said as we walked into a crowded saloon.

24th February 1904

I showed Ed that I could cook a dinner like my mama. What surprised him the most when he arrived was that I had invited my family over for the festivities. I prepared enough food for an army. Of course, the size of the family is like a small army. The venison was delicious.

He is such a tease. He whispered to me that he knew why I invited them over so that I could have help cooking the meal. Of course not, I insisted, and then said it was so I could have help in the cleanup. He laughed, and as he hugged me, he twirled me around in the air. I was giddy with happiness. Oh LJ, I just want to pinch myself and see if this life is for real or not. I have dreamt of this for most of my life.

Have you always wanted something for so long that when it finally happens, you question yourself as to why you wanted it in the first place?

CHAPTER THIRTY-FIVE

1st March 1904

Ed came over in the early evening and stayed with me until the wee hours of the morning. He fulfilled all of my desires, moving very slowly. He seemed to take as much pleasure out of the encounter as I did. Then we slept, wrapped in each other's arms until he woke me with a passionate kiss. I could stay here forever like this. His touch was soft and pleasurable. Why did the sun have to rise today and take my pleasure from me? He promised to return and dared me to stay in bed, awaiting his return.

2nd March 1904

I stayed in bed all day yesterday, awaiting his return. Sadly, when he did appear, he was as drunk as he could be. He hurt my feelings when he mocked me for taking on the dare. Trust in this relationship is quickly fading. My elation has turned sour.

3rd March 1904

Ed is gone to a Rancher's Association meeting in Prescott. He left this morning on the train. I told him I wanted to go down and see him off, but he insisted that I stay home in bed. I have slept alone for so long now in my life that every minute without him seems like a bottomless empty cavern. I do not like it when he is away. I am not one to take orders and stay home when all I really want is to go off with him. Can I trust him? Maybe he has grown tired of me already.

I know I will go crazy these next few days.

4th March 1904

I have been so bored. I have a plan. I am not sitting here in Williams alone. It is George's birthday, and I am going to Bellemont and visit him. If Ed thinks that I will be here waiting for him as he departs from the train, he is sadly mistaken. He can find me.

6th March 1904

A heavy late-winter storm came in last night. There must be a good five feet out there. Lucky for George, I am here to help him. We ran the pigs into the barn, which was a big job. The storm gave no warning and the days prior had been almost like summer.

I sense that George is not as young and able-bodied as he once was in his younger days. He is nearing the age of my parents at their death. I will not let myself think of George as old. I pray for a long life for him.

7th March 1904

The storm stranded me at the farm. It was déjà vu to me. I felt like I was back up North. I had no longing to return, if that is what you are thinking, LJ. We played cards all day, and he listened intently to my stories. I realized then that besides my sisters, no one else ever wanted to hear them. Everyone is too busy, I assume.

9th March 1904

I made it back to the world. Amazing how the sun comes out here and warms the ground so quickly. One would never know except for the mud that we had a big storm. Another warm day and the snow will be all but gone. I would have given anything in the Yukon for it to be like this.

The first thing I did was to go to the telephone office and make a call to Tillie. She was glad for the news. She was happy to hear that George was not alone on his birthday. We discussed having dinner for him soon. Food always made him happy. I made my way home, finding the place empty and cold.

There was no sign that Ed had been here. Even my doorstep was clear of footprints. In all of those days, he did not yet attempt to check on me. I am dumbfounded. My curiosity as to whether or not he returned from Prescott will not get the better of me. I will wait to hear from him.

Yes, I am stubborn.

10th March 1904

After an entire day of no news, George came by to see me. He informed me that George B had been by to see him. The Association meeting went well because he told me everything. After a few moments, I questioned him as to if there was anything else he wanted to say to me. He looked up and away from me only to whisper that Ed was in jail in Prescott.

I showed no emotion. I thanked him for telling me, but I insisted that it was none of my business. He is safe and sober for the time being.

15th March 1904

He received ten days in jail for drunk and disorderly behavior. He got off lucky because there is some influence in being on the board of Ranchers. I gave him no sympathy, not that he expected any. It is the dark cloud in our relationship. It saddens me deeply.

I had a nightmare last night. A black horse was dragging me away from something that felt evil. The horse appeared to be protecting me. Was that it? Is the horse, my protector, and the man my enemy? Silliness, I must stop this nonsense. It was years ago, and I am safe. Nothing has harmed me so far.

30th March 1904

Ed has stayed sober when he is with me. He has obligations to attend to for the Rancher's Association. He is also readying the cowboys for the spring move. He has invited me along to watch. Does he know that I am itching to learn all I can about ranching? I do not intend to sit around cooking and sewing. If I could mine for gold and run a roadhouse, subsequently, I can herd cattle. Should he be against it, we are through. I shall get my own ranch. My life is leaning towards boredom and monotony. I am itching to do real work.

1st April 1904

We awoke early to catch the train north to Anita. We rode in the caboose. Jesse, a friend of ours from Williams, has worked the line since it opened and offered us a bench in the back with him. He knew us and said there was no use in us sitting with the Easterners.

We arrived in familiar sights. It is somewhat desolate in the open prairie. A small depot which houses the local post office and a few cabins and that is about all that is around. The wind seems to blow every time I have been in this place, tumbleweeds roll down the dirt street as if hurrying on a journey to nowhere. The grasses were bent over, headed northeasterly, apparently in the direction of the wind.

Women and children came out of the cabins to greet Ed. He eagerly hugged them and introduced me to them. It was as if he were the great leader returning home.

We walked toward the largest cabin and then made our way to the back. To my surprise, he lived in one of the smallest ones. The largest was a bunkhouse for the unmarried men. Inside there was a chair, a table, and a bed. The room was sparsely decorated. He informed me that the wives were in charge of dinner for everyone. I said nothing. He then included "No work, no eat."

We are a family, he said. There were families from other outfits who lived here too. Over the years, they had settled into this routine.

Most of the men were out with the herds and did not live in the small community.

Ed told me to join the women while he rode out to find the men. He was gone before I could protest. I was met with a warm greeting inside the tent that housed the kitchen. In talking to the women, they all seemed to know what their job was in the meal preparation. Several were either pregnant or nursing infants. The older children were in school inside one of the cabins.

Eagerly, they questioned me about who I was with today. When I said my maiden name, they all recognized it. My brother Bert was a regular here. Johnny worked with many of the men for the Hashknife Ranch. I instantly felt at home.

When the children were dismissed from school, the teacher came inside the tent and introduced herself. Immediately she insisted that I stay with her tonight in her cabin. I thanked her, not knowing what else to say. I had not thought that far ahead to be worrying about where I would sleep. For today, I was a guest and treated with respect. I knew that if Ed and I married, my position here would change.

They questioned me on my life in the Yukon and kept saying how I was the bravest woman they had ever met. I thanked them and returned that I thought they were courageous. Gasps of disbelief went around the tent.

I told them that to live out here and survive the cold winters were no different from me in the roadhouse. I could surmise that the women were amazed that I called them brave. I went on to explain that they are raising a family out here on the plains away from civilization. That takes a courageous person to do what you ladies do for your families. You are allowing your husbands to be cattlemen and family men.

"I have brothers who have been cattlemen but have chosen a single life as Ed has done," I said encouragingly.

"Why, Liz, you make us feel valuable, and we never feel relevant. When are you and Ed getting married? We'd sure like to see you be a part of us here and at Spring Valley," the women said in agreement. "I guess I need to explain to you that I am a married woman. Married to another man; however, I am in the process of getting an annulment," I tried to explain.

One of the women let out a little gasp and clarified, "You mean, since you are Catholic, you cannot get a divorce." The other women gasped at the woman's rude remark.

I explained that it was all right. "I am Catholic, and I know that the church does not believe in divorce. The relationship between my husband and me is that we have moved on from each other. He wanted to return to Alaska, and I did not want to spend the rest of my life away from my family. If the church does not agree, then I will leave the church, but not by choice. I will do what I can do to convince the church that I had no choice and hope they will understand." I have never had to explain my position before to anyone. It was awkward for both the women and me. Preferably, it was a relief to me having it out in the open instead of hiding who I was from others.

"You're in love with Ed?" asked a woman, dying of curiosity. She was acting as if she did not care. I laughed. "I think I have been in love with Ed Geddes my whole life or at least a good part of it," I said dreamily.

Ed and I spent the evening together sitting around the fire trying to keep warm. One of the women even brought out a blanket for us to snuggle up in. The women giggled as they enjoyed watching the two of us together and remembering back when they courted. All the women were somewhat envious of our relationship.

3rd April 1904

I watched the camaraderie of Ed with his cowhands. There seemed to be mutual respect. The banter of teasing went back and forth. I love this man. The ranch is where he is happiest. I have to prove to him that he can have both worlds.

Ed remarked back, "You're just jealous because you can't get a woman to look at you. Now, saddle up the horses for us, you lousy cowboys. Liz and I are going to take a ride." Ed said he had never had a woman accompany him on a ride before that he felt so comfortable.

Usually, he was trying to make sure they did not hurt themselves, or the horse runs off.

Ed showed me how to check the cattle for the brand. He felt proud of teaching me how to become a stock woman. I have much to learn. We rode to where the juniper and Pinon trees started. We dismounted the horses, giving them a much-needed break. I walked away and hid when he began to chase me. I was an easy find.

His well-defined muscles revealed themselves as he removed his shirt to cool himself. My hand immediately started rubbing them, which turned into making passionate love there on the cold ground. Nothing fazed us for hours until we realized that we had to return to camp.

6th April 1904

The next afternoon I boarded the train headed home to Williams, the women, telling Ed to bring me back soon for a visit.

When two hearts join in mutual interests, they become one.

CHAPTER THIRTY-SIX

Proving Myself, Again

8th April 1904

I returned home alone on the train. I could feel Ed's anxiety begin to build over the move to Spring Valley. I was the one who suggested that he stays, and I return. He seemed to be impressed that I understood the task involved in moving the cattle. After all, I am the daughter of a rancher.

I look back at my father and admire him even more for his tenacious desire to succeed. He had such difficulties with his leg but persevered to create a beautiful life for us all. I have more respect for my parents now than when they were alive. God rest their souls.

After a long hug and kiss, he told me that I was welcome anytime. If he were not in Anita, he would be out on the range and return shortly. As the train was pulling away, he shouted, "Don't be a stranger." Then I saw the women, waving good-bye to me. I felt as if I were a part of them.

I am happy.

20th April 1904

I received a message from Ed, through Jesse, our friend on the train, which stated that he would be leaving Anita soon with the herd. *"Please come "*How could I say no? I am off on the next train to the Grand Canyon.

21ˢᵗ April 1904

I arrived at a scurry of people dismantling the camp. Ed was out on the range and would return before nightfall. He left specific instructions for me to wait in the kitchen tent, as it would be the last thing taken down.

I could not sit without offering help. I was quickly given a huge pile of potatoes to peel. As I was making my way through the spuds, a familiar man came up to the table. He asked me if I was Ed's, new woman. The women gave him a glare that could stop a train. He quickly apologized, and I accepted, holding out my hand and introducing myself as Lizzie Shroyer.

Then he introduced himself as Tom Harvey, fellow rancher. I laughed and told him that I was Lizzie Hoffman. We had gone to school together. It instantly broke the ice, and we began reminiscing. He got a whiskey bottle and started drinking.

As time went on, he sat nearer and tighter to me, so close that I could smell the liquor on his breath. Being a bit repulsed, I rose, pretending to be looking for the potato pot. When I returned and tried to sit to one side of him, he grabbed my arm and pulled me down to the bench beside him. I tried moving and managed to pull myself away from him. Not wanting to make a scene, I walked elsewhere, knowing he would follow me.

He immediately took it as if I were egging him on. He nuzzled his face in close to mine and asked me why I would want to be with someone as old as Ed. After all, he and I were the same age; Young and vigorous. When he was near enough to me, I put my hand inside my pocket, placing my hand on my gun. My mind raced back to the Roadhouse and the old trapper. My finger went inside the trigger.

"Why don't you and I go off together and get naked. See, you have aroused me. You can't just leave me like this."

I could feel the cold steel barrel push against his tight frame.

"Is that a gun, Lizzie?"

"Yes, and you would not be the first man I have shot. Consider this a warning. We will see lots of each other, so let us both forget that this happened today. You wouldn't want to rile Ed, now would you?"

Sweating and visibly shaken, he immediately stepped back and exited the tent. Later, after Ed arrived and we were eating, he introduced me to his fellow rancher and his wife, Sarah. I wondered if she performed her wifely duties to him earlier in the day.

I quickly explained that we had met earlier and that we had known each other years back. Tom relaxed, and I knew that I would have no problem with him in the future.

A giant bonfire was burning, drawing us toward the flame like a moth to the light. The ranch hands were playing several guitars and handmade instruments. It had a festive feel to it. We sat huddled together, enjoying the entertainment. I felt like I had come home, reminiscing in my mind of my memories of my first cattle drive. It seemed so long ago.

Tom and his wife soon joined us, acting as if nothing had happened between us. The men discussed the move, deciding that they would begin at first light in two days. Sarah and I would go together on the train back to Williams.

Sarah was not one to live out on the range. She was a city girl and had her home just outside Flagstaff to the southeast. A chair was brought out for both of us, but I chose to be on the ground beside Ed.

Visiting led Tom to question me more about my life in the Yukon. The stories were new to Ed since he refused to talk about my previous experience. Surprisingly, Tom asked me, specifically about my shooting a man. I felt Ed's attention awaken. He sat up a little straighter as I began to tell the story. I left out no detail, not wanting to lose his focus. He listened intently but refused to ask me any questions.

"Damn, Ed, that is quite a woman you have there. You must be very proud of her." I sat waiting for a compliment but sadly, one did not come.

24 April 1904

Tom caught me before Sarah and I boarded the train home. He apologized to me for his behavior the other day. I accepted, and I knew that he and I would have a good friendship. I also know that Ed will learn more about me through my stories to Tom. He is captivated by my tales. Funny, he told me I could write them down. He was surprised to learn that I have kept you all these years. Ed does not know about you.

An apology from the heart is priceless and earns great respect.

CHAPTER THIRTY-SEVEN

Spring Valley

14 May 1904

My mind has been distracted with the twelve years since that awful day my mother died. It must have occurred to Ed since I received word for me to visit him today. I am happy for the distraction.

I can take the train to Chandellar, where he will pick me up. It is another eight or so miles up to Spring Valley. My first sight of the valley was of the beautiful Cienega surrounded by mountains. Ed explained that they called the big one Kendrick Mountain, and another nearby mountain is Government Mountain.

There is a lovely view to the north of the San Francisco Peaks. As I gaze out over the valley, I think this is one of the most beautiful places I have ever seen. I have seen many places in my life. There is an abundance of deer, rabbits, turkeys, and other birds. Of course, it has its predators like the coyote, the Mexican gray wolf, bears, bobcats, and rattlesnakes, just to name a few.

The winter runoff has left tanks full of water for the cattle and the pastures green. There is a calmness here. I am in love with this place.

Ed was especially proud of his ranch. Since it was my first time in the area, he wanted to show me everything. He tried to run off with me to the top of Kendrick Mountain and make beautiful love to me under the rustling of the aspen trees.

I knew that like all of Northern Arizona, the summer rains and lightning could get intense. This was nothing new to me since I had spent a good deal of my life here. When I asked Ed about cyclones, he laughed and said, "No whirlwind would dare to take on the likes of my little Cyclone." The endearment in his voice touched me.

I noticed that there were more cabins and fewer tents. People were spread throughout the valley. I asked where the kitchen tent was, and he laughed at me. He explained that here most meals were eaten separately. They did have a fire pit for larger gatherings. He showed me where he cooked his own meals outside, not wanting to heat the cabin in the warmth of summer.

Ed's cabin was small, with little decoration. I could tell that it needed a woman's touch to make it more of a home. My mind was already racing with ideas on how to decorate. If things worked out according to plan, this would soon be my cabin also. The small windows did not have curtains, but I could quickly remedy that.

Ed excused himself politely, telling me that he had chores to be done. I could go with him if I liked or stay in the cabin. I chose to remain behind arranging the small kitchen in a useful way. My new friend Catherine, or Cat as she prefers, lives across the valley and to the south. I finished my work and walked across the Cienega to her cabin. The children saw me walking, and all came running to greet me. I had many questions for Catherine but did not want to seem as if I were over-anxious to become a part of their lives.

"Ed went out on the range?"

"Yes, yes, he did, and he asked me to go, but I decided to stay back at the cabin. I don't want to interfere with his work in any way."

"You two seem like an old, married couple even though you are not married yet. I have never seen Ed so calm and relaxed before. You are a good woman for him. It takes just the right woman to make a man like Ed settle down. Many have tried, believe me," Cat said in such a way that it made me wonder if she had been one of Ed's many women.

"Yes, I have known some of his women. Did he bring many of them out here to the ranch?" I had asked the question; now I was not so sure that I wanted to hear the answer.

"Out here? Why no girl, he ain't stupid. He knows that none of them would live out here on a ranch with him. That is what makes you so special. You have ranching and adventure in your blood."

"I grew up on a farm in Kansas and a ranch in New Mexico. I lived in a roadhouse out in the Yukon. I can handle life on a ranch," I boasted.

"Have you ever branded a calf before?" Cat asked.

"Yes, when my dad was teaching my brother Johnny. My brother used to work for the Hashknife Outfit."

"No wonder Ed has his eye on you. A good ranch owner knows that he has to have the right people to make a ranch run smoothly. Sounds like you have some things to teach him," Cat said as we both started to laugh. It would be good to have a friend like Cat around. I missed the friendship of women like her.

5th September 1904

Today is my 28th birthday. I have spent my summer in Spring Valley, Williams, and Flagstaff; however, seldom out of the company of Ed. It was terrific, LJ. I have more women as friends than I have ever had in my entire life. True friends. I now see what I was missing. I was trying so hard to be a boy that I lost out on being a girl. These are hardy women, like my mother.

4th October 1904

We were all caught by surprise when early this morning, there was a loud screeching sound and then a crashing noise coming from the railroad yard. A train from Seligman headed into Williams hits a stopped train. Two men were killed right there in town. Our ease of train riding has been disrupted by the reality of the danger involved.

My prayers to the families of those hurt and killed.

Thanksgiving, 1904

My family says that I am too distant. Ed and I will spend the day with them. My sisters will make me out to be the biggest sinner in the country. They remind me that I am still a wedded woman. They think nothing of Ed being with a married woman. I find that interesting.

New Year's Eve 1904

I am looking forward to next year. I hope that by this time I am married to Ed. We are starting our New Year's in Flagstaff, and then we will hop the train to Williams. We are such a popular couple that everyone wants to see us. I am having fun, if nothing else.

I will be myself, but I also recognize that I can learn from my new friend.

CHAPTER THIRTY-EIGHT

Where is Johnny?

2nd January 1905

I am still in bed. I overdid my partying. We did not get home until late yesterday afternoon. It must have been the punch. Everyone had to add to it until it almost straight liquor. The party just kept going. I danced all night and well into the day. I thought that writing might help my head, but alas, it seems to be making it worse. My feet hurt so bad; I must look for a new pair of shoes next time I am in Flagstaff.

15th January 1905

We are taking a trip to see Nellie. She has moved to San Bernardino. Warm California weather. I cannot wait. Fresh citrus and seafood, my favorite. It reminds me of when Bill and I were there. Mr. Jealous does not want to hear about that, though. Am I with Bill? What does he think? If I were going back to him, I would have already been gone.

26th January 1905

LJ, I had so much fun. We went to the beach and played in the sand. Ed actually had fun. He let down that cowboy tough fellow guard. Ed in a swimming suit is a sight. He refused to have his picture taken. We played games up and down the boardwalk and rode a wooden roller coaster. For a man who can ride a bull, his face was as white as a ghost. He claimed that it did not bother him, but he would not ride it a second time.

Little Georgie is a grown man. He has a lovely girlfriend. Nellie is hoping they get married. Imagine, I have a nephew who is twenty now. I feel old.

Nellie and I went to church. She had a difficult time explaining Ed and me to her friends. She finally started calling him my traveling companion.

Silly, Nellie. She is so prim and proper.

30th March 1905

Time flew by, and before we knew it, we needed to begin making plans to move the herd back to Spring Valley for the summer. Again, it works like a well-oiled machine. We are staying out at Anita until the roundup. The women included me in all the planning. The solitary person to object much was Sarah Harvey. She thinks she gets all the say since she is the lonely wife of a rancher. The women do not like to be looked down on, and she treats them, well, let us say she is somewhat snobbish. Uppity up. The women tell me that they trust me and not her. I try not to get in anyone's way since I am an outsider.

15th April 1905

Wagons are loaded, and the cabins are all packed up for the summer. I am excited to be a part of the big expedition to Spring Valley. It will take several days to reach the Valley going overland with the cattle. Everyone must do his or her part to make it a successful move. Even the children have a job to do; Just like when I was a child. When all is prepared, the roundup will move out at first light. We pray for a smooth and safe journey.

16th April 1905

Since it is staying light later, we could travel a reasonable distance today. Travel was slow but steady. Clouds were rolling in, and we were all praying for good weather but knew what life is like in the high mountains in the spring. It would not be unusual or surprising if snow fell. Everyone was prepared for what lay ahead.

18th April 1905

Ed had to double back, taking a couple of the men with him looking for eight missing cattle. The wind was blowing so hard you had to keep your head down. I wish I were with him. If I had my own horse, I would be of use. I am feeling very anxious because of the weather. I yearn to be helping him out. Instead, here I sit. Next year will be different. I will not let him talk me into sitting in a damn buggy or wagon.

19th April 1905

We pushed our way east, not stopping to wait for Ed and the others. We met Bert headed home from the Canyon. He gave us an update on Ed. He found six of the cattle and will return later to look. I say you cannot risk six animals for two. We could always go back and search for the two later.

25th April 1905

This trip for me was an easy one. Comparing my life now with my life in the Yukon, there is no likeness. At times, I think it is hard for Ed to imagine how difficult life was for me. Riding in a wagon on a trail was much easier than driving a dog sled over the frozen earth in a blizzard. I told my stories to Tom and the others. They listened intently.

Maybe by the time Ed and I are too old to herd cattle, he will let me tell him my stories. They are now more fun to tell than experiencing it firsthand. At times, it seems so long ago, and even I am amazed at what I accomplished. 'Gold Dust Lizzie, the lady of the Yukon!'

20th May 1905

I received word that Johnny would be calling Tillie today. I sure miss him. He has news for us that he wishes to share with all of us. Johnny plus surprises are not two words you use together. Is it good news or bad news?

Johnny is following in my footsteps. Well, sort of. He is going on a gold-mining expedition in Mexico for the summer. This professor person is leading them, and Johnny will be the mule packer and cook. The professor knows about some gold that is on an island in the Gulf of California.

Johnny did not want to say much about it for fear others would get the word. I understood the matter of secrecy entirely and did not press him further.

Tillie was worried. She said one miner was enough in this family. He will not have ice and snow to deal with. I asked him if it was dangerous, and he said no, they planned it all out with the Mexican authorities. My thought was, so did the people on the Chilkoot. Never underestimate Mother Nature. Go over-prepared.

We laughed and agreed that we would compare notes when he returned in August.

10th June 1905

Life here in the valley is peaceful. Every direction that you look at, you can see a mountain. We walk up to the top of Kendrick and are in awe of the view. Spectacular! Is all we need is a light show from the Northern Lights!

6th July 1905

Tillie expected to hear from Johnny. She is fretting. He is fine. I am sure– there is just no way to get word home. I told her we would not hear from him until he drops those bags of gold at our feet. She does not think I am funny.

I rode over the Beale wagon road to her place; it is just a jump, bound, and a leap away. It would be perfect if I had my own horse. I have to borrow a horse from the ranch. Ed promises me that one of these days he will buy me a gelding.

15th August 1905

Jesse called down to the sheriff of Morenci and asked him if they had any word from the gold-mining party. Not a word he said. The professor's brother arrived the other day, preparing for the homecoming. The sheriff says he will keep him posted.

5th September 1905

I am twenty-nine today. Maybe my birthday will bring news from Johnny. That would be a good present.

16th September 1905

No word yet from Johnny, Please God, let him be safe and return to us. Everyone is beginning to worry since they are a month overdue. The Professor was to be back to start his term as Principal of the Morenci Schools.

1st October 1905

Nothing. No word. I am beside myself. The Professor's brother wants to go and try to trace their steps. Tillie said something about cannibals down there. We are in daily communication with the sheriff. He checks the trains coming in and out of Mexico and posted flyers in Spanish.

15th October 1905

Not looking hopeful. Two months late. They will be out of supplies. *"Please, Lord. Help him."*

16th October 1905

The family is meeting with the Priest today. The families of the other men on the expedition are gravely concerned, as are we. Jesse remains in contact with the Sheriff of Graham County. I need to be with my family.

I keep thinking that if I were in Alaska with Bill, I would be beside myself. No, I would be traveling home to be with them. I pray that Ed understands my needs. LJ, why are men so hardheaded? Ed assured me that we are worrying needlessly. If anybody can make it back, it is Johnny. I agree with him, but I also know the perils of gold mining. It is never safe.

Bill taught me to take nothing for granted. Do not let your guard down. I will go and pray for our instincts to be right. Amen

5th November 1905

He is alive! Thank you, Lord. We will travel south later in the week to Morenci to see him. He is weak and no bigger than a beanpole. His beautiful black hair has turned white. They say he looks like an old man. No one else in the party has returned.

My beautiful Johnny. Ed wants me to stay behind and not go. He thinks we have made too much of this. I told him not to make me choose. Will he ever learn that I am not a typical subservient woman?

I have always followed my own path, and I will never give that up.

Begrudgingly, he has allowed me to go see him.

25th November 1905

What a trip we had. Johnny was recuperating after weeks of dehydration and sun sickness. It will be a slow recovery, but the main thing is he is alive.

We were shocked to see his skin and bones. We are lucky because none of the other men have returned. I fell in love with the Morenci area. They mine for copper in the hills around here. Although, the mountains in the east must be loaded with veins of gold. You get gold in your blood, and it is hard to deny the urge. I reminded myself that I have a different life now.

Ed missed me profusely. He has too much time on his hands during the fall.

If it is not your day to die, you shall be spared. Prepare to do well.

CHAPTER THIRTY-NINE

Wedding

28th December 1905

Word came from my attorney in Flagstaff that my annulment was complete. Ed played Santa Claus for the local children this year. He surprised me by proposing in his Santa suit. Never, would I have imagined that? He suggested we elope, but I have other plans. I want a wedding, intimate with friends and family will suffice. We have such kind friends. John Selman and his wife Rose had suggested that we get married at their house. The ladies of Williams have offered to help plan the wedding. I know it will be beautiful. We set the date of January 25, yes, in just a month. I will be quite busy from now until then. Nellie and Tillie will be disappointed that it is not in the church, but I prefer to have a small ceremony.

4th January 1906

I chose a gray satin material and lace for the dress. We had it shipped out all the way from Chicago. I had in mind a beautiful dress that I once saw from Paris while I was living in Dawson City. When I first saw the dress there, I could imagine myself as a bride in it. I would sketch a great drawing of how I remembered it looking. Mrs. Gardener, the seamstress, would be very capable of re-creating such a dress. Plans are coming together nicely for the big day.

Rose went with me to the dressmaker. It was so cold today. Mrs. Gardener had tea ready for us to warm up after being out in the weather.

"Why you ladies must be icicles being out on a day like today," she said. "Come in and get warm before you go trying on a wedding dress." We were grateful for the hot tea. We removed our hats, gloves, and coats and proceeded to the comfortable sitting room. The little shop on Main Street was adorned in a very feminine fashion. Lace curtains were hanging from the windows and beautiful lace doilies on the tables. In a corner was a stylish display of hats and gloves. Mrs. Gardener brought the nearly completed wedding dress, which exactly matched my drawing. When I saw the dress, I let out a small gasp of delight. It was even better than I had imagined. She was very meticulous in its creation. That left the dress to be sized to fit my petite body. She carefully pinned the back accordingly and had me stand on the table so that she could get the exact length of the hem.

"There must be hundreds of little beads on the dress," Rose said, never having had such a beautiful dress herself. Rose's wedding dress was very simple and inexpensive. Her husband, after all, was the meat cutter for the shop in Williams and the surrounding ranches.

Mrs. Gardener replied, "No, there are five hundred and thirty-two little beads in all. I counted each one as I sewed them on."

"Mrs. Gardener," I said enthusiastically, "your dress is much more beautiful than the one from Paris." She was thrilled with such praise for her work. She could not stop thanking me for the compliment. I can scarcely wait for the day of my wedding. My thoughts went to Ed, and if he will think I am beautiful.

17th January 1906

Now is all that is left to do is to purchase the undergarments. That consists of crotchless bloomers (you know LJ, for ease in the lavatory), and a corset that is laced tight. I have to look very skinny because it is all the rage. Before I can fasten the corset, shoes go on the feet first. Once you fasten the corset, it is almost impossible for a woman to bend over to put her shoes on. Then a chemise will go on down to the knees. Followed by several petticoats, leggings, garters, and the bustle pillow for the back of the dress. All of these things go on before the dress. It takes a woman quite some time just to put clothes on.

Ed, on the other hand, will be wearing a pair of long johns, followed by a silk shirt, black wool pants, and a silk tie, double-breasted vest with the dress coat. In his vest pocket, will be a monogrammed handkerchief with the "G" showing.

Gentlemen carry handkerchiefs to offer to the women when they cry. At weddings, men need several hankies. It seems as if all women cry when someone gets married. Ed's boots will have a square toe made of patent leather. Women's boots had pointed toes. Flowers were ordered from Los Angeles and will arrive on the train on the day of the wedding. A cake made by the local bakeshop. The wedding rings have been specially created in Chicago and are scheduled to arrive just in time.

24th January 1905

Johnny cannot make it. He is still weak and needs to keep his strength. He plans to return to Mexico soon to retrace their steps to see if he can locate any of the party. I am sad, but I understand. George is giving me away. It seems appropriate that he steps in for our father. The Selman house was decorated for the wedding. It will be a candlelight evening wedding with the Justice of the Peace, Mr. Crawford presiding. The Selman's son, Ronald, is just a baby. I was concerned about disturbing his routine, but Rose assured me that things would be beautiful. After all, the house would be filled with my nieces and nephews.

25th January 1906

It is here, LJ, my wedding day. I am so excited, and I have to wonder if there has ever been anyone more excited than me. This is the day I have been dreaming of most of my life. I pinch myself, and I am here, so it is not a dream. I know I should arise from my slumber.

However, I just want to lie here and savor every moment. This day must not hurry for this is the most important day of my life.

I wish that my mama and daddy could be here to witness my marriage. I know that daddy would be proud of me. Would mama think I was beautiful? I know that I am older than most brides. Now that I think about it, it was ten years ago that I went to the Yukon. I was so young and fearless.

I take more time now in making decisions in my life.

Ed and I have a six o'clock appointment with Mr. Crawford, the Justice of the Peace. I do feel sad not having a priest officiating. This time it is a real marriage with the vows being consummated.

I am spending my day preparing for this evening. I plan on soaking in a hot bath of rose water. Then I will nap a bit before the girls start on my hair and face. Luckily, they have not arrived yet, as I am enjoying this time of being by myself.

Lunch will be served to us. I have asked for those little finger sandwiches that have salmon and cucumber on them. I specifically ordered salmon as a rare treat for today. It is the one thing I miss the most from the north. I wonder if Ed planned anything special. Lord, do not let him indulge in too much liquor today. I do want him to be upright. Men. Anyway, I plan on being pampered with fine chocolates and wine, a good merlot, along with our luncheon.

I have left others in command of preparations. I ordered delicate paper napkins that remind me of onion skin paper. I had our initials placed on them with the date of our marriage printed in gold, My favorite color. Ed would think that it was a waste of money. I call it sentiment. When we are old and gray, I will bring out my velvet photo album, and we shall have a keepsake.

Tillie loaned me pearl earrings for something borrowed. I would have loved to have worn something of my mama's, but nothing was left after the fire. Do not start crying now, Liz. For blue, I am wearing a blue Safire pin in my veil. Just for good measure, the black onyx horse is in a pocket in my pantaloons. That is what is old, and of course, my dress is new.

Speaking of my dress, it has been delivered, and it is so gorgeous. I hope Ed likes it. He told me that I could wear nothing at all and be the most beautiful woman in the world. Why do women even bother?

I hear the girls arriving, so my day has officially started. I now have butterflies in my stomach. I suppose maybe I sampled a little too much merlot already since I am giggling and do not know why.

I am now fully dressed and am waiting. I can hear people gathering downstairs. I am sequestered in the upstairs of the house and am not allowed to even peek. My patience is running thin. The next time I write in you, I shall be Mrs. Ed Geddes.

30th January 1906

Blissfully, I will tell you that right now I am the happiest I have ever been in my whole life. It was a beautiful ceremony. The candlelight evening made Rose's house look so charming. We ordered extra flowers from Los Angeles, expecting some to be wilted. However, they arrived in perfect condition. So, there were many bouquets spread around the room. The smell was heavenly. Guests were thrilled to share the arrangements after the service was over.

Of course, it was a short, simple ceremony. We gazed lovingly into each other's eyes as we said our vows. In sickness and in health until death do us part. My body shivered at that part. I do not recall at my first wedding, even reacting to those words. I was young, I suppose. I am not a naive bride. I am past the prime of my life. I wonder which one of us shall die first? He is older than me. I could not bear that after being apart for so long at a time. My wish is for a lengthy, happy life together. I do not ask for much in this life now. I am content to settle down being Mrs. Geddes.

Everyone braved the winter weather. We used George's sleigh to get people back and forth in town. It just made it that more festive. My brothers seemed to delight in the fact of my marriage. I am sure my life put them on the spot at times. Now I am a duly married woman.

Ed was a charismatic groom. We have stayed here in the hotel since the wedding. We lavished in tasty meals and time for us. We have not allowed ourselves to think of the ranch, for spring feels a million days away.

I will end this now as I hear someone coming up the stairs. My cowboy returns.

In a wedding, the vows are only the beginning.

CHAPTER FORTY

Earning the name, Boss Lady

4th July 1906

Ed signed up for the yearly calf-roping relay race. Three horses were strategically placed a quarter of a mile apart, three calves, and a saddle on the ground beside each horse and a rope.

Ed saddled up the first horse and rode as fast as he could to the calf, jumped off the horse and chased the calf, hog-tied the calf's feet, saddled up the next horse, and proceeded to be the first rider onto the following calf. This process was repeated a final time. The winner of the race would be the first rider to return to the start. Ed successfully moved on to the second horse and calf and then on to the third. Ed was the winner. The crowd loved it. I was so proud of him.

A hearty cheer went up. "Give Mr. Ed Geddes a hand, folks, on his remarkable race," said Mayor Nellis to the crowd of onlookers. Of course, he was my favorite cowboy. He has come a long way from the tenderfoot I once knew. I ran up to Ed and placed a big kiss on his lips. He quickly picked me up and put me on the horse with him. The crowd roared. Ed was definitely a showman. As the winner, he received fifty dollars.

"Drinks are on us at the saloon," Ed chirped, oblivious to the look on my face. I would have used the money for a honeymoon instead of flaunting it at the saloon. I know that he won the race, and, it is his prize money and not mine. We are so different when it comes to money.

The party moved to the ballroom above the saloon. It was obvious that Ed was settled in for the duration of the festivities. I knew that I needed to stay to keep him in line. I felt good; I steered him away from two fights. The party lasted through the night; as we were leaving, the sun was rising in the eastern sky. As we proceeded home, a drunken Ed slurred, "I love you, Cyclone." I love him too. I thought that life with him was like a cyclone. There was a significant difference in my life with Bill.

7ᵗʰ March 1907

Spring is just around the corner. I always feel so good in the spring. Ed and I have decided to increase the number of cattle on the ranch. We will travel to the stockyards of Los Angeles to purchase more head of cattle.

We intend to double the size of the herd.

12ᵗʰ March 1907

Ed purchased a beautiful black gelding for me as a late anniversary present. I named him Noble after the black onyx horse. I said he looked very regal and deserved a name like that. I am thrilled to have my own horse. There is nothing to the prediction of the little girl at Loretto. I was childish. Although, I have to admit that at first, I thought it odd that he would buy me a dark horse. We returned home on the train to Williams with cattle and the horse in hand.

I was prepared to ride Noble alongside Ed and his horse, but Noble seemed to have a different idea. The horse was still on edge from his ride on the train. Ed explained that it would take time before I could saddle him and begin to ride. I, instead rode in the buggy.

We moved the new herd to Anita. As Ed said, it was wiser to take them ourselves than change trains and unload twice.

14th March 1907

Our return to Anita was the perfect reason to have a celebration. The cowboys themselves provided the music for the dance. They did not have any local or military band playing for them. They provided their own group with a couple of guitars, washboards, and brown jugs. A couple of the men did the singing, and everyone else, including the children, danced and clapped along with the music.

Life is perfect right now.

10th April 1907

I had that nightmare again. Ed and the horse were in it. Ed was yelling at me about Noble. He was angry with me. I was scared he would shoot my horse. I wish I would stop having those awful dreams.

11th April 1907

We were out at the corral working with Noble. He seems to be very skittish around certain men– Ed being one of them. He paces and stomps his hooves. Ed left, and Noble was fine. I got him tethered with a walking cinch on him. I can get him rideable if Ed just leaves me alone with the damned horse.

12th April 1907

I made the mistake of telling Ed that Noble was well behaved around me. He went into a tirade and said we need good dependable horses, not a high-strung one. He has threatened to sell him. I will not let him. Noble and I are a good team. Besides, he was given to me as a gift. You cannot take a gift back.

14th April 1907

Bert stopped by to visit with me today. He was making deliveries to the Grand Canyon. Bert will always drink a cup of coffee when offered. He is so peculiar; he sits on the floor to drink his coffee. One day, I asked him why he never sat in a chair. He laughed and explained that at his house, there were not enough chairs for everyone, and being an old cowboy, he was used to sitting on the ground.

He began telling me about a fire they had on Sunday afternoon. He and Nora were enjoying a peaceful afternoon when they suddenly smelled smoke close by. Bert went to investigate and found his three boys high tailing it out of the barn and down the street. His son Floyd had found tobacco and was showing the younger boys how to smoke. The barn was a total loss, and lucky for them; it did not involve the house.

I laughed until my sides ached, picturing my little nephews (the oldest one was a mere six-years-old) running down the street to escape punishment. Bert was getting a lot of his own medicine back. He was so ornery as a little boy.

21st May 1907

Ed has not come in yet from the range. When I went to inquire as to his whereabouts, I was told that a cow was giving birth, and the calf was breech. I knew that meant he would not be home until the calf was delivered safely. It could take hours to deliver the calf.

"Take me out to where he is," I ordered one of the men.

"I don't know if the boss would want me to take you out there. It's so dark that we could have a hard time finding him," he protested.

"I am a capable horsewoman. You just show me what direction to look for him, and I will find him. If you do not take me, then I shall go out on my own. I think that would upset the boss more, don't you?" I said smugly, knowing that the men were afraid of Ed. "Now, let's stop wasting time and get going." We saddled the horses, and I took a basket of food and extra blankets with me. Ed was not as far away as I had thought. The men had a bonfire built, so they could see and be seen in the dark.

Ed, not surprised by my arrival in the middle of the night, even though most men would have been by their wife's intrusion.

However, he just shook his head and said: "That's why I love you, baby."

I stayed by his side for the rest of the night. Finally, close to dawn, we managed to pull the baby calf from inside its mother. As the calf stood to take its first steps, I let out a sigh of relief. Ed and I stood arm in arm watching the miracle of life unfold in front of us.

"I sure am glad that I did not marry a sissy. It takes a special kind of woman to be married to a rancher. Mine is as unique as they come," he said embracing me with a strong hug and a passionate kiss. "Let us get back home now, darlin. There will be plenty more times to see calves born."

"Oh Ed, I am so happy now. This is what I always wanted," I said kissing him passionately.

"We had better be gettin' home before we embarrass the men. We don't want to make them jealous of us." I knew what Ed was thinking and giggled at him.

"I love you, Mr. Geddes," as we rode towards home.

"And I love you, Mrs. Geddes. My life was never right after you left. Every dark-haired woman I would see I would think it was you. I thought I had lost you forever. I know my drinking gets the best of me at times. I never want to lose you again."

"I don't want to lose you either."

My position as "boss lady" secured, I had been tested, judged, and accepted by the hired hands as a member of the ranching community. This made me very happy. I traveled to parts unknown and become a rancher. I have done what I set out to do with my life.

Sometimes you have to do unexpected things to receive the approval of your peers.

CHAPTER FORTY-ONE

10th June 1907

Ed came in yesterday and told me that he had to go searching for cattle that had strayed. He asked me if I was interested in going along. You know me if, someone offers a possible adventure, I accept. I am just afraid I will miss something. At least, that is what mama always said about me.

Quickly, I changed into my leather riding pants and donned my beaver felt hat. Ed laughed, saying that I was so pretty even the bulls would be jealous of him.

"You don't need to dress up all pretty to go out riding," he teased me. "I suppose you got dressed up to go pan for gold, too."

"Of course, and don't go bringing up my past when you won't tell me a thing about yours. We agreed that we would leave the past behind us. Besides, you go and get all jealous of poor Bill," I scolded him.

"I am sorry, Liz, but a man who won't even tell his own mother that the two of you were married about eight years has a problem. I just do not get that. Did he take a vow of celibacy?" Ed went on complaining about Bill.

"I am ready to go now, Ed," I said, trying to get his mind off Bill. "I want to think about us and how much I love you."

We left following the Beale Wagon Road, its deep ruts entrenched in the earth. The wagon road goes right through Spring

Valley to Law Springs. We followed the wagon road until we could look out and see a mountain far off to the east.

"That mountain over there is the old volcano, Sunset Crater."

"It looks so small and far away from here. I think all of these mountains out here are old volcanos. I know the San Francisco Peaks are volcanos. We learned that in school. Why look, Ed, we are on volcanic rock."

We dismounted our horses at Law Springs. Ed was anxious to show me the stone marker that said, Law Springs. He explained that when Lt. Edward Beale's men stayed in the area, one of the men carved the name into the rock. Ed heard that the man cut headstones along the journey.

We saw the petroglyphs also scribed into the rock walls by Indians long ago. The pictures showed animals and men hunting. We knew we were looking at something ancient and unusual. We followed the trail on horseback back to Government Mountain.

"There are springs all over this area. A good place for homesteads, I see why more ranchers are moving farther out this way," I said. "You would not believe all the water in the Northwest, Ed. Why you can put your hand down in the water and snag yourself a nice big salmon. Oh, Ed, I wish you could taste a fresh salmon," I said, not seeing his face as he was bent over washing the dust off his face in the cold spring water.

"Liz, quick look down here in the water; what do you think this is?" he said while picking me up and submerging me in the cold water. My arms flailing as I was drenched and looked like a drowned cat.

"What did you go and do that for?" I said, pushing back a piece of wet hair from my face.

"You were talking about cold water like you missed it and well… this water is cold." He could not help but laugh at me.

My wet blouse was stuck to my skin, revealing every line of my undergarments.

"If I had been with you in Canada," he said, kissing me, "I am afraid the gold would still be there because I could not stay away from you. We would have just stayed indoors with each other, wrapped in a bear coat."

We spent the rest of the day riding the wagon road and exploring the area. I enjoy being with Ed. The two of us have so much in common. Ed was only serious about his cattle; the rest of his life is about having fun. Ed is so different from Bill. All at once, I could see it: Frank was not like my brother Johnny, as I had always thought. Frank was more like Ed. I could understand immediately why I was so attracted to Frank. Why did it take me, until now, to see it?

"Your mind is a million miles away, my dear," Ed said to me as he was helping me down off Noble.

"I was just thinking of someone I used to know in Canada. I will tell you about him one of these days when we are old and gray. You don't need to get jealous though, and he died in Canada a few years ago," I explained.

"Did you love him?" he asked, not wanting to hear the answer.

"Loved in a way that I love my brothers," I said. "I miss him; he made me laugh and cry. He was there for me when I needed a friend. But you, I love you more, and you make me laugh and cry."

"You are a beautiful person, Liz; I love you too," he said, gently touching my face and kissing me on the lips. We shared a very personal sensual afternoon at the top of Kendrick Mountain overlooking Spring Valley. As we made our way home, I thought to myself; I needed a sign made for over my front door that said 'Here' to replace the one at my roadhouse in Canada that read 'On To.'

I am happy and content. As far as I am concerned, if I was here at the ranch in Spring Valley for the rest of my life, I will be elated.

15th August 1907

A puppy was barking nearby. I kept looking out the little cabin window to see where it was coming from. I could not see a thing but definitely heard a puppy. My curiosity got the better of me, and I went outside to look. There was nothing but a wooden crate sitting near the front door. I approached it and saw that inside the container was a black-and-white border collie puppy. I opened the box and saw the bow tied around the puppy's neck.

"Are you mine? You are so soft and cute; I could just hug you all day long," I said, holding the puppy near my face. "Oh, you have puppy breath and puppy teeth."

"Will you hold me all day long?" Ed said, coming into the cabin.

"Oh! Ed! You shouldn't have… but I love him," I said excitedly as I held him up for Ed to see.

"What is his name?"

"You get to name him. Remember now; he will be a working dog. He is a border collie, and he will help us herd the cattle," he reminded me.

"Yes, I know, but not for a while. He is so little. His name will be Bo," I said, laughing as Bo licked my face. "Thank you, Ed," as I kissed him quickly, taking the dog indoors.

"I'm jealous now," he said, "but I have work I need to do today."

"Bo just left his mama; he is still a baby." I put him down, and he ran off to explore the cabin.

"You spoil him all you want; I got him for you. If he does not end up herding cattle, that is all right too. They are good dogs for protection," he said.

"I know; I had my sled dogs. Those were working dogs, and I do know how to teach a dog how to behave," I explained. I was reminded of my husky's protection. Bo stayed near me for the rest of the day. I was happy and content.

My brother Bert stopped by the cabin to visit. I proudly showed off the dog. I offered Bert his usual cup of coffee, and he promptly sat on the floor by the settee.

"Oh, sis, you know me," Bert said as the little pup crawled onto his lap and proceeded to go to sleep.

"You have patience with babies that I do not have. You are a good father. Our parents would be proud of you."

"I had a salt delivery today for George B. I heard he and Ed are going to Needles to sell some of their cattle. Fine looking cattle you two are raising out here. We have had enough rain this season to keep the cattle grazing well," he mused.

"Yes, there are just too many cattle in the area. Ed and George hear complaints all the time about an overabundance of ranchers," I replied.

"The good ranchers will hold on, and the inexperienced ones will move on. I have seen that since we came here. Ed knows that also. He never puts more cattle out there than the land can feed. Nora's family has been ranchers since the sixties. They went into the Tonto with a herd of cattle, they brought all the way from San Diego in Seventy-Five. Brought the herd up the Gila River after crossing the Colorado at Yuma," Bert told me. I could sit and listen to Bert's stories all day long. He was quiet most of the time, but when he told a story, people listened. He got around all over Northern Arizona, so he knew many stories.

Bert got up from his spot on the floor, placed the pup in my lap, kissed me good-bye, and made for the door. Ed was coming in at the same time.

"You are not leaving, are you, Bert?" Ed said, disappointed that he had missed seeing his brother-in-law. "We will be in town next week; maybe we will all have Sunday dinner at Tillie's house." "I will look forward to that," Bert said as he was leaving.

Bo barked his ferocious puppy bark as Bert's horses and buggy were heard driving away, making its way back to Flagstaff.

10th September 1907

Ed went to Needles this week to sell some cattle. He returned, having sold them for top dollar to a fellow rancher. Ed then wanted to buy Braham's from Kansas. George B. had a connection in the stockyards in Kansas City. They have planned the trip for later in the month. Most of the time, the women stay home. I have to train Noble while the weather is still warm. We do not have much time until winter comes again. I will surprise Ed with how well I am doing.

14ᵗʰ September 1907

Noble and I had a fall. I decided to take him out of the corral and down the road at a full gallop. Something spooked him, and he bucked. I went down under him, hitting the ground with my total weight. Nothing seemed broken, and I had to make sure that Noble was all right. I realized that my ankle was injured. We limped back together to the corral. Is all I can think is that I am glad Ed was gone. It would surely be Noble's fault. Is he jealous of my attention to a horse? He seems to despise this animal for some reason.

15ᵗʰ September 1907

I had the same dream except that it was Ed, who was on him when he bucked. Ed was so angry, and the gypsy kept saying, "I warned you about him." Ed should be back in a couple of days. I sure miss him. I am still pretty bruised. If I am lucky, he will not notice. I have asked the men not to utter a word about the incident.

10 October 1907

Ed never noticed my swollen ankle or the bruising on my arms. I kept myself well covered. His trip was a success. I told him about an invitation from Mr. Percival Lowell. Mr. Lowell built a massive stargazing telescope inside a big observatory on top of the hill westward above the town. He had extended an invitation for the ranchers and their wives to come for viewing after dark at the observatory. He balked at first, then he agreed to attend. I am so excited.

15ᵗʰ October 1907

A large group from the city, dressed in warm clothes, made our way up the windy road in carriages to the top of Lowell hill. Mr. Lowell was there to greet us as we approached the observatory. There was a significant opening on the roof. Gazing up, I saw the large telescope standing ominously inside the room. The long tube was eyeing the night sky.

Mr. Lowell took his seat upon the wooden stool that sat on a platform high above the floor. He positioned the scope towards Mars. Each person took his or her turn, viewing the stars and distant planets. It was exciting, but I like the skies in the north.

I was fascinated and caught up in Mr. Lowell's lecturing. I sat transfixed on his every word. I did not take notice as the room emptied, leaving only Tillie and me. Mr. Lowell was always eager to have captive audiences. We searched the night sky as I told Tillie about the Aurora Borealis in the northern hemisphere.

Mr. Lowell was quite impressed with my story and colorful description of it. He was more traveled than me.

"You tell the story so beautifully, Mrs. Geddes. It makes one feel as if one were there looking at it with you," Mr. Lowell said complimenting me.

"Why, thank you, Mr. Lowell. I tell the story with my heart."

"I could listen to your stories forever. Your voice is captivating," he told me. As we began looking for the men, we realized that they had left us up on the hill without a way home. Tillie, discreet, motioned for us to go.

"It is getting late, Mr. Lowell, although I understand that you spend your nights up here studying the sky. To the rest of the world, it is time to call it a night. Thank you for your gracious hospitality, Mr. Lowell. We will be looking forward to visiting with you again."

"Ladies, I will take you home in my motorcar since it seems that the rest of your company left you stranded up here."

"Mr. Lowell, how very kind of you," we said as we sat down in the motorcar. It was a night of firsts since neither of us had actually been in a motorcar before. The speed at which we raced down the mountain was exhilarating. I wondered how Ed would react to my being in a motorcar with a man I hardly knew.

When we arrived home, it was no surprise to find that Ed had not stayed with Jesse. Ed told Jesse that he had business downtown, which on this night was at the gambling table. He had money in his pocket that was itching to get out. I went to bed disappointed that Ed had not stayed and enjoyed Mr. Lowell's company.

I rose to find the puppy playing with the children.

"I hope you don't mind them playing with Bo. The children love dogs," Tillie said to me.

"No," I said, rather distracted. "Bo loves children. Is Ed outside with Jesse? Did he come home last night?" I asked, concerned.

"We haven't seen him today. We thought he was still asleep with you," Tillie said, not wanting to alarm me.

"No, he must have stayed over in town. There are times that Ed forgets that he is a married man."

Tillie offered to send Jesse into town to look for Ed. I expressed that I was planning on going in later to shop for a new dress.

Ed was nowhere to be found on the streets of Flagstaff. My longtime friend and saloon owner, Sandy Donohue, came to my aid. He told me that the Sheriff arrested Ed last night after he was causing a disturbance in another saloon. Ed had too much alcohol and fired off his gun into the floor.

"You know, Lizzie; the law is the law. Ed always thinks he is above the law. Guns have to be removed and left outside. Now, let us go see what shape he is in."

"Thanks, Sandy, you are a good friend," I said as I hugged him, eyeing the scars on his arm from our house fire years back.

Ed paid his fine and was let go, the Justice of the Peace warning him that if he repeated his actions, he could be asked not to return to town. We went home without speaking a word to each other.

Evening

He is taking his anger out on me. He says for me to stay out of his business. He called me a bitch and said that I was a spoiled woman who has always gotten her way. I could not help myself and told him, "No, I am a woman who stands up for herself."

He then tried to slap me. I ran out to the barn. I was leaving. I did not feel safe staying here with him in the mood he was in tonight. Jumping onto Noble, bareback, I rode off towards George's farm. Ed has a mean streak in him that scares me.

16th October 1907

I do not want that happening again. He followed me to George's. Noble seemed to understand my fear because he started bucking as Ed tried to come near me. That made him mad, and he began striking Noble with the reins. Noble reared up with me on him. I had nothing to hold onto, and Ed knew that, but he kept spurring him on.

George appeared, and Ed stopped. He actually pretended that it was Noble's fault and that he was just trying to help me get off. I was visibly shaken, and it was not Noble's fault. Ed was trying to hurt me.

George came to my rescue and helped me off. I clung to him tighter than I had in years. He knows me well enough to sense my fear. He walked me inside, leaving Ed. When I realized that he was alone with Noble, panic struck me. Would he kill him, as he has threatened in the past?

17th October 1907

George went out to talk to him and try to calm him down. After some minutes, he returned alone and said that Ed had left, but not before he made it clear, he was not up to discussing it today or anytime shortly. It was over, and that was that.

I began crying and explaining to George precisely what happened. He listened intently as I laid my head on his lap and cried myself to sleep. I am lucky to have him for my brother.

George was not there when I awoke. When he returned, I did not have to ask him where he had been. He told me that I should go home and work things out with him.

My nightmares have gotten more regular. I pray for them to stop. Ed's face appears. He is angry with me. I will remain strong. Right or wrong, I will not return home for several days.

Why do certain people feel that the law is for everyone else, and it does not include them?

CHAPTER FORTY-TWO

Mr. President

28th October 1907

I prepared for the onslaught of anger; he was the exact opposite of what I was anticipating. I will not cower down to him. He acted as if nothing happened. Is it me, do I expect too much from a man who has spent most of his life alone? I have to talk, and he chooses not to speak of it again. I am so confused. Bill did not have a temper, and neither did Frank, at least not like Ed. Of course, they did not consume alcohol the way he does.

3 November 1907

Life is normal. He has been exceptionally kind to me. I think he is a changed man. I pray.

I just heard the news that President, Theodore Roosevelt, will come west to the Grand Canyon. He is trying to make the Grand Canyon into a National Park. There was quite a commotion in town, knowing that there would be hundreds of people attending the ceremony. There were people for it being designated a National Park while others were against it. Those against were mainly business owners and budding entrepreneurs wanting to make a quick dollar at the Canyon's expense, though, to me, the Canyonlands being so honored, would draw more people to it.

The date was set for January 11, 1908, for the President's visit.

2nd January 1908

Tillie asked Ed and me if we would attend the festivities with her. This will be a historic day for the Grand Canyon. The President was coming again; he had been there before in May of 1903. Tillie did not attend that ceremony and would not let anyone in the family forget it. Tillie will arrive at my house in Williams a couple of days before the event. We will then ride the train to the Canyon. Arrangements have been made for the trip; we have secured tickets for the train and will stay with friends at the Canyon. It is always good to have connections.

9th January 1908

Ed is not going to see the President. The men are upset that the government will make a National Park in a territory that the legislators have yet to make into a state. I agree with them. However, I am going no matter what.

11th January 1908

We dressed in our best attires and hats, covering it all up with heavy coats. Women are so funny. It was a winter's day, and it was cold. The wind blew miserably. There was much talk among the spectators on the loss of mining. I understand the loss of the Grand Canyon to the miners. Being a miner, I knew what precious material lay buried in the canyon walls. It was rich in uranium, coal, copper, and zinc. However, this is not a typical place. No one can argue the overwhelming beauty of the Canyon. There are other places in the world to mine. We need to preserve the land for our future generations. The President respects the beauty of Mother Nature.

Everyone in attendance was spellbound with the President's speech. There were news reporters and photographers. The excitement of meeting the President was overwhelming. I have never met such a famous person. The anticipated day was a total success.

Now I see the importance of making it into a National Park. It will protect it for future generations to enjoy. Save the Grand Canyon is my new motto.

30th May 1908

Keeping three homes has been challenging for me; the house in Williams, a cabin in Anita, and a cabin in Spring Valley. Balancing life on a working ranch is hard work.

2nd June 1908

I have to tell you this funny story, LJ. Ranch hands come and go, with only a few staying on for the long haul. Then there are the ranch hands that come on for the roundup and cattle drive only to gain experience. These are young boys, tenderfoots, that leave home to learn the art of ranching. Out in the world seeking work, much like my brothers and Ed once did.

A horse or bull will set the young men straight quickly. Bragging and fabrication of past work experience are usually revealed on the first day. The senior cowboys highly anticipate a crop of young tenderfoots as their form of entertainment. They purposely make everyday jobs more complicated to harass the recruits.

One young tenderfoot from the east needed to relieve himself. Being shy, the young man approached Ed and asked him where he should go to relieve himself. Ed, enjoying a good joke himself, pointed to a small shrub and said, "You can go over there by that scrub brush and squat down."

"Way over there, sir? That far away?" the young man stuttered as he crossed his legs, trying to hold it in.

"If a coyote or mountain lion smells human feces, son, they start moving in for the kill. Just make sure you do not stink it up.

Cover it up as it comes out," explained Ed, acting very serious. "You get the idea, don't you, son?"

"Coyotes and mountain lions, out here?" he said, looking around the open grazing land trying to spot the animals.

"Yes, and when you squat, look first for jumping scorpions and rattlesnakes," Ed added.

"It's okay sir. I think I will just hold it for a while." The young man's face was turning white.

"I'll keep a watch out for you. You go on now and do your business," Ed said, feeling rather bad that he had scared the wits out of the young man. "You'll be okay."

The old cowboys knew from experience what Ed was about to do. They got in on the act by waiting until the kid squatted down. Roscoe, who could sound just like a coyote, began howling. The young man jumped up, ran like a bat out of hell, all the while trying to keep his pants up. A safe distance away, the sound of amusement made him realize he had been sucked in by cowboy humor.

The young man gathered his belongings and began walking towards Anita. The last anyone knew, he boarded a train and headed for home, seeking a less dangerous life. As Ed told the story that night at dinner, he and the other cowboys laughed until they could not laugh anymore. I felt sorry for the young man.

10th June 1908

Ed and I took a business trip to Flagstaff. Ed had to attend a Cattleman's Association meeting. We try to not seen since the newspaper tells everyone when we have been in town. Sometimes you would like to go into town without reading about it the next day. One of the areas of business was to discuss the on-going depletion of the grasslands in Northern Arizona. The cattlemen were being told to move their herds from Anita the following winter, to let the land recover.

When Ed told me that he had offered to winter our cattle in Spring Valley, I wholeheartedly agreed. "That is what I love about you, gal. You are always ready to do what it takes to make our ranch work," he said to me as we walked down Aspen Street holding hands.

"Oh look, it is our happy couple," said one woman to another as we passed on the street.

"They make such a nice couple. Don't you agree? It is so nice to see that kind of affection towards one another."

We smiled at the two women and kept walking. As we passed an alleyway, Ed pulled me aside and began to kiss me zealously.

"Ed, you are so bad," I laughed.

"Let us enjoy the rest of the day and go bicycle riding. The mesa is so pretty this time of the year. We could take our dinner in a basket," Ed suggested. We borrowed bicycles from some local friends and rode to the top of the mesa.

"Look how it has changed, Ed. Do you remember how it was when we first moved here? There are so many people here now. It used to be when you came up here, is all you could see was a forest. Now, there are houses and businesses where the forest used to be. The Greenlaw Lumber Mill looks so much bigger than it used to from here."

"They say change is good, but sometimes you have to wonder," Ed said, trying to hang on to the bicycle.

"Are you having trouble riding that wild bull? You look like the cowboy clown in the rodeo who cannot ride," I laughed at him as he tried to stop the bicycle and ran directly into me. I tried to tease him about the first time I saw him in a rodeo; he did not ink I was humorous.

"Did you do that on purpose, so you could get me down on the ground? Ed, you are a bad boy." We watched a herd of deer meander through the grasses, and we lay under the ponderosa pines. I found myself hunting for horny toads as I used to do as a child. I learned that if you can get them turned over and massage their bellies, they become hypnotized and lay very still.

The afternoon was relaxing and sensual. I loved the quiet moments with Ed, which were not often enough for my liking.

20th September 1908

History repeats itself: he did it again. He got himself arrested for drunk and disorderly conduct again. This time in Williams, and it is in all the papers. I have to go bail him out. This time he shot the gun. Not at anyone, but he shot it. To him, that makes it right. I told him I was tired of his trouble with the law. He was angry with me too. We are not speaking to each other right now. I have done this before. He had done so well. My disappointment with him shows. When will he learn not to get into fights and do not take his gun? When will I learn that he will not change?

Humans have difficulties in learning from mistakes they make, I being included in that. We are surprised when the outcome is the same.

CHAPTER FORTY-THREE

A Man, A Mountain Lion, and A Cave

30th October 1908

Winter has come early to Spring Valley. We are somewhat isolated in our beautiful valley. It is not new to me, having been in the Yukon.

However, Ed is going stir crazy.

31st October 1908

We purchased a new Kodak camera in town one day on a whim. I wanted to learn to take photographs of my animals. I suggested we take the camera out and take pictures of the snow. Bo, being small enough to sit on my lap, always accompanies us on our rides.

"Let's take a picture of Bo in the snow," I suggested. Ed caught sight of Bo and me standing together in the snow. He thought of how beautiful I looked in my bearskin skirt and lamb jacket. I had brought these with me from the Yukon and did not often need such massive warm clothes in Arizona. Today was an exception. The wind was cold, and my outfit would keep me warm.

As we were concluding our ride, Ed noticed mountain lion tracks in the snow. He was immediately concerned for the cattle. He knew that the lion would be looking for a hardy meal on such a cold day. We have to protect the animals. Returning to the ranch house, Ed grabbed his rifle and bullets.

"Are you going out after the mountain lion? Let me go with you. Two eyes are better than one," I said. Ed would not hear of it.

"No use for both of us to be cold. You stay inside and make us a good dinner. I will be back before dark," Ed promised me.

"Leave good tracks to follow," I said, thinking back to the day my father went missing in New Mexico.

"I will. I love you," Ed said, walking out of the door quickly as the snow was blowing in the doorway. He saddled his horse and rode off in the direction of the mountain lion tracks.

I am trying to comfort myself by doing mending and ironing. I prepared a dinner of root vegetables and meat in broth. I baked cornbread and worked hard to keep myself occupied. All the while, my mind was on Ed and his return home. As the afternoon was fading, my heart was pounding hard.

He should be back by now.

Grabbing the lantern from the corner of the room, I heard a thud on the wooden floor. I reached down into the dark corner and pulled an empty whiskey bottle off the floor. Ed hid it away from me. Disappointed but afraid for Ed's safety, I would just have to discuss this with him later. I have no choice but to go and try to find him. It is not the first time I was in a snowstorm looking for men. Most women would have waited it out... not me. I dressed quickly in my warmest clothes, packed blankets, food, and water. I returned for my Winchester rifle. I saddled Noble and rode off, following Ed's tracks on the snow. I know how to follow tracks. The snow had covered some of them, but it was not deep enough snow to hide them completely. I could see both Ed's tracks and the mountain lions; it was evident that at this point, the mountain lion was alone.

I traveled east toward Flagstaff along Government Mountain. I was used to going on horseback in this area. The sun would peek out of the clouds, and I could feel the warmth on my face. This was a typical snowstorm in the high country. There was suddenly the sound of a rifle in the distance.

'Ed', maybe he killed the mountain lion. I wanted to respond by calling his name or shooting my rifle into the air, but experience had told me to keep riding in that direction. Bill had taught me that hunters, so caught up in what they are hunting, could mistake a sound for an animal and shoot towards the sound. Not wanting to put me in harm's way, I rode silently. As I came closer, I saw that the white snow turned red. Blood was everywhere and lots of it.

"Too much of it for just one mountain lion," I said, talking aloud. Then I saw it; Ed's horse was dead and lying in a pool of blood from a gunshot.

It was apparent as I examined the area that there had been an altercation with the mountain lion. The horse had deep claw marks on his flanks.

As I continued riding east, I approached an opening in the earth. There were large volcanic rocks in the area that riders avoided for fear of the horse's hooves becoming damaged. Today, however, it was apparent that Ed and the mountain lion had traveled towards the rocks. I dismounted the horse and began leading the horse through the area.

"Ed," I said aloud, praying that he was nearby and could hear me.

Suddenly, my heart pounded; I was having flashbacks of Frank and the moose. Tying Noble to a tree, I made my way over the boulders. I followed the trail of blood that led to what appeared to be an opening between the boulders. The path of blood went down, descending into the earth.

"Ed," I called out his name again. I was praying that he was alive. I listened for any audible sound. The forest was eerily quiet.

"Ed," I said again, only this time a little louder. Was that a sound coming from deep inside the earth? I would need my lantern to see. I returned to the mouth of the cave-like opening and climbed through, picking my way over the boulders. It was pitch black ahead of me. The cave smelled musty and damp. Suddenly, it opened up.

Where was he? I spotted what appeared to be a large dark figure lying on the cold rock. It was Ed, and he was injured. I could hear him breathing and moaning. Quickly, I went to him. The glass bottle rolled away as my foot kicked it in the dark.

"Whiskey."

I brought the lantern down close to his body to see where he was injured. Due to the amount of blood on his clothes, it was impossible to determine the severity of his injuries.

"Liz, honey, is that you?" He said, both relieved and surprised as he tried to lift himself up to look at me. "I got that son of a bitch mountain lion, but he got Red. I had to put him down."

"I know Ed, just lie still and don't move. Where are you hurt? We have to figure out how we are going to get you out of here. We need help now because it will soon be dark.

"It's my right leg. I am clawed and bitten. My pants are ripped."

"Don't speak; save your strength for getting out of this place. What is this place, anyway? Is it like the ice cave out at the Crater?" I asked, more thinking aloud and not expecting an answer.

It was so cold in there. "I have to go and get a blanket and supplies off of Noble." I made my way out of the cave and over the boulders. I was surprised at how much the sun had set already. I carefully led Noble around to the front of the cave. I removed the supplies from the saddlebag and rubbed his long nose.

"Good boy, you signal me if there is trouble out here." The beautiful horse whinnied as if understanding everything I said. I made my way back through the large boulders, throwing the supplies ahead of me as I stepped. I then proceeded to build a fire in the cave. I gathered pine needles, moss from the trees, and leaves. Using a limb, I lit it on fire with my lantern. When it did not take, I doused the needles with a little kerosene. I blew on the fire until it had a good start. The stone room immediately filled with light from the fire.

I continued to comfort Ed. I reached into the pouch and brought out a flask of whiskey.

"We need some to put on your wounds."

"You are going to want me to drink it, so you won't want to kill me. I am not a good patient. Since when do you carry whiskey in your satchel?"

"Ed, Lizzie, are you in there?" The man's voice echoed inside the cave. The dog barked again in rapid succession.

"Back here, inside the cave. Watch your step; it is slick," I instructed. A rush of thankfulness swept over me. Bo came running and sliding on the slick rock floor. I picked him up quickly so he would not jump on Ed.

Enrique Sedillo, our ranch foreman, has worked for Ed since he started ranching. He and his family live in a cabin down the road from us.

"I was walking over to talk to Ed when I saw Bo sitting on the porch, looking east. Then I could see a rider on a horse and the tracks through the snow. I knew it was you, and I knew there was a mountain lion in the area. When Ed's horse was gone from the stall, I knew that something was wrong," Enrique said. "Bo was frantically pacing back and forth on the porch. He did not follow you, Mija?"

"I told him to stay, and he is trained to stay. Otherwise, he would have followed me. Now, how do we get Ed out of this trap?" I asked him, hoping he had an idea.

"We need to make him comfortable and stay until morning. It would be too dangerous to get him outside tonight. I could barely get over those boulders myself, much less carry a man as large as Ed. I tell my wife, if I do not come home by dark, she needs to tell the men to come to find us," explained Enrique, hoping to convince me to wait until morning. He then proceeded to the front of the cave, where he would keep watch over the horses and his boss.

I ate the dried meat from the satchel. I then proceeded to lie next to Ed to keep him warm. He was shaking from cold and shock. I kept running ideas through my head as to how to get him out of the cave. The morning was hours away. Once out of the cave, getting him back to the cabin was no problem. There was light from the moon, and the snow reflected the light making it easy to see around you. It would not last forever, though. Once the moon moved behind the mountain, it would be dark again. Time was of the essence. I drifted off to sleep, fitfully.

A commotion outside the cave awakened me; it was the other ranch hands. They are a loyal group of cowboys who will do anything to help their boss, even by risking their own lives to save his. As the men entered the cave, they were amazed by the size of the underground opening. A volcano in the area hundreds of years before had caused a gas pocket to explode- it left an opening in the earth.

The men took immediate charge of getting Ed out of there. There were enough men and whiskey to lead him on his own strength. The most laborious and tedious was at the cave's opening because of the incline leading out. It was slick ice. Ed cussed and shouted profanities at the men; the men ignored his ramblings. At one point, he refused to attempt to move any further.

I promised him more whiskey when they got him outside. Ed accepted my offer and exited the cave. I mounted Noble while Ed was put up on a horse with another man. The caravan maneuvered slowly through the forest towards home. The light from the cabin was a welcome sight.

15th November 1908

Ed's recovery has been slow. My patience is wearing thin. He continues to drink heavily, blaming it on the pain. I am frustrated with him as his temper becomes more enraged. I thought of Bill and compared the two men. Bill was definitely easier to take care of when he was sick or wounded.

26th November 1908

Thanksgiving came and went with little ado. Enrique shot and killed turkeys in the area and brought one by for me to cook for our dinner. The snow turned to rain. Then the storm came back with fury as if it had to prove it was more powerful. It is quiet and lonely in Spring Valley. If we had just been in Anita this year, we could have escaped periodically on the train into Williams or Flagstaff. The only people we saw were a skeleton crew of ranch hands and a few passersby.

11ᵗʰ December 1908

A man driving a sleigh said that he was out checking on remote areas of the county. He was stopping by to see if we needed anything. "The snow is so deep people cannot get out of some areas. You folks look like you are doing okay. You are much better off than some people in the area," he said.

"Can we ride with you into Flagstaff?" I asked anxiously.

"You and your husband? Sure thing, I could use some company. I need to go to a couple more cabins to check on people. I will come back by for you," the man said as he drove away.

I offered to pay the man for his services; he just motioned with his hand, saying no. I was excited to ride on a sleigh again.

"Ed, I just arranged for us to get a ride in a sleigh to Flagstaff. You need to see the doctor for your pain. We can visit with Tillie and my family for a few days. This is just what I need right now to get past the winter blahs," I said, waiting for an answer from Ed. He did not answer, as he was too drunk to acknowledge me speaking to him.

Oh, brother, I will get him ready, whether he likes it or not. No use me even waking him up.

I proceeded to lock up the cabin and pack. I arranged for Enrique to watch the ranch.

"We will be back in a week or so if there isn't another heavy snow," I told him.

Ed could barely walk on his right leg, and the whiskey made it nearly impossible to load him into the sleigh. I bundled him up and prayed that he would be incoherent on the trip. Ed woke up after a few miles of riding and angrily protested to the man.

"Stop this damn thing, I say; I need to go home. Where are you taking me?" Ed said, becoming angrier. I had no choice but to remove the flask of whiskey and coax him into being quiet for the rest of the ride into town.

We arrived at Tillie's at dusk, surprising her without warning. Tillie always kept an immaculate home but always felt like she was not ready for the company.

"Come in, come in. Get in out of the cold. I am so surprised to see you. It feels like a long time since I have seen you," kissing me on the cheek.

"Ed is in the sleigh. He is not doing well. I will need some help getting him out and into bed," I explained; I was a bit embarrassed.

Tillie went to the back door of the cabin and rang the bell for Jesse.

"Lizzie is here, and we need your help with Ed," she shouted to him. "Bring some help with you."

"I hear you, my love. I will be right there," answered Jesse. Jesse would do anything for anyone, especially Tillie and me.

"He is such a good man, sister. Do you know how lucky you are to have him?" I asked, thinking of all the trouble I had with men.

"Yes, yes, I do. Jesse is my life, along with my dear children. Now let us go get that back room warmed up for you," Tillie said. The men helped get Ed indoors, got his boots off, and put him on the bed. Jesse noticed the cuts on his leg as he pulled his pants off. The wounds had not yet entirely healed after all these weeks.

"Lizzie, you need to take him to Doc Raymond tomorrow and get those cuts on his leg checked out," Jesse said, quite concerned. "I have known of men losing their leg from gangrene. What happened to him, anyway?"

"We had a mountain lion attacking the cattle. Ed went out after him alone," I explained. "I'll tell you the story after dinner."

"Dinner is ready now; let's eat so we can hear your story," Tillie said, placing an extra plate on the table. The meal and dishes were finished, and the kids tucked into bed when the three of us sat down to talk. I began telling the story of the mountain lion and the cave. Tillie and Jesse were transfixed on my every word.

"It is certainly the most interesting story that I have heard in a long time," Jesse told me. "I agree about keeping the cave a secret for now. Come spring, you would have an infestation of people looking for it. Half of them would have no business out there in the first place."

Jesse was on the board of County Supervisors and an authority figure of the county business. Jesse said his goodnights and went off to bed, leaving the two of us alone to talk. Tillie had been waiting all evening to get me by myself.

"Tell me what is bothering you, Sis," said Tillie in a concerned voice. "I have watched you all evening, and I know something isn't right with you. You are not acting like yourself." I agreed and began crying as I opened up to her. I explained my situation with Ed's drinking and angry outbursts.

"I just cannot make him happy anymore. Is all he wants to do is drink. He says his pain is bad, but I think he is just using it as an excuse to drink. Oh, Tillie, what am I going to do? I am hoping that come spring, he gets better," I said as I wiped the tears away with my lace handkerchief.

"Tomorrow, you will take him into Doc Raymond, and he will help you. These men and drinking, I do declare, is a real problem. Jesse has to go into town to the saloons all the time to bring the help home, so they are not thrown in jail. He is always bailing someone out of jail. Then the men cannot work the next day, and you have wasted an entire workday," said Tillie.

"I hope Doc can talk to him, man to man. It sure does not do any good for me to say a thing," I explained.

"Has he hurt you?" Tillie questioned in a worried voice. Before I could answer her question; Ed had come to and began yelling at me. I was so embarrassed knowing that Jesse would never speak that way to Tillie. I quickly rushed into the back room to quiet him down. "Hush now, Ed, you'll wake the children." "We do not have children," Ed retorted.

"Tillie's children, silly. We are at Jesse and Tillie's house. Now be quiet. I can fix you some dinner. Tillie made good potato soup," I said to him, hoping he would eat.

"Soup? I want a big juicy steak. What time is it? Take me into town, woman, and eat steak with me," Ed commanded in a loud voice. "Get all decked out, and we will make a night of it, just you and me."

"Sounds good, Ed, except that we have no way to get into town. We came here in a sleigh. Do you remember?" I asked him.

"Woman, if you are lying to me to keep me away from the saloons tonight, I will have to tan your sweet little hide. Now, get dressed up for me," he demanded.

"No, Ed, not tonight," said Jesse, standing in the doorway.

"Do not interfere, Jesse, with my business," Ed said as he turned around, swinging his fist towards Jesse.

"Ed," I yelled, "do not lay a hand on him." I moved in between Ed and Jesse to protect Jesse and hopefully to prevent Ed from doing any harm.

"Just get me a drink of whiskey," he said as I pulled the flask out of the satchel, and Ed took a big swig of the brown liquid. "Now, leave me be," Ed barked at them.

I dozed in a chair in the room where Ed was sleeping. I had a fitful night in anticipation of another incident. I slept with one ear open, listening for Ed to awaken. Again, I was awakened by my recurring nightmare. Morning came with no further incidents.

"Why are you sleeping in a chair, Aunt Lizzie?" Asked my niece, Betsy.

"Your uncle Ed isn't feeling well," I explained.

"Hurry and get ready for school, or you will be late." At that moment, Tillie appeared and distracted the children. I made my way to the kitchen for a cup of coffee.

"How did you sleep?" asked Tillie after the children left the table.

"Awful, it was my fault. I kept listening to Ed instead of sleeping. I am haunted by nightmares lately. Thanks, Sis, for listening to me. I missed you."

"Do the nightmares seem real?"

I started to open up to her when Ed appeared in the doorway to the kitchen. He sobered up some from the previous night.

"Do I smell coffee?" asked Ed, apparently not remembering his outburst in the night. Tillie and Ed began talking. Ed had respect for Tillie, and he sat and listened to her. He agreed to go to Doc Raymond's office with Jesse.

"Thanks for your help this morning with Ed," I told my sister as we were leaving for town.

Tillie smiled and hugged me.

"That's what sisters are for. Say hello to the Doc for me."

The trip into town in the buggy was quiet. We arrived at Doc's office on Leroux Street with a hearty greeting from him.

"What can I do for you today, Ed," said Doc Raymond, a tall, gray-haired man with glasses. "I never see you in here."

We explained what had happened, not mentioning the cave.

"Let's have a look at that leg," the doctor ordered. "Looks pretty angry to me. I need to incise the wound and clean it well. I will give you a little something for the pain and this strap to bite on while I clean it. Lizzie, it would be better if you left us alone while I do this. Ed, I will return after I take Lizzie up to the Mrs."

As we walked up to the stairs to the living quarters, I told the Doc about Ed drinking so heavily. The Doc shook his head and said he was sorry to hear that I was dealing with that problem on my own.

"Liquor can take a good man down. I have seen it happen to a lot of men around here, especially in winter, when they are not as busy with work. I will give him a good talking-to before I start treating him. Now, you and the Mrs. visit while I go to work."

Mrs. Raymond took her job as a distractor very seriously and engaged me in conversation while screams could be heard from down below in the office. Suddenly, they heard laughter coming from the two men, signaling us that the procedure was complete. The Doc wanted to see Ed again the following day.

"Let us stay at the Weatherford tonight. We don't want to inconvenience your sister again," Ed suggested. I was caught in a tight spot. I knew if we stayed downtown, Ed would drink in the saloons. If we stayed at my sister's house, he would still drink but disturb them again for the second night. I agreed after some hesitation. I would just have to hope that his leg was too sore to walk on. Ed passed out cold on the bed of the hotel room. I took the opportunity to go tell Tillie our plan and gather our belongings.

Ed had a time of it following his procedure. He developed a fever and sweats. The Doc had told me that it might happen after he worked on his leg. He explained that the fever was right, as it would kill the infection. The saloons went on as usual without Ed that night.

After a visit to the Doc the next day, the leg was improved. He bragged about my skills as a nursemaid, and I told him I had much experience in my past life. He told me that he would love to hear my stories. Telling my stories makes me happy; why won't Ed ask me to tell him?

Ed became better day by day. Doc showed me how to clean the wound when we went home. We will return home after Christmas. This has been quite an ordeal for both of us.

When hunting prey, pray that you do not become the hunted.

CHAPTER FORTY-FOUR

Liquor, Fighting, and Jail

12th April 1909

Ed traveled to Albuquerque with some other ranchers, including George B, to buy cattle. He left with a promise to behave himself while he was away.

"This year is going to be different. You act as if that is all I do is drink. I guess I had better go since you are going to start on me again. Honey, I am a changed man. Trust me," Ed said as he rode off towards Chandellar to catch the afternoon train.

I have grown accustomed to disappointment. It will be a win for our side if he does not spend time in jail. I was missing my home in Williams and decided to go there instead of staying on the ranch alone. It has been a long hard winter.

I love it when the wild iris is in bloom in the forest, along with the beautiful grasses sprouting. If the summer rains come early, the cattle will have plenty to eat this year. Fat, healthy cattle meant more money coming in. We, women, agreed that even though we did not have the move from Anita this year, it was better to winter there than be isolated all winter in Spring Valley. I guess we have spring fever. Ha, Ha!

I busied myself around the house during Ed's absence. He would be gone all week. I was surprised to have a visit from my brother George.

"I ran into Ed as he was leaving for Albuquerque. I told him I would come out and check on you," George said, feeling somewhat silly telling that to me. I had been too far more places in the world than he had and experienced more things.

"Thanks, George. Did you plant potatoes? Jesse said he got his in last week," I said as I prepared a cup of coffee. "Cream and sugar?"

"No," he replied stroking his long white beard. George was looking older these days; however, he was fifty-eight years old.

"I am thinking of selling the farm and moving into town. Get me a little place that does not take as much care. I am looking for a place in town on Phoenix Avenue, just under Mars Hill. The damn railroad runs right past it though. It may pay off to be deaf."

I told him it sounded as if he had thought this through and should act on it. He was grateful for my blessing. George stayed through lunch and visited with me. We enjoyed each other's company and could talk on any subject. He left to head back to his farm in Bellemont. I wished he could have stayed longer but understood that he has a way to go to get home. A damn stubborn man will never learn to take the train. He cannot be without his horse and buggy.

Independent, old cuss.

15th April 1909

The days have gone by slowly. I cannot help myself when it comes to worrying about Ed and his drinking. I keep telling myself that he did promise to keep it under control on this trip. Is all I can do is to have faith in my husband.

17th April 1909

Bo began barking one morning. He was quite excited when we went outside to feed the chickens. Bo loves to chase the chickens around the yard as if he were herding them. There was an unfamiliar sound coming from the south. Then we heard the sound like a horn from a motor car. Bo barked and ran toward the sound. It was George B in his motor car.

"Good morning to you, Lizzie. Sorry to surprise you without notice, but I thought I should tell you about Ed," he started to say.

"Ed, is he in jail?" I asked in a worried voice.

"Yes, he is in Albuquerque. I am sorry, Lizzie. We got word yesterday. He told us he was staying for a couple of extra days. It seems he does not want you to know about his predicament. He was drunk when he got into a fight with a man down there. He pulled his gun and would have shot the man had he not fallen off the sidewalk. He barely missed a man who was walking on the other side of the street.

"What do I need to do?" I asked, trying to contain my emotions, and not burst into a tirade.

"Can you get over there to bail him out? The Judge says he will not let him leave the jail without talking to you first," he explained.

"Yes, I can go now. Let me settle things here first. Are you headed down towards Bellemont? I can ask my brother to go with me."

"Yes, I will wait," he said. I found George on his farm. The two George's have been friends for many years– both having come to Flagstaff at about the same time.

19th April 1909

George and I arrived in Albuquerque. It was late in the evening when the train pulled into the station. I decided that another night in jail just might do Ed some good. George and I took our time; visiting daddy's grave while we were there.

I met with the Judge. We had met before under similar conditions, and he wanted to help me as much as he could. He explained the seriousness of Ed's actions to me. I agreed with the Judge and paid the bail. I also promised him that it would be some time before Ed would return to New Mexico.

Ed left jail a humble man. He could not stop telling me how very sorry he was for breaking his promise to me. George would nudge me anytime I would start to go easy on Ed. He was not buying the man's excuses for drinking. George and the family were concerned about my safety around the man. His drinking was becoming worse.

He expressed what I was thinking: how am I going to handle this problem?

The trip home on the train was quiet. I was glad when we finally returned home. Luckily, the ranch kept us busy, and we could continue our own for a few weeks following the catastrophe. Ed sobered up and tried to make up for his mistake.

"I love you, Liz. I do not know what I would do without you. Please, promise me you will never leave me. Please," he begged, actually getting down on his knee to persuade me.

"Only if you promise to never do that again," I answered, praying that he meant every word he said. I know that Ed will travel without me, but I will try my hardest to go with him in the future. There will be times; however, that he will have to go alone. I cannot stop him, but maybe I can keep him from killing someone.

Love tells me to protect you with my body and soul, for as long as we are on this earth.

CHAPTER FORTY-FIVE

The Buick Runabout

Summer, 1910

Ed has insisted on going into Flagstaff for the day. He promised me that he would be home before dark. It is a big day for us. He is no longer a homesteader but a landowner. I am so proud of him, and he has worked hard to accomplish this deed.

I have been nervous all day. After lunch, I took Bo, and we went for a ride around the pastures. Noble needed a good ride. I rode the horse hard and fast through the tall grasses. It felt good to be riding and free. Once again, there was the sound of a horn coming up the road. My heart sank, and I rode Noble toward the sound. What could it be this time, I wondered, as my heart raced in fear. It was not familiar to me. Then I saw inside the automobile was Ed, driving proudly and waving. I waited for the motor car to stop before approaching it on horseback. I did not want to spook the horse with an unfamiliar object.

Dismounting Noble and tethering him to a tree, I approached Ed. "What is this?" I asked.

"I think," I said hesitantly, "I think this means a race to the cabin. I on Noble and you in the Buick.

"Little cowgirl, you are on, and may the best person win," he said. Ed was relieved that I was taking the automobile so well. The race began with a shout out from Ed, "Go!" I was determined I would win. Noble rode fast, with Bo running alongside as quickly as he could go. We ran through the pasture and up to the cabin door, leaving Ed behind traveling over the makeshift road.

"We won!" I said, patting my beautiful horse. Bo jumped from the ground upwards and into my lap. It was an exciting win. When Ed arrived, he quickly explained that he could have won except for the ruts on the road that had been caused by too many wagons traveling over it on muddy days.

"Let me drive," I said impatiently.

"I have to show you how to drive this contraption. It is not like a horse. You need to learn how to handle her," he said.

"Maybe I want it to be a boy instead of a girl," I laughed. "I shall name him Hermes."

"Hermes, what kind of name is that?" asked Ed.

"Hermes is the son of Zeus and Maia. He is the Greek God of travel," I said, showing off my knowledge of Greek mythology.

"Something tells me that you have driven an automobile before.

"Am I right?" he asked.

"Well, maybe, once." I would not tell him that I had not.

I leaped into the driver's seat with him and Bo sat next to me. We drove over the familiar roads that we had ridden together on horseback. I was in love with the automobile. We stopped in a pasture full of iris and spent time alone just as we had done in the past. It was the most beautiful, loving day that we have spent alone in a very long time. Our passion for each was renewed. It was as if we had to make up for lost time with each other. The automobile brought us together again. I realized that I had not accepted the fact that we had grown so far apart from each other until today.

"I love you, Ed," I said as we climbed into our feather bed. "I love you too, Cyclone," he said lovingly.

Is it the elation of the race or the winning that we enjoy the most?

CHAPTER FORTY-SIX

A Black Horse and an Ed

Summer 1911

The summer lightning storms have been so intense. We have lost several heads of cattle due to electrical strikes. Ed's temper was short.

Any rancher knows you cannot prevent Mother Nature from doing what she will do. We moved some of the cattle up on to the Peaks. We placed a big canvas tent in the woods. I began telling some of the men about my experience living in a tent in the summer of 1896 in Canada. They were transfixed and encouraged me to tell more stories. Ed sat quietly by, allowing me to continue. I do not need much encouragement to tell my tales. It seems so long ago. Luckily, LJ, I have you, and if my memory gets too faded, I can go back and read the story of my life.

Ed never moved. He expressed that night in the tent that he was afraid to hear my stories. When I asked him why he said that his life was nothing compared to mine. He is fearful that I am too strong a person to be with him. How can a man live with that? It should be him telling me those stories.

15ᵗʰ July 1911

He resents me, so it seems, for my life, as I have chosen to live it. He has become distant. Who did he think I was in my past life? I am no different than before.

30ᵗʰ July 1911

I am moving off the mountain. I cannot stand to be treated as if I am such an oddity. The men try to comfort me from his disgust. Has he always seen me as an ordinary woman? Is seeing me for whom I am such a disgrace to him?

5ᵗʰ August 1911

The rain and lightning continued. Everything is under mud. We have had several trees hit by a flash in front of us. It is so scary and surprising when that happens. I have made the decision to move the cattle out of the pasture and up to Kendrick. Ed continues to stay at the mountain. Tomorrow we will begin the move with or without his approval.

26ᵗʰ August 1911

I attempted to remove a cow from barbed wire. I worked and worked on the fence to free the animal. I was giving up when I decided to give it one last try of tying the fence to Noble and pulling it off the cow. The hail was hitting my back hard so hard that it felt like I was being stoned. I got on Noble's back and began pulling on the rope. A huge crack of lightning came through the sky and seemed to touch down right beside me. The hair on my neck stood up. Noble reacted by bucking me off. The good news was that the cow got loose from the wire. In doing so, the flying fence hit me in the head. I blacked out.

I lie here in bed, recovering from my injuries. I am thankful for the good men I work with. Moving cattle in torrential rain is not easy. I think in the future, I will leave that for the men. I confess that they are more muscular than I am.

I knew of nothing until I heard Tillie talking. Waking to my family standing over me as if I had died is disconcerting. Everyone was excited to see me open my eyes and talk. Apparently, I was out for a couple of days. How and when I was rescued, I have no memory. The fight with the fence, cow, and the mud was slowly returning in my mind. I searched the faces for Ed. He was not here. Heartbroken, I closed my eyes to keep the swell of tears back. I felt like an empty shell. My love was not here with me. It was more comfortable to sleep than to deal with the reality of our demise.

I awakened to a familiar snore. The room was dark, but I could make out his frame, asleep upon a chair near the bed. Was I dreaming? I tried to move my arm and realized it was in a sling. I reacted to the pain with a pitiful whimper. He was by my side, immediately asking me what I needed. Keeping tears back, I told him since he was here by my side, I had everything I ever desired. He kissed me softly, not wanting to hurt my scratched face. I have never seen him with tears until now. He was genuinely concerned for me.

He told me that they searched for some time for me. Each time a posse returned without me; his fears grew. They found Noble before me. Of course, that did not help his mood. Every cowhand around, from every ranch, assisted in the search. I was thankful to have him beside me. I healed faster because he was there. However, I also wanted to get well to see Noble. He discouraged me from moving too quickly. As soon as I could walk, I pushed myself harder each day. I saw what lying down too long will do to you.

One day, when Ed was out of the house, I asked George about Noble. He told me that Ed blamed him for my injuries. I argued that it was my fault. I could feel his apprehension in telling me. George had never been one to lie. I should not have forced him, but I had to know where the horse was now. I let out a scream when he said that Ed sold him.

I was beside myself. That horse was no different to me than a child to its Mother. It seems that I talked aloud while I was ill. Ed learned of the black onyx horse from my family. He knew of my nightmares from sleeping beside me for years. He took offense to the man in the prediction. I persuaded myself not to think that Ed is the man of the prophecy.

George promised me that if I kept quiet, he would find a buyer, and he would get Noble back for me. It would mean keeping a secret from my husband. I agreed, knowing that I could not persuade Ed to let me keep him. We had a bargain.

I decided that it would be best if I did not bring Noble up in front of Ed. I did not want to bring attention to our plan. What am I to do, LJ? I cannot live without either one of them. I love them both equally. If he agreed to stop drinking, I would be willing to give Noble up. He would never do that for me. I know that in my heart to be true.

1ˢᵗ September 1911

I will be up and running in time for my birthday. I have to be. George has promised me a trip to see Noble. I cannot wait. He has hidden him close by. Bert seems to be in on the scheme too. I love my brothers. I am blessed.

4ᵗʰ September 1911

I have had the best birthday. Life is good. Noble is at Bert's barn. The future is uncertain as to how to convince Ed that I must have my horse. I sat on him to prove to everyone that I have no fear. He nuzzled me when I fed him a carrot. When I left, I could hear him whinny. If I did not know better, I would have thought that he was calling my name. Next time, I will go on a ride.

6ᵗʰ September 1911

I received a warm welcome when I returned to the ranch. It was good to be home where I belong. The roundup had begun, so Ed was busy. I took a buggy ride down to see George. The plan for Noble to be at George's house today worked. I saddled Noble up, and we galloped away, my brothers praying that I return unscathed. It was courageous of them to go behind Ed's back. I rode for some time, making sure to let them see me every few minutes. I felt rejuvenated.

Thank you, Lord, for watching over Noble for me.

9th September 1911

Ed came storming in from the roundup, yelling profanities at me. He said, "Damn you, Liz. Why do you fight me on everything? I should have known you were up to something by not mentioning that damn horse to me. You are a conniving bitch. And your brothers are as bad. I have too much to do right now, but I am telling you it is the horse or me."

I sat silent. I knew that anything I said right now would go unheard. He took his aggression out on me that evening by having his way with me. I said nothing as he pushed himself into me. I was lucky when he fell asleep right after.

Never underestimate the love between a cowgirl and her horse.

CHAPTER FORTY-SEVEN

Destiny at the Coconino

10th September 1911

I am amazed at myself for bouncing back so quickly. Generally, after a fight, I feel sad. There seems to be strength in standing your ground. I have decided to force the issue of keeping Noble. We will come to a decision that I promise you.

Ed announced that he was selling a significant portion of the herd and is to meet with a buyer in Flagstaff. He wants to set an example for the other ranchers and have less in the winter and increase it over the summer. Too risky if they get sick. I think he is over-selling. My vote did not count, even though half of this ranch is mine. He decided that he and the men would drive the cattle to Flagstaff instead of at Bellemont. Too many nosey ranchers hang out there. He seems to think that the more prominent ranchers control the market. He was never this way before. Did something happen, and has he had a falling out with them? Men carry grudges differently than women.

I am nervous about him going to Flagstaff. However, he has assured me that he will return right after the cattle have been loaded on the train. It will mean the world to me if he is telling me the truth.

The women and I shall do our wifely duty and remain behind to close up the cabins for winter. It takes all of us, plus the older children to load wagons for the move back to Anita. After all, he has promised me a trip to Coronado Island. It is all the rage now since a few of the other ranchers have taken their wives there.

I am in much need of a getaway before we face winter again. The ocean is so relaxing.

I said good-bye to him as the cattle were driven down the road towards Bellemont. We kissed, but it seemed to lack any passion.

I thought he would drop it, but he reminded me again to "Have that damn horse sold before I get back, or it will be taken to the glue factory. I mean it, Liz. Don't make me show you who is boss around here."

12th September 1911

I began frantically pacing up and down the kitchen of the cabin, nervously checking the window that looked down the road. I am wearing a path on the wood floor. I knew what had happened to Ed– drunk, just like all the other times when I did not go with him.

His purpose in life right now is alcohol.

"The man is like a child in the candy store."

"Yet," I disputed myself, "A man who works as hard as Ed is allowed to celebrate his success."

As quickly as I was accusing him, I turned to blame myself. I did not care If he drank. I am jealous of the fact that he is there, and I am here. Quickly, I changed into the satin dress Ed liked so well, fixed my hair up in a bun, and hurriedly closed up the cabin. Packing can wait for now. I would surprise Ed and have dinner with him in town. I got the automobile out. I needed to hurry. It was getting dark earlier that September day. I headed east into town. Bo began to follow me as usual when I left. He soon lost interest and turned around to go back to the cabin.

I can get the runabout going quite fast over the back trail from Spring Valley to Fort Valley.

"Damn," I shouted. A big buck was standing in the middle of the road. There were several deer and fawns there too. They were blocking the way. I made a loud screaming noise and honked the horn to scare them off the road. The herd broke up quickly and ran to the shade under the aspen trees. To my dismay, the big buck stood his ground, looking very regal. I did not have time for this, not today. Patiently I waited in the Buick for the deer to make his way under the shade with the others.

I was topping out over the hill into the valley below where Tillie and Jesse had their farm. I could see Jesse and his workers in the field. The oats were ready for harvest along with the wheat and potatoes. Tillie was fixing dinner. The men would be coming in from the fields soon and be hungry.

I told myself this to make my excuse for not stopping to visit with her.

As the Buick neared the cabin, I could see Tillie outside. "Hello," I said, waving as I drove past.

"Lizzie, what are you doing out this time of day so far from home," said Tillie.

"I'll come by tomorrow to see you, Tillie," I said hurriedly, not wanting to be caught up with gossip. "Ed is on another binge, and I am going into town to find him."

Tillie waved as if she understood.

"See you tomorrow then, Sis. I love you. Be careful."

"I will. Love you too," I said.

13th September 1911

I went into Babbitt's Mercantile as soon as I arrived in town. I saw Gladys. She said to me, "What brings you to town so late in the day?" Everyone knows your business. Then she proceeded to tell me that Ed was on a binge. I was feeling a little embarrassed, so I turned towards the display of hats.

I picked up a cute gray hat with lots of lace and feathers on it. It would go with my gray coat. "Beautiful," said Gladys realizing she had caused me some embarrassment.

Another woman, overhearing the conversation, spoke up and said, "He's on a good one, alright." "You, his little lady? He has gotten into several fights in town, and the Sheriff threatened to put him in jail to sleep it off. His lady friends at the saloon got his mind off fighting if you know what I mean?"

The other girl in the shop, named Lettie, had come up to where we were talking. Lettie is not one to keep to her own business either. My blood was boiling at these women. I have met plenty of this type in my life and have no use for them.

"Lizzie darling, did you come to town to scrape Ed off the ground? Heard he's on a bad one," Lettie said, laughing.

"No, we had arranged a late dinner tonight to celebrate the end of cattle season," I said. A small little lie will not hurt; Reminder to self: go to church later to confession.

"He should be cheery company for you, drunk and all," Lettie said, continuing to enjoy herself at my expense. "If he keeps it up," and then she giggled at her own joke and said, "you can take him dinner in jail."

"Stop this right now, Lettie," Gladys said trying to protect me.

Lettie took the hint and went back to the counter where she worked.

Looking apologetic at me, Gladys said, "Lettie's just jealous because she will be an old maid."

"Ed is taking me to California next week," I blurted out without thinking.

"Really Lizzie, you are so lucky. Where will you go?" Gladys asked.

"San Diego, to the Hotel Del Coronado."

"Lucky lady."

"I'll take the bonnet and a bottle of Jasmine water," I said, restless to get away from the store and to find Ed. "Just put it on our tab." Gladys took my old bonnet and placed it in a box.

"You will look pretty tonight, as always." I am lucky to have such good friends in town.

"Thank you, Gladys," said I am picking up the box and hurrying out of the store.

I dashed toward the Buick and nearly ran into Deputy Sheriff Pulliam.

"Have you have seen Ed in town?" I asked, knowing that he would tell me where he was.

"Not for a few hours now. Someone thought they saw him go into the saloon again."

If he is in the saloon, then he can stay there. I am angry. How dare he spend the evening with a prostitute? On that note, I went to the boarding house and asked the Mrs. if I could have my old room for tonight. Luckily, it was waiting for me; she smiled, grabbing the key.

She offered me tea and cake that I readily accepted. I explained my situation, and she let me cry on her shoulder. A lady can always use a friend. I felt better and went downtown to see if I could see him. I returned shortly, disappointed that I could not. I am going to drink this shot of brandy and sleep.

14th, September 1911

No nightmares last night. The brandy helped me sleep like a baby.

Well, I saw him. Whether or not he remembered is something else again. He showed me the Colt pistol he bought this morning. He said something to the effect of having forgotten his at home, and he may need it to clean up this town. When I protested and asked him if we could go home, he changed the subject to Noble. He said I was gonna have to choose between that horse and him. When I refused to answer him, he grabbed me by the arm and squeezed my wrist. I pulled back and told him he was hurting me. He laughed sinisterly.

I pulled my hand away, and with the cup of my hand, I slapped him on the cheek. Typically, I would not have been afraid, but this was a man who was apparently not himself. He glared at me and told me that I would be sorry for striking him. A shiver ran down my spine as if someone had just walked on my grave. I turned and walked away.

Surprisingly, he let me. He was obsessed with what I did with the horse. I shall have to threaten him with divorce if he does anything to him. I will settle this argument before we leave town – that I promise.

Nellie O'Brien and I are going to the picture show. She and Chick Nation are dating, and he will come too. When I saw Ed, I politely invited him to attend. He accused me of two-timing him. I will let him go to dinner with me at the Coconino Restaurant. Woo-Yen always cooks a good meal. Wish me luck in calming him down tonight. I love you, LJ.

To my readers: Unfortunately, this is where Lizzie's story ends. The adventurous, brave, intelligent, tenacious woman whom we grew to love lost her life that night in the Coconino Restaurant at #3 Railroad Avenue in Flagstaff, Arizona.

Ed did not sit with Lizzie at the picture show. When he arrived, he sat several rows back from her. They later met up with a very drunk Ed. He went inside the restaurant only to order his chicken dinner and promptly left with Chick Nation.

The men went down the street toward the saloon, where he continued playing poker and drinking. He arrived back at the restaurant in time to eat his dinner. A ruckus that had begun earlier in the day involving Ed's friend Jim followed them to the restaurant. The men were taunting Jim to come out and fight. Jim went out of the restaurant. Ed, Lizzie, and Nellie O'Brien stayed behind. When Ed got up and proceeded to follow Jim and Chick outside. Lizzie stood up between Ed and the doorway. She was trying to convince him to sit down and stay out of the argument. She was protecting the man she loved. A defiant Ed refused. Having his finger on the trigger, "accidentally" shot Lizzie in the leg. She went down, holding onto him and a chair. He told her that she was fine, and it appeared as though he kissed her. Onlookers realized that she was bleeding out...he had struck the femoral artery. Dr. Raymond's office was around the corner on Leroux Street. The time was Ten o'clock.

By the time he appeared, Deputy Sheriff Pulliam had also arrived. They immediately arrested Ed. Several bystanders helped to carry her to Doc Raymond's office. She died shortly after that, alone. Her last words were Ed…. You…. Shot….me. (1)

May you rest in Peace, dear Lizzie. Your story has now been told.

Love you with all my heart, JKH

Letter From Ed Geddes, 30th September 1911

My dearest Liz,

My heart is heavy with grief and sincere remorse. I have wronged you worse than any man has to his lady. When did I last tell you that I love you? Why were those three words so difficult for me to say? I could blame it on being an old cowboy too set in his ways, but it makes no difference now. I found your journal that you left under your pillow at the boarding house. That old lady that runs it did not want to let me inside your room to gather your belongings. I just finished reading it. I feel the need to fill in the blanks. You made me out to look like a villain, baby. Why did you do that to me? I never did you no wrong.

Remember our meeting the other day in town? Parts of my memory are as blank as can be in my mind. Your family and friends have helped me to remember what they know to be true. So, here goes with the story. My head was swelled up big; kind of like that horse we had who had the colic really bad. You begged me not to shoot her, but I did anyway. I never listened to you. Hell, you know more about ranching than I ever will. I brought 500 head of cattle into the stockyard here in Flagstaff, Monday two weeks back. I took most of the money to McMillan's bank and pocketed two hundred dollars for my indulgences, including poker and drinking. I told myself that I deserved it. I work hard for a living. Besides, it is what I have always done. I was not about to change my way of living entirely for some woman. Pardon my honesty; I just want to tell the story as it should be said.

Tillie said you went scooting past the farm in such a hurry, and you did not even stop to say hello. You just gave her a wave and said you would talk to her later. You looked so darned pretty driving that horseless buggy of ours. You had such a big grin on your face when you first saw me on San Francisco Street. I never will forget that grin. Then, came the disappointment on your face when you reached up to kiss me and realized that I was drunk. You turned around and stormed off so fast that I did not have time to get my wits about me.

They tell me that I walked back down to Donahue's Saloon. I cannot remember any who, but they say I stayed until Sandy kicked me out. One of the girls kept good care of me while I was sobering up. I heard that you went into Babbitt's Mercantile and bought a really pretty hat and some of that Jasmine water I like to smell on you. See, I remember, Eau de toilet, its French for something.

You told Gladys about my surprise for you... a trip by train to the Hotel Del Coronado in San Diego. I knew how much you had wanted to go stay there since Nellie told you about it and you saw those pictures at the movie house. I never could keep a secret from you, my little cyclone. It was gonna be a trip without any business involved. Just me and you, sugar pie. I wanted to treat you to something extraordinary this year. Did I ever tell you that you are the strongest, bravest, selfless, smartest, pig-headed woman that I have ever known?

Any who, I know'd you went and got a room at the boarding house. Were you trying to hide from me? Otherwise, you would have gotten a room at the Weatherford. You know, it is where we always stay when we come to town. We indeed are not destitute. I know it is where you stayed when you first came to town and after your house burned down and the Mrs. always gives you your old room back.

You went up to your brother's house to visit with him and Nora. You missed him the last time he stopped by to visit out in Anita. I had to find that out from somebody who saw you drive up Humphreys and turn onto Dale Street. You and Bert could visit about the darnedest things. I could never keep up with the chatter. Bert refuses to talk to me. It is okay, I do not hold it against him.

Some people swear that you and me had dinner together that night. Only you would know. People say we did, also say we got into an argument. Knowing us, we probably had words. You slapped me, now I can remember that. You can belt a man pretty hard.

I went to Babbitt's the next morning after I was sort of sober. Of course, I am never without my liquor. I carry my pocket flask with me wherever I go. I bought a little pistol. I am not sure why only that I had left mine back in Spring Valley. You know me, hon, I feel naked without a gun on my person. I only bought six bullets. We had rounds at home, just none on me here in town. I went back to Donohue's to play some poker. It relaxes me. I guess I was kind of mad at you for following me and not trusting me. I needed time away from you, I think. You always nagging me about my bad habits. I know, I drink and smoke like a fiend. I will never change, I cannot.

Like I said, I want to be honest with you. No use now, not to be. Oh, I could lie to myself, I guess. When I saw you later, before I passed out in the alley over by Doc Raymond's office, you begged me to go to the picture show with you. You were with those friends of yours that always look at me like I am some sort of madman. They make me uneasy. Ah, I know they are your friends and all, and you do not get to see them much. I did go inside, but you did not see me. I sat on the other side. That was probably what got your tail feathers ruffled at me. I half expected to see you sitting by another man. I sat in that picture house and thought about that damned horse of yours, Noble. I should have never given him to you, my fault. He is the stubbornness horse I have ever seen. I should have shot him that first time he bucked you off to the ground. The only horse that would not let me within ten feet of him. I don't know what I ever did to him 'cept give him a good home. That creature did not deserve the good life he had.

You love him. I know, then there was that damn black onyx horse from when you were a kid. You wanted to prove that premonition wrong. I am guessing that I am the one who made it come true. When I left the other day, I told you to get rid of Noble before he hurts someone. When you told me, you took him over to George's house in Bellemont, I got real angry with you. You even threatened to leave me for a horse. Holy shit, Liz, do you know what that does to a man's ego? No matter what I say, or do you are always telling me what you think I should do. Well, no matter now. Water under the bridge, right Cyclone? You always did wear the pants in this relationship. Anyway, Chick Nation and I were meeting up with Jim Burke for some poker. You and Chick's girlfriend Nellie O'Brien begged us to meet you at the Coconino for dinner. We knew if we needed lovin' later, we had better do that one thing for you gals. In the meantime, these two men started picking a fight with Jim. He thought he got things settled with them, so we left him at Donohue's. When Chick and I arrived at the Coconino, Woo-Yen escorted us to the back room. He makes all the drunks sit back there as to not scare off the decent patrons. So, I was riled by that too.

We ordered dinner, chicken as I recollect. There were many people around that night so we knew it would take a while. No use wasting a good poker hand just sitting around, so Chick and I left to go play. Then, I understand you and Nellie disappeared too for a time. No bother now, anyway.

When we got back and started to eat, we heard noise coming from out front on Railroad Avenue. Jim came back in and said that the same two men were calling him out for a fight. Apparently, they were not happy with the settlement that Jim had made with them. I had a gun, and I would go take care of them. I got up to leave when you pushed in front of me. My finger automatically went to the trigger. I can still feel the cold steel in my hand. You had to go and do that thing you always do to me. You know, stand right in front of me like you were my mother. I warned you to never do that to me again. I got so mad my blood boiled, I could not think. You told me not to go out there and to let Jim handle his own affairs. Hell, I do not need no woman telling me when I can fight, and when I cannot.

I was just pulling out my Colt revolver from my pocket when the gun went off accidentally in my hand. Next thing I know is that you are grabbing hold of me and you fell against the chair. You said to me that I shot you. I argued with you for a time when I realized there was blood everywhere. Nellie was screaming, and people were pushing into the room. You turned pale, and I thought I could give you air, so they thought I was kissing you when I put my mouth on yours. Then Doc Raymond and Deputy Sheriff Pulliam come in and push me out of the way. Someone grabbed me and held me away from you while they carried you off down the street. Woo-Yen was shouting about the mess and complaining that people left his restaurant without paying.

Next thing I know is that I am being dragged off to jail. I asked what for, and they said for killing my wife. I informed them that it was an accident. I told them that I would work all of it out with you later on. I just remember asking for a smoke, and I damned near got slugged by this man helping Pulliam.

The whole nightmare did not even seem real to me until the next day at the coroner's inquest. Jesse Gregg got on the stand and said real nice things in my defense. Along with several other people. I was sure happy when they let me off and said it was accidental. I cannot get your last words in this world out of my mind… Ed, you shot me. I am going to miss you, Cyclone.

ED

EPILOGUE

Monday, September 17, 1911: 3 PM

The crisp fall rain was coming straight down from the heavens above, and dark black afternoon clouds created an ominous sadness in the mountain town of Flagstaff, Arizona. Beaver and Cherry Streets were lined with automobiles, horses, and buggies; sitting apart in front of the church was the funeral hearse. It was the usual number of mourners at the funeral of a prominent person in the area. This day's funeral was of no exception. The townspeople turned out in full force to support the Hoffman family. They all came seeking comfort from the tragic death of one of its own.

The family had been anxiously waiting for the train to arrive, bringing the deceased's brother from the mining town of Morenci, Arizona. A few days earlier, he received a telegram informing him of his sister's death. Distraught and horrified he began making his way to Flagstaff. Johnny was about as tough as they come. However, this tragedy struck deep. "Why Lizzie?" the words kept repeating in his head. "Why wasn't it me?"

Inside the ornate Catholic Church, mourners filled the pews. People were even standing on the wet wooden steps and sidewalk outside the church. The cold and rainy day did not stop people from coming. In attendance were also Dr. Raymond and Deputy Sheriff Pullium, who had attended to the deceased at the time of the shooting. There was one crucial member of the family and community missing from this sad event. Even though no one expects her husband, Ed Geddes, to be present, his absence struck a chord with everyone. Ed was a favorite rancher in town that everyone had grown to know and love. On this day, his presence would have been unwelcomed, if not explicitly denied; armed men waited outside the church to prevent him from entering.

A few days before this funeral, Flagstaff was its usual bustling western town. Lives went about as usual. Usually, this town would welcome this man warmly. However, today, Ed was a man who was not welcomed. If he were grieving, he would have to do it alone.

Lizzie Hoffman Geddes was one of those people from the community, until her premature death at the age of thirty-five on the night of September Fourteenth, Nineteen Eleven. Now, her lifeless body was lying silently inside the casket, resting at the front of the church; a church that she so eagerly helped raise money to build. A life accidentally cut short by the man she loved.

The Priest conducting the mass on this day had known Lizzie from the time she was a young woman. Her family had moved to the mountain town the same time that the Church had sent the young priest to this town to conduct monthly mass at parishioners' homes. This family was a respected part of the congregation.

The Priest's voice cracked as he conducted the service. He had to work hard to hold back his own emotions. The service was about strength, forgiveness, and healing. He knew this all too well, as he had spent the last several days consoling the immediate family and friends. He spoke of Lizzie's life from his heart. He knew her to be a courageous woman.

She was a wife, sister, aunt, and friend to members of the Northern Arizona area. She was a rancher, gold miner in the Yukon, and entrepreneur. Strong and courageous to face her adversities as well as comfort others in theirs. A life cut short protecting the man she loved with her own body.

With those words, the parishioners began sniffling and crying. Her two sisters' faces were buried in each other, trying to comfort the other, mourning the loss themselves. Children rustled about in the pews, unsure as to what to expect.

The rain continued as the mourners prepared to exit the church and make the final journey with her to the cemetery south of town.

Noble, Lizzie's own horse, led the hearse, guiding the procession majestically as if he knew that this was his most important journey.

Onlookers bowed their heads as the procession made its way down Beaver Street, across Railroad Avenue and down Mike's Pike Street. It passed homes and businesses, including the Riordan's house and mill, a home that she enjoyed visiting throughout her life.

A fitting burial place for her was at Calvary Cemetery in a grave beside her mother. Safe and secure beside the woman who made her what she was. She taught her to be strong, courageous, and loving. The surname translation of Sturn means to be strong, which was her mother Mary Josephine's surname. Her mother instilled in her three girls to be strong; a trait all three had excelled at, especially Lizzie. Had that philosophy played a role in her death? No one would ever know the exact circumstances of her death. Her two sisters agreed she would not have done anything different that fateful night at the Coconino Restaurant.

The trip back to town seemed to last an eternity. Everyone's hearts were in angst, and it felt like nothing could ever fill the empty space. Would anyone be as cheerful or loving as Lizzie was, or as independent and fearless as she had demonstrated? How they all could survive without her, the family wondered. It seemed as if everyone walking had the same thoughts. Everyone in the procession walked with his or her heads bowed, looking down to the ground. All of these things would take time to heal.

Will they ever be able to look Ed in the eyes again and find forgiveness in their hearts? This was inconceivable at this particular time. Hate for the man consumed them, and disgust filled their minds. All of these things will work out in time; however, the overwhelming truth was that Lizzie was gone forever. Nellie experienced the loss of her parents as well as the loss of two of her own children. She was familiar with grief after the tragic death of her parents and the unexpected loss of her 4-year-old son and 12-year-old daughter, 11 years ago, still haunted her. Unexpectedly, without any warning, her baby sister, Lizzie, departed from them. How cruel this life could be, she thought? Nellie's thoughts were at a shallow point when suddenly she felt a strange warmth surround her. It was the sun breaking through the clouds and shining down on the path of mourners. "Look up at the sky," Nellie spoke excitedly as she gazed up to the heavens, "a double rainbow!"

"A true sign from God that Lizzie is home," the priest exclaimed to the crowd of people. He crossed himself enthusiastically as if he had foreseen that God would make the sun come out.

The mood of the crowd lightened as they made their way back up the muddy streets to downtown Flagstaff. A man in the group began singing a familiar hymn. Soon everyone was singing as the mourners walked north to town.

No one noticed the figure, the pitiful remains of a once good man, hidden and walking alone on a side street: Ed Geddes. His sorrow ran deeper than anyone could ever imagine. He kept repeating to himself as if hoping that Lizzie could hear him, how sorry he was that he shot her. "I didn't mean to do it, Liz, I love you, and I cannot live this life without you. It should have been me, not you!" Ed fell to the ground, crying pathetically as he opened his coat and pulled the whiskey flask from his pocket.

As the years passed since her death, she became forgotten. As if, she never existed. Resurrected from microfiche in the Flagstaff Public Library one summer evening, her story will be live on forever.

Ed Geddes was acquitted of the murder of his wife. He sold the ranch at Spring Valley two weeks after her death for 32,000 dollars. He roamed the country drinking and fighting, only to return to Kansas where he came down with measles. He died from complications of the illness just four years after her death.

Lizzie was buried in Calvary Cemetery beside her mother. The beautiful, woman of character soon became Flagstaff's Forgotten Cowgirl.

Jesse Gregg died a year and a half after Lizzie's death in a saloon downtown. He went downtown to bring a farmhand home when the man bludgeoned him in the back of the head. Tillie was at his side when he passed days later.

(1) Coconino Sun, Friday, September 22nd, 1911 page one.

Readers, if you enjoyed Lizzie's story or have a young reader, you will enjoy my next book, "You Can Call Me Lizzie. A Collection of Short Stories." She continues to fascinate my imagination. I have compiled more stories of Lizzie when she was a young girl.

This book is a series of short stories that you could enjoy all together or each story is a quick read with itself.

So, follow along with her early life in Kansas, New Mexico, and Arizona as she experiences life with the same excitement she did in Forgotten Cowgirl.

Also,

Destiny at Tiburon Island

Meet Marcus, a young ambitious newspaper reporter on his first assignment. The editor-in-chief of the prominent Phoenix paper is only helping Marcus to please his sister. World War II is raging across the world and Marcus was given a 4F rating due to rheumatic fever as a child. He had a strong desire to prove himself worthy of escaping military service.

His uncle sends him on an assignment that is over Marcus' head. The editor predicted failure for the young reporter.

Marcus arrives at the Pioneer Home in Prescott, Arizona with only a week to get a good story.

After meeting with his subject, a crotchety old cowboy called Jack, he realizes that the job will be tougher than he expected.

The year is 1905, and a hard-hitting cowboy takes on a job as a cook and packer deep into the Mexican desert with a gold-mining expedition.

Jack is as experienced as they come. After twenty years of running cattle with the Hashknife Outfit on the Colorado Plateau, he has seen it all. Cattle rustlers, Indians, blizzards and scorching deserts, and the war between the Grahams and the Tewksbury's known as the Pleasant Valley War. The Hashknife is known for its tougher than nail's cowpokes. When offered a job cooking and packing for an opportunity to go to Mexico in search of gold, he jumps at the chance. He has a fierce competitive nature with his youngest sister, Lizzie, who has spent eight years in the Yukon during the gold rush. It is his chance to prove that he can come back with more gold than she did.

Did unforgiving summer heat, a lack of water, inferior maps, and an Indian guide known to other Indians as a detrimental man all play with the fate of the prospectors?

Travel with us as we take you, deep down, the Mexican coast on a journey of peril and death motivated by gold fever. Witness a possible betrayal of loyalty when their situation becomes dangerous. This is based on a true story of a man's determination to make it home alive.

Captivated by the man, the story, and Marcus' determination to be a success he learns to play by Jack's rules. At times, experiencing life as he had never done. Drawn in by the man's tales he writes his life story.

I hope you enjoy the stories as much as I do writing them.

ABOUT THE AUTHOR

JK (Judy) Hoffman was born in Prescott, Arizona to Ray and Edabelle Crawford. Her parents lived in Mayer, Arizona where they owned and operated Ray's Market. She enjoyed a fun-filled early life in many little towns in Arizona. She experienced Arizona in the fifties and sixties shaping her life in the knowledge of western life. Moving from Mayer to Phoenix, then on to Holbrook and back to Phoenix. She often lived with her grandparents who loved to spin tales.

At the age of nine, the family moved to Sedona where her parents lived for 33 years. Sedona brought an array of fun with the height of moviemaking at its highest. She observed as movies were being filmed, which inspired her creative mind. A story was always created in her head as if she were writing scripts.

At sixteen, her family moved to Tuba City on the Navajo Reservation in Northern Arizona increasing her life experiences. A painfully shy girl gained confidence in herself by immersing in school activities. There she worked as a clerk in the "Navajo Trails Trading Post." She learned to embrace life and accept each day as it was given to her.

She then attended Northern Arizona University where she met her future husband, Garry. Life nudged her to become a dental assistant and make her home in Flagstaff in the early Seventies. Together they had three children whom they raised in the beautiful mountain city. The majority of her career was having the pleasure of working with James Mast, DDS for twenty-eight years. Upon his retirement, she worked for Bryan Shannahan DDS for two years.

After a diagnosis of stage three renal cancer, and two hand surgeries, she decided it was time to write the book of her dreams.

She had been researching her genealogy for several years when, after the death of her mother, she began work on her husband's family. Excited to do local research, she went to the Flagstaff Public Library where she discovered Lizzie Hoffman. This fascinating woman at the turn of the last century captivated her imagination. She could not let go of her and her life in early Flagstaff. So, in the winter of 2016, she began to put her story into words. She found a very creative writing coach named Jacques LaLiberte, who encouraged her to change the book into a journal.

She lives in Flagstaff with her husband, son Justin, two cats, and a dog named Bo. She is lucky to have her oldest son, Chris, living and working in Flagstaff. Her daughter Heather is a teacher in Winslow, Arizona where she lives with her husband Randy and Judy's two handsome and talented grandsons, Riley, and Aiden.

www.ingramcontent.com/pod-product-compliance
Lightning Source LLC
Chambersburg PA
CBHW061558190726
48288CB00007B/2081